Reader Reviews

"This well-written and very imaginative book will enthrall sci-fi readers, especially those who enjoy time travel. The characters are well-drawn, and if the method of time travel eludes readers, it doesn't matter. At times humorous and at other times scary, the story speeds along at a frantic pace. Tag along with Dan and Freddie, but watch out for Chantelle - you don't want to mess around with her! A great story for anyone who wants something far different from their ordinary lifestyle."

***

"When I saw *Time Travel for Fun and Prophet* described as Douglas Adams meets time travel, I was skeptical as he pioneered a genre with his unique wit. If you've explored the entire Hitchhiker's Guide, you will enjoy this book. The book, bordering on older-young adult, offers an easy yet fun read with well-developed characters and spot on humor. Each chapter unfolds a new adventure. As a promising debut in the time-travel genre, the author's universe-building sets a strong foundation, and left me eager for more adventures. With hopes for a series, I hope the authors take more risks, venturing into some of the more 'alien' worlds and expanding their universe. In their first foray into the genre I look forward to their time traveling universe where the next stop is only a jump away!"

***

"This fun book will be an easy read as you laugh the way through time."

"Fun. Fast. Witty. Charming. This book was an entertaining, quick read. I would sneak-read a couple of chapters, put it down to do chores and then do a few more in stolen minutes. It was like a compilation of short stories but with the same great characters throughout. You never knew where the next chapter was going to land you (literally) and what mayhem Dan and Freddie would encounter. Sometimes it would go to the absurd, but that all made sense based on Dan and Freddie's time travel abilities. This will be one that I'll reread on a hot summer day, sitting poolside with a nice cool drink."

***

"I wholeheartedly recommend this read. It is fun. It will take your mind off the tragic 24/7 news cycle we live in. For a short time you can smile and leave reality behind you."

***

"I give it a YA-thumbs-up."

***

"Who knew being a professional plumber could be a valuable skill to have while time-traveling? It works in this book. A fun read, especially for fans of Dr. Who and Monty Python."

***

Read more and share your review at

www.CineHunden.com/review

Time Travel for Fun and Prophet

by Terry Willey and Carol Baker

ISBN: 978-1950755011
Library of Congress Control Number: 2023919993

Certificate of Registration

This Certificate issued under the seal of the Copyright Office in accordance with title 17, *United States Code*, attests that registration has been made for the work identified below. The information on this certificate has been made a part of the Copyright Office records.

United States Register of Copyrights and Director

Registration Number
TXu 2-165-713
Effective Date of Registration:
September 30, 2019
Registration Decision Date:
November 12, 2019

Cover Design by Miladinka Milic
Edited by Zoe Quinton, Literary Strategist.

r24-0819

TABLE OF CONTENTS

– Chapter 1 –
Lunch and the HFM

For humanity, it was time for regression or for enlightenment.

For nations, it was time for reconciling differences or for waging war.

For the planet, it was time for insanity or for reason.

For Dan Baker, it was time for lunch.

It was lunchtime in the valley and the restaurant was humming. Not just busy, but humming, an annoying hum that was pushing Dan to an unpleasant place. The hum would have been offended by that, as they thought it was quite musical, but they were not a telepathic hum. Luckily the smell of fresh baguettes soothed him slightly, even though the baguettes were not even trying.

Dan was sitting at lunch with his best friend Ambrose. Ambrose wasn't his legal name, but that's the name he insisted everyone call him. Until he was twelve Dan knew him as Jim, but Jim thought that name was dull and so Ambrose was born. This made it easier seven years later when Ambrose came out to his parents—Jim wasn't gay, Ambrose was.

No surprise there for Dan; he figured that out when he was six. He had watched an old movie and wanted to play "Knights of the Round Table" with Jim. Jim wanted to be the beautiful princess. If Dan was Aquaboy, Jim was Aquagirl. By the time Jim became Ambrose, the only question Dan had was whether Ambrose was gay or trans.

Dan shook his earlobe. "Can you hear that?"

"I swear the waiter is flirting with me." Ambrose glanced at said waiter.

"No doubt."

"Because I'm so hot." Ambrose really was hot. Cary Grant hot.

"Or because he wants a big tip."

Ambrose smiled.

Dan clarified. "A gratuity."

"What do you know?"

"I know waitresses." He had attempted to date quite a few that had been friendly.

"Yes, but you're not me."

"The hotness factor."

"Yes, I am hot and you are not."

Dan was not unhot—but not actually hot either. He was the kind of guy that people have a hard time identifying in a lineup. He was 30's (32) with no observable scars or tattoos. He did, however, have a smile that made women melt—if they were close to the sun.

"I'm not saying you couldn't be," Ambrose said, "but you don't take my advice."

"I like my look."

Ambrose gestured to the world. "You want *them* to like your look. No one is looking for a man in coveralls."

"Unless they need their toilet fixed."

"Yes, but if you looked good while you did it… Could you imagine how the ladies would fall for a gorgeous 30-year-old man making plumber money?"

"And alimony payments."

"They'll settle."

"It's not a romantic job."

"The hot waiter's looking at me."

"He's not that hot."

"What do you know? You don't have a gay bone in your body."

"I gotta get back to work. Don't let him break your heart."

"Worry about *his* heart."

Dan tossed money on the table to pay his tab. He hated leaving the quaint sidewalk café where he and Ambrose met for lunch on irregular occasions. The café had the ambiance of a Parisian bistro right in the heart of a bustling American cosmopolis. Dan knew this because Ambrose had been to Paris and told him so. One day Dan hoped to go to Europe, but probably not this decade. Maybe in the 1940s.

Dan climbed into his car and headed to his next job. He had to fix a toilet.

Typical job—broken ball cock. He hated to tell her the diagnosis as he always felt like he was sexually harassing women when he mentioned it. And he had heard every comment every man, or occasionally woman, would make.

On the other hand, it was an easy job, a cheap part, and ultimately the customer was very happy. He'd just replace it with a fill valve and avoid the language issue.

When he got to his car, he found he had gotten a text from Ambrose. "Are you okay?"

He texted back. "Why?"

"You were acting weird."

"That's just me."

"True. Oh wait, the waiter's calling. Call me tonight, bye." Ambrose hung up before Dan had a chance to respond.

Dan couldn't remember a call with Ambrose when he had a chance to say "bye."

Next up: clogged drain. Simple, but messy. The hard part was listening to the man explain why he hadn't fixed it himself. This was nearly universal. Men needing to reclaim the masculinity they had lost falling before the mighty drain.

Dan used the words, "Uh huh," here a lot. For the ones who really needed an excuse he'd explain:

"Modern drains are made with inferior metal, so they wear quickly, break easily, and clog impossibly. A homeowner just can't afford the tools to handle a job."

Just like cars. Way too complex with computers and hybrid systems. Most men can't even change their own oil.

Rationalization makes them feel better.

Now he was on to his last job of the day, and of course being the last job of the day it was also the most annoying. Although to be fair, the work was only mildly annoying—the annoyance came primarily from the well-dressed brunette who had hired him.

The work involved replacing a calcitrant kitchen faucet in a rather calcitrant kitchen sink belonging to a recalcitrant hedge fund manager (HFM). He considered the sink merely calcitrant, due to his only having the urge to hit it with his wrench one time.

The HFM's expert supervision of his work was impeded by her inability to disconnect from her assistant. Her cellular umbilical cord kept her constantly in contact with the beleaguered Chuck. And since she was yelling at her assistant more than Dan, he was grateful for the distraction. From underneath the sink he could see her $500 designer shoes pacing angrily through her perfect kitchen.

"NO! I said the Armbruster account; Hollingsworth can wait. Chuck, if you don't give me those numbers in the next ten seconds, I swear I will… Oh… Then give me the Hollingsworth numbers NOW!!" She pushed the off button of her phone with an unsatisfying deliberate tap.

She paused to breathe and placed her phone in her holster. With Chuck sufficiently abused, she would turn elsewhere. Dan readied himself.

"How much longer is this going to take? Just being here to make sure you do this job correctly has cost me at least twenty thousand this afternoon."

"Why didn't you make Chuck do it?"

"Because Chuck doesn't know shit about plumbing."

Dan had a hard time not laughing to himself as he had been done for twenty minutes and was deliberately wasting her time.

Dan was dark haired, average height and weight. He was pretty much average everything. You could say he had a large nose, except for the fact that he didn't. But in order to give him a distinguishing feature, we'll say it anyway.

He had a large nose.

Or not. Make up your own mind.

Dan began to slowly put away his tools.

The HFM tapped her foot. Not in the cool Fred Astaire way, but like a rabbit signaling the herd of approaching danger. "It's about time. I should have just done it myself."

Dan turned to wash the oil and grime, and for some reason sardine, off of his hands, which left a considerable layer of filth on the pristine white sink. Interestingly, there was no grease needed for the job, so he was forced to grab some from the can he kept for just such emergencies.

The HFM thrust a wad of bills forward. Interestingly, all of the bills in her wallet were crisp, right side up, and sorted numerically by worth and serial number, so she was forced to wad them up for just such emergencies.

Dan grunted and walked away. He grunted because he had learned if you engage certain people with actual language, they will invariably speak back and this was not ideal.

He stepped across the porch and down the steps toward the sidewalk of a nondescript upper class neighborhood of identical townhouses. Only the street numbers and colors of the BMWs were different.

As he hopped into his Toyota, Dan checked off the last box on his job sheet for the day. Being the last job, he didn't really need to check it off, but it felt so damn good doing it. Normally he would have pulled off his tool belt before driving away, but he couldn't risk the HFM finding some reason to stop him in her driveway.

Dan's Toyota was a lot like Dan: it was the first new car he'd ever owned and had aged into mediocrity. When it was new, it was marginally above average. Dan had promised himself his first new car would be American made, but he wanted a car that was better than average, so that didn't happen.

Driving home, Dan felt good. Very good. It was a beautiful September 27th at 5:27 p.m. (this will be important later). He'd had six calls, all resolved—people could go on with their lives unhampered by flood or dehydration. The reason Dan felt so good was, in fact, that he was not average in one area—he was a very good plumber.

He was listening to Procol Harum and all was right with the world—other than an odd odor of gunite.

The next thing on Dan's agenda was to think about all the things he was not good at, like spelling, making curry, and marriage. While this may not seem like the best use of one's time, it is, nevertheless, quite human.

Dan's mind went to a series of inedible meals, failed tests, and one spectacularly unsuccessful relationship. While he and Jeneane had been hopelessly in love, they were also hopelessly mismatched. Several shouting matches and a visit from the local constabulary were enough to convince the couple they would be better off living in separate cities.

At 5:32.05, as Dan was preoccupied with making his formerly high self-esteem plummet to its usual depths, he noticed something seemed to be slightly off in that he was no longer in his Toyota but rather outside of it looking in. The visual of his vehicle, driverless, beginning to slow in traffic and veer to the right, was the last thing that he saw before winking out of existence entirely.

And that's when time began to turn inside out.

– Chapter 2 –
Plumbers and Saints

When one enters the timestream with no vehicle for protection, as time begins to unravel, so does one. Dan began breaking down into strings of time. Later he would try to describe the experience but would find it extraordinarily difficult as his brain had been broken down into strings of time at the time. From outside of the phenomenon, one could best describe the sensation as having your body and mind shoved into a paper shredder, taken out, and then having the process repeated until the universe said *Stop*.

From inside Dan's perspective, he could best describe it as *Owwwwwwwwwww!!*

When everything finally stopped shredding, Dan found himself not on the freeway, but rolling down the side of a soft green hill. The rolling continued until it didn't.

One of the blessings of time travel is that it prepares you for whatever you may find by leaving you in something akin to shock. What would leave a normal person panicking, screaming and running for the hills, instead leaves you like listening to Led Zeppelin—a little dazed and confused.

Standing up and looking off to the distance, Dan saw trees and possibly some sheep. He was tired and felt not unlike he had spent 45 minutes in a paper shredder. He remembered being outside of his car and wondered if he'd had an accident. He checked his arms, legs, and body for wounds and found none. He checked his head a little more carefully as it was obvious there was something wrong there. But again, there was no sign of trauma.

"Perhaps I've hit my head so hard that I only *believe* I'm fine."

He checked his head even more thoroughly for any sign of lumps and bumps, gashes, abrasions or any other questionable sensations. He found none.

Dan looked around to get his bearings. The green rolling hills and the deliciously breathable air left him flummoxed, as neither were part of his daily experience.

"The freeway must be over the crest of the hill," he thought, and began to climb the slope. When he reached the crest, it was completely bereft of freeway.

"Now I know I've got a concussion."

From the hilltop he could see more hills, more sheep, and what looked like a man in the distance. He shouted.

"HELLO, I'VE BEEN IN AN ACCIDENT."

The figure, which looked to be wearing a heavy coat on a warm day, turned and headed toward him. The heavy coat made Dan question his choice of calling to the man.

"Oh great, I've just called to a crazy person. Of course, I'm concussed so we'll probably get along fine. I hope he has food—I haven't had my dinner yet."

Dan was quite hungry. Didn't he have a candy bar in his coveralls? He found it and wolfed it down. Funny, it made him think of kippers—and he had never really eaten or even seen kippers.

Dan heard the sound of Procol Harum and wondered if his car was nearby.

Almost immediately his world turned upside down.

– Chapter 3 –
A Missed Opportunity

Dan and his thoughts unraveled. When he was once again raveled, he was in a concrete structure being blasted by music, The Beatles' "I Feel Fine" to be exact. And shrieks.

Loud, feminine shrieks.

"Great, now I'm hallucinating."

Dan was not aware that visual hallucinations are much more indicative of brain damage than auditory ones, but since this was not the case the point was moot. Although with the volume of the music Dan would be happy if it was mute.

Moot/mute—know the difference.

Dan froze in his steps. He smelled hotdogs.

Looking down the concourse, Dan saw a concession stand and realized he was in a stadium. And there was food. And no one was in line.

Dan made a beeline for dinner. "Can I have two hot dogs and a coke?"

"Sure thing." The concessioner looked pleased to do something. "That'll be a buck."

"Wow. Is this a special promotion?"

The vendor put the dogs on the counter, laughing. "Sure, a Beatles dog."

Dan pulled four quarters from his pocket, which the concessioner scooped up. Dan grabbed his supper and headed to see what was going on in the stadium. Walking through the tunnel, he noticed the screaming was louder than the music.

Looking down to the field from the lower level, he noticed a stage in the infield diamond and four musicians playing. They were dressed like the Beatles.

"Must be a tribute band," he thought. "Wait, maybe this is an anniversary thing—the Beatles' Shea Stadium concert. When was that? The sixties sometime."

He noticed a sign: "Shea Stadium."

"Must be it."

Dan watched for a few minutes while eating his dogs. He made it through "Ticket to Ride" then headed to look for someplace quiet as the screaming caused a ringing in his ears and a headache. He wondered if they'd play "In an Octopus's Garden."

Walking through the tunnel, he popped out of existence.

Well, out of time, but he did cease to exist in 1965.

- Chapter 4 -
Bogged Down

Given the cacophony of where he was and his belief he was concussed, Dan's jump into time did not bother him quite as much. It still felt like going through a cheese grater, but at least the transition wasn't quite as jarring.

Between the jump's muddled acceptance effect and his own sense of denial, he had no idea what was happening. Concussion, dream, or hallucination were his best guesses.

He knew something was wrong, he was just wrong about *what* the thing was.

He felt like he was getting closer to the truth.

With each jump things seemed to make more sense.

Or maybe he was accepting the senselessness.

Dan's return to time was not much an improvement to his situation—he fell into someplace dark and rather wet.

If not for the fact that he was cold and damp, he would've preferred to take a little nap, but circumstances being what they were, he felt perhaps he should actually try to figure out what was happening.

He was spectacularly unsuccessful at that.

However, he did find that his clothing was dripping from being in the wet; his wallet and all of his credit cards and cash were at best very damp; and a few of his best wrenches were now missing and the rest were in danger of rusting.

"Best to get moving." He began trudging through the muck. A strong earthy scent swirled around him. There were gnarled trees like shadows in the dark.

As his boots sloshed, the soles began to stick in the suction of his steps and, conversely, his feet began to slip inside the leather. If he hadn't been wearing work boots, normal shoes would have been lost in the mud. There are physical laws as to why something can be slippery and sticky at the same time, but mostly it's the universe's perverse sense of humor.

Dan spotted a light in the distance and it made sense to walk towards it. He knew a little bar—Henry's—that should be around here, or it would have been had he been anywhere near Pacoima. As he approached the light, several more lesser and lower lights became visible. The first light originated from the church steeple and the others from individual homes.

Besides the flickering light, all he could make out was vague shapes. He didn't spot any landmarks. There were structures but none of them were Henry's. Eventually the muck got less muckish and he was walking on dry ground, then a dirt road.

Of course when I say "road," it was more of a path with ruts in it.

Upon reaching the town, Dan struggled to recognize the houses and buildings; in fact, they did not resemble anything he had seen outside of history books. These were simple cottages, not modern homes and apartments. There was ample evidence (that Dan was trying to avoid stepping in) there would have been cows and chickens out had it been daylight.

What's more, the lights inside were not incandescent or fluorescent but candle or lantern light.

If Dan had thought he was confused when he woke up shredded and wet, he was sadly mistaken. That was less confusion and more timestream pacification. Now this, *this* was confusion. Up to now his hallucinations had taken him to places that were plausible; now he was in a place that did not exist in his time—at least that he knew about.

He looked for anything he recognized. Failing that, he looked for a building he could identify. Failing that, he looked for a building that looked inhabited. When he heard voices, he knew he was on the right track. As the voices got louder, although he could not quite make out the words, he could make out the universal sound of drinking.

When he spotted a rustic tavern, all was right in the world. He would get directions, a beer, and perhaps a doctor, then things would return to normal. Entering the establishment, he saw this might not be the case.

The interior looked like something out of an old movie: it had wooden tables, exposed beams, and was lit by lanterns and a fireplace. The patrons, all men, were wearing simple rough-hewn clothing, and they were all staring at him.

"Can someone help me? I seem to have been in an accident and I'm a bit lost."

The funny thing about time travel is that time travelers transported to a new era somehow absorb the language and speech patterns of the area they have traveled to or perhaps it's just too much work for your near omniscient narrator to research language and speech patterns of ancient civilizations every time Dan changes location time.

That being said, what the bar patrons heard and what Dan actually tried to say were quite different, but they did get the message.

One of the patrons responded: "Good sir, have you been injured?"

What Dan heard was: "Are you all right, buddy? Anything broken?"

"I don't think so, but I crashed my car and I don't know where I am."

"Well let's see if we can find your wagon."

It doesn't always work precisely the way one would expect.

"We should take him to the doctor." That's what Dan heard, although the stout man actually said "apothecary."

"We should take him to the sheriff."

The barkeep leaned in. "Apothecary first, sheriff second."

That choice saved Dan from spending the night in jail.

– Chapter 5 –
Ready Freddie

In no time Dan was hustled over to a building at the other end of the road to see the apothecary, who had been eating what Dan could only assume was mutton, as it smelled slightly lambish. Dan himself would have been quite pleased to learn that it was indeed mutton.

The patrons gathered round to listen as this was the most interesting thing that had happened to them since… well ever.

First, Dan stared at the exam room with trepidation. There were shelves filled with jars with things inside them that vaguely resembled body parts or tiny rodents of some kind. There was a cupboard filled with lots of little vials of unidentifiable powders and liquids. In the lantern light, shadows leaped over the walls like grasping fingers.

Second, Dan stared at the little grey bearded man with trepidation. The man wore baggy clothes, shabby and disheveled. He was small compared to the tavern patrons, and yet confident in his trade and ominous in his frumpiness.

"So, doctor, I've been…"

"Call me Freddie."

"Freddie?"

"Yes. Frederick, actually, but that's always seemed a bit stiff to me so how about we go with the informal. And your name is?"

"Dan. Well, Daniel, but if we're going with the informal…"

"So, Daniel, you had a bit of an accident."

"A bit."

"So what happened?"

"That's just it. I was driving along the freeway and suddenly I was someplace else and eventually I found myself here, soaking wet and lost."

Freddie raised an eyebrow. "Well, the moors will do that to you. You're lucky you made it out at all." He looked at the tavern patrons. "Gentlemen, don't you think you should be out looking for whatever happened to Daniel's wagon?"

The men hemmed and hawed, but slowly filed out. Dan thought they probably wouldn't find anything. Freddie was positive they wouldn't find anything.

"So, Dan, where are you from?"

"Pacoima."

"Is that in the New World or the Old?"

"New World?"

"Yes, the Americas."

"Americas? I'm from the United States."

Freddie repressed his excitement. "Of America?"

"Uhhhh, yes?"

"What year?"

"2018?"

"I forget, do you have space travel?"

"Space travel?"

"Are you going to put a question mark after everything you say?"

"Me? You're the one asking all the questions." Dan was becoming peevish.

"Yes, but you're answering my questions with questions."

"Perhaps I'm confused."

"Not perhaps," Freddie said under his breath.

"Look, this is not helpful."

"Then how about this: have you ever time jumped before?"

"Time jumped?"

"You're doing it again."

"Sorry."

"So, you've never time jumped before?"

"I don't even know what that is."

This particular series of fairly useless questions and answers went on for some time and has been edited to save the reader from excessive boredom. Suffice it to say that eventually Freddie came to the point.

"You, my friend, are a time jumper. You move through time with the ease of someone walking across the street."

"If crossing the street means you feel like you've been ripped into pieces, swallowed, vomited, and then tossed into a bog."

"Granted, but if the process of traveling several hundred years back in time really leaves one fluish and moist, that seems a rather small price to pay."

"So you're saying I traveled through time?"

"Yes."

"Without a ship?"

"Yes."

"On my own?"

"Well you did get some help from the universe."

"Still."

"Yes, yes, quite impressive."

"Wait a minute." His eyes narrowed. "How do you know about all this?"

"I'm one of you."

"A plumber?"

"A time jumper. Well, I used to be."

"So you're not anymore?"

"I seem to have lost the knack. I was happily traveling through time and then I spent more time here than I should have and the timestream wouldn't let me back in."

"How long have you been here?"

"Twenty-seven years."

His eyes widened. "Is that going to happen to me?"

"I doubt it. You probably won't live that long."

"Thanks for that."

"Time jumping is supremely dangerous. Most jumpers don't survive the first year without help."

"Where can I get help?"

"That's where I come in. You can take me with you."

"Can I?"

"You can. I merely have to be in physical contact with you when you jump."

"Physical contact?"

"Touching you."

"Touching me—how? This isn't some kind of medieval come-on, is it?"

"Like holding your hand. I can go with you when you jump. Show you the ropes."

"That would be great if I knew when I was going to jump."

"I can teach you that."

"I had no warning."

"You did."

"I think this is the third time I've wound up somewhere without moving and I had no idea it was coming."

"You did, you simply didn't know what to look for. Before you jump, you may get a mild headache, ringing in the ears, an odd smell, and a brief thought of fish."

"Thought of fish?"

"Or at least some sort of marine creature. Could be a dolphin, or maybe a platypus."

"A platypus is not a marine creature."

"Well it should be. They do like the water."

"So do Labrador retrievers but they're not marine creatures."

"Regardless, you can learn to recognize when you're going to jump."

"Crap!!"

"What?"

"I walked out of a Beatles concert!"

"Who hasn't?"

"I could have used my phone to record it!"

"That would be great. An hour of screaming."

"Yes, but, still." He frowned in consternation. "How long will I be here?"

"Could be a day, an hour, or a few minutes. It all depends on the timestream. After you get some practice, you may learn to control when your jumps happen. That's what I did."

"And then you stayed too long in one place."

"And the timestream forgot me."

It's a terrible thing to be forgotten by the timestream. It's like that time when you were seven years old and your parents were supposed to pick you up after band practice but forgot and you sat for two hours waiting because the school was closed and your parents wouldn't let you have a cell phone. And when they did finally show up, your father claimed your mother was supposed to pick you up and your mother said it was your father's job and the eventual apology they gave you was half assed and you were never quite sure they felt bad enough that they wouldn't do it again.

Only with the timestream, they might never pick you up at all.

In the history of the universe there have been thousands of time jumpers. Well, to be fair, the universe is infinite: there have been an infinite number of time jumpers. To make it clearer, we'll just say that every planet gets one every hundred years. It's probably not true, but that's what we'll say.

No civilization possesses any kind of time technology. The timestream does not allow for just anyone to enter; it makes the choice. This has led many to believe that the timestream is a sentient being. The timestream, however, has stated on numerous occasions that it does not believe this to be true.

Dan's mind was filled with a thousand questions—or more specifically, 1,763 1/2—but it was getting late; he couldn't quite formulate the final question. Freddie showed him to a room where he could sleep.

Dan did not want to seem ungrateful but believed the use of the word "room" in regards to the medium-size closet Freddie put him in was rather generous. There was a bed of sorts, but if you shut the door it was pitch black with what felt like a limited air supply. Dan turned on his cell phone for light while he prepared for sleep. It was then that he was struck with the most fearful thought he had thought in years.

He did not have his cell phone cable… or charger.

Later, he would realize he couldn't get one for another four hundred years.

– Chapter 6 –
Lessons, Just in Time

Time is an elusive thing. You can't hold it in your hand; it seems to slip away from you; you never have it when you need it; and when you don't need it, you have too much of it on your hands. So maybe you can hold it in your hand... or maybe it's just sticking to your hand like peanut butter.

Waiting in the doctor's reception area lengthens time. Playing World of Warcraft shortens time. This is known as the Elastic Interval Enigma.

Although Einstein called it relativity.

Dan's life was now to be completely controlled by time; all of his thoughts, actions, and plans could be interrupted at any time, by running out of time.

Kinda like the rest of us.

When Dan awoke the next morning, the first thing he noticed was the crick in his back from being folded into a closet. The second thing he noticed was how good the air smelled. There was a smell of burning wood, but beyond that the air was fresh and pure—at least compared to what he was accustomed to breathing.

Then Dan noticed other smells: bacon and eggs and fresh bread. He had never remembered breakfast smelling this delicious before. Perhaps it was the very clean air or the fact that he was very hungry; very, very hungry.

Being reduced to one's component bits and traveling 500 years into the past tends to put an edge on one's appetite.

When he entered the dining area, Dan saw Freddie sitting down to breakfast. By the light of day the little old man looked a little less old, but undoubtedly still little. Definitely under 5' 4". Dan remembered that a hundred years ago people were smaller, but of course that is one of those things every generation says about the last century's inhabitants as a way to make themselves feel better about the crappy era they're living in.

"Good morning, Dan. Join me for breakfast?" The little man gestured at the plates of eggs, bacon, and bread.

"Absolutely. It smells delicious." He sat opposite Freddie at the sturdy table.

"I was getting ready to make porridge when I remembered the post-jump hunger."

"That's normal, is it?" Dan was already stuffing a piece of aromatic brown bread slathered in butter into his mouth.

"It is. When all of the nourishment in your system has been drained to power the jump, it takes a toll. If you travel thousands of years, *that's* when you get really hungry."

"Is that all the energy it takes to jump? I mean, I was thinking some kind of quantum, fusion, plasma, nuclear, wormhole thingie."

"Exactly. Your understanding of time travel is better than I expected."

"Is it?"

"Yes. The atoms of the food are drawn into the quantum vortex, transformed into pure plasma by nuclear fusion, and that powers the wormhole you travel through."

"Of course." Dan slathered more butter on the bread, and then some jam. "Where did you learn all this?"

"From other jumpers. When you travel long enough, you're bound to run into a few."

"Given the size of time, it being eternal and all, I would think that very unlikely."

"Ahh, but you've forgotten the human element, you see."

"Have I?"

"Yes. Jumpers have, at the very least, unconscious influence on their destination. Do you think it's a coincidence you landed in a bog outside of London, not far from the Globe Theatre?"

"Shakespeare lives here?"

"Not here precisely, but he does have a flat nearby. And yes, out of all the backwater, nothing's-happening-in-a-hundred-years places you could have landed, you came here."

"Is that why you came here?"

"In a nutshell."

"What's he like?"

"Who?"

"Shakespeare."

"I don't know."

"You don't know?"

"I've never met the man."

"You've been here for 27 years."

"You know how these things go. When I first arrived, I went right round to the Globe to ask him pointblank, 'Did you steal your plays from Bacon?'" (At this, Dan grabbed a fistful of bacon.) "But he was on holiday and not in. Realizing I was going to be stuck for a little while, I set up shop here, so I wouldn't starve until I could meet him."

"And?"

"It dawned on me he hadn't even written most of his plays yet and I should probably ask Bacon instead anyway." (At this, Dan grabbed another handful of bacon.) "But there's not even rudimentary public transport and it takes forever to earn enough to buy a horse."

"After 27 years you haven't accumulated enough income to buy a horse?"

"The wages here are outrageously low. I mean, the guilds used to regulate wages, but then all these Huguenots and Flemish started coming in and setting up their workshops outside the city limits and, well, wages are in the toilet. Damn Hugies taking jobs from good Englishmen, creating inflation and unemployment. Why don't they stay in Hugieland, where they belong?"

"So, no horse. You could walk there."

"On these roads? Do you know how long it's been since they've been properly maintained? Not since the Romans left. And don't get me started about walking on roads traveled by horses and oxen."

"But don't you make good money as a doctor?"

"Apothecary."

"That's a physician, isn't it?"

"An apothecary is *not* a physician. Wow, if I was a physician here, they get all the respect and customers. Mind you, I can lance and bleed a person as well as the next guy, but with the tools available I choose to do no harm. Plus, I didn't want to be accused of witchcraft by actually healing people. So in short, I never made it to London again."

"Never?"

"Never got around to it."

"You traveled through time to get here and never got around to it?"

"Kind of."

"Brilliant."

"Look, I had to wait for him to write the plays and then I lost my connection to the time field and the plays didn't seem that important. But now that I've got you here, I need to finish up."

"About time."

"Yeah, about that. You need to empty your pockets."

"Why?"

"Because you don't want to get caught with anything anachronistic, do you?"

"No, we wouldn't want that."

"Remember they hang witches around here. Well, maybe not here, but not far from here. You need a reasonable explanation for anything you're carrying."

Dan dutifully emptied his pockets—wallet, comb, Chapstick, pocketknife, and cell phone.

Freddie scrutinized each item carefully. "You should be able to get away with the knife. The comb is whale cartilage imported from the islands. Chapstick is softened beeswax for softening the skin, but the plastic container." Freddie scooped out the balm, placed it in a tiny wooden box, and tossed the plastic into the fire. "The wallet you can keep as well, but the cash, credit cards, and driver's license have to go."

"But I'll need money."

"Not that money you don't. There's no 'Bank of Chronology' to exchange it in. In the fireplace with it."

As Freddie tossed the cards and bills in the fireplace, Dan leaped up to retrieve them.

Freddie blocked him. "More trouble than it's worth."

"You've never tried replacing a driver's license."

"Out of all of time this is only helpful in four specific years."

"But I'll need that when I get home."

"That won't happen for some time."

"It won't?"

"You have to learn how to navigate time and that takes a while."

"How long?"

"Probably hundreds of jumps. Maybe thousands."

"Thousands." Dan was stunned.

"It should go faster if I help."

"Can you get me home?"

"I wish I could, but it's your jump. I'm only along for the ride."

"Thousands."

"Now the phone."

"What? It's brand new!"

"It's so new it hasn't been invented yet. We need to dispose of your phone."

"I need my phone."

"Until it loses power, then it's a paperweight."

He regarded the $1,000 phone. And thought of the missing charger. And lack of electrical plugs. "An *expensive* paperweight."

"Still. Well, could be useful." Freddie looked at the phone. "What does it do?"

"Do? It makes calls."

"Not here it doesn't. The problem with most technology is it's only good in the era that made it. Except brooms—always useful. Even when purification systems clean the environment to the microns, brooms are still the most humane way of driving away the hordes of purification system salespeople roving across the planet."

"It goes on the internet." He nodded in realization. "Right, no internet. It plays music. I've got thousands of songs in here."

"Right, because a portable orchestra won't get you stoned."

Freddie didn't mean stoned like you get at the tavern or in shops in Denmark.

"It takes pictures."

"That could be helpful. Does it have a disintegrator?"

Dan frowned. "On a cell phone?"

"Excuse me for forgetting what year your technology was adopted. There's too much. Even the big stuff gets muddled. Do you know when the electric light was invented?"

"I know it was invented by Edison."

"No, it happened before Edison was born."

Dan instinctively pressed Google to verify that claim—but there was only a blank screen. This created a level of signal loss anxiety that continued to grow as the conversation moved on.

"So does your phone have a disintegrator?" Freddie asked.

"No."

"Too bad. A good disintegrator is always useful to a time traveler."

"Wait—are you saying cell phones will have disintegrators?"

"For a while."

"Why?"

"Someone decided the only way to stop criminals and psychopaths was to arm everyone."

"Did it work?"

"Hundreds of lives were saved when criminals were stopped cold by disintegration."

"Hmmmmm."

"Unfortunately, thousands of lives were lost by drunk college students and angry drivers stuck in traffic. Accidental disintegrations alone killed more people than sharks, lightning, and splinters. Imagine sitting on your phone and instead of butt dialing Peru, you vaporize your lower extremities."

Dan shuddered and his sphincter tightened, which is the typical reaction of a sphincter at the thought of being vaporized.

The time period in question was later compared to the Old West, except rather than just draw and fire, there was turning it on, using a password and/or facial recognition software, and bringing up the app, then firing. Everyone wanted to be the fastest thumbs in the west.

Eventually, as in the Old West, people realized when everyone carried a weapon, the angry, mean, and unhinged terrorized everyone all the time, so they started taking measures to discourage anyone but the police and trained criminals from carrying killing devices. Just the way the Maker intended.

"What else does the phone do?" Freddie asked.

"Uhhh, it has games, clocks, timers, calculators and a flashlight."

"Flashlight? Excellent! Why didn't you start with that? There's a reason it was called the Dark Ages. Well not now, but it's still pretty dim."

"So I get to keep my phone?"

"For now. If anyone asks, it's a phosphorous glass from the Orient. Now. We need to get travel satchels ready."

"To go see Shakespeare or Bacon?"

"No, to time jump. Shakespeare will only take a couple of hours, but we need to be ready to jump."

"After 27 years you think you'll jump now?"

"No, I think *you'll* jump now. Jumps happen quickly until you learn to control them."

"How quickly?"

"Are you still here? Quickly. The first few time jumps usually last less than a day."

"Then I've got..." Dan had never been good at math under pressure. Wait, the phone had a calculator—

"We've got less than twelve hours, yes."

"What if I'd jumped last night?"

"I was listening outside of your door. You never jump while asleep."

"Why?"

"Not sure. Some say it's an alpha wave thing, some say the timestream is protecting jumpers."

"What do you say?"

"I say time jumping awake is dangerous enough."

The anxiety of the light bulb reasserted and Dan fondled the screen as Google tried futilely to connect. "Really. Who invented the light bulb?"

"Humphry Davy."

"Who?"

"Maybe we'll meet him sometime. Prioritize, Dan."

Freddie pushed a cabinet aside, revealing a hole in the wall. Reaching deeply into the gap, he pulled out a metal box, then removed a key from inside his shirt. Carefully opening the box, he extracted a collection of trinkets and doodads, stuffing them into his pockets.

Then Dan saw something he recognized. "Are those—computer cables?"

"Computer, cell phone, printers, and devices of all kinds."

"But you don't have the devices?"

"No."

"Then why do you have them?"

"Why does anyone?"

It's a well-established fact that once a civilization reaches the computer age, it begins drowning in obsolete device cables. The device breaks and the cable goes into a drawer, with a belief you will reuse or recycle it.

This will never happen.

As a result, millions of cables are eventually jettisoned into space, which means, according to Einstein, they are also floating in time.

Freddie handed Dan a cable. "This may fit your phone."

"Great. Show me the nearest outlet and we're in business."

"We may have one by tomorrow."

"One can only hope."

"Of course, there could also be cannibal mutates."

"There could?"

"Yes. Just one of a thousand good reasons to have a disintegrator in your phone."

Point of fact: on every planet, there are, sooner or later, cannibal mutates. There is always some causation involving toxic waste, radioactive material, insects, or mystical forces beyond our ken. Don't bother fighting against the idea, it's just how it is. The same is true of the living dead.

It happens.

Luckily, neither experience lasts long: if they are unsuccessful, they are all killed; if they are successful, they run out of food. This is true of every world but one. Tennore is a living dead world, where the terminally ill go to continue to exist. The planet is protected by a satellite projected anti-technology field and new citizens take a one-way pod trip to the planet where they are soon either infected or eaten.

You would think this option wouldn't be taken often, but with an infinite number of beings in the universe, the planet is well stocked with new citizens and fresh entrées.

In addition, many major health insurance companies now require this, rather than expensive terminal treatment. They consider it a humane solution to the problem of high cost health care.

Freddie produced shoulder bags for them both and stowed dried meat, firm cheese, a small bed roll, and a water pouch inside. Soon they were both outfitted with the finest of time jumping gear the early Renaissance had to offer—which it turns out was not much.

Next, he provided Dan with time neutral (relatively) clothing and a hooded cloak. Dan put them on over his coveralls.

Geared up, they walked out of Freddie's home. Dan had not seen the building well the night before, but it was a stone structure with a thatched roof. Dan thought it looked a little shabby for an apothecary until he recalled the low wages situation.

Freddie turned back to regard the place that had served as home. "Well, house, thank you for keeping me mostly dry and nearly warm in the winter and out of the sun in the summer."

"Do you always talk to your house?"

"Yes, but usually it talks back."

Dan thought of his Alexa back home and felt a twinge of melancholy at never speaking to her again. Perhaps the thought of losing Siri as well was why he didn't want to give up his phone—if his phone ever functioned again.

Two townsmen rolled up to the pair in a small wagon pulled by a small donkey. The smaller of the two men spoke.

"Well, sir, we couldn't find hide nor hair of your horse and no sign of your cart. The bog must have swallowed them up."

Freddie answered for them. "Likely. Arthur, you've always liked my house, haven't you?"

The man nodded. "Aye, you're lucky to have a home of your own."

"How would you like to live here?"

"I couldn't afford it."

"Sure you can. I'm going away for a while, gonna travel the world. If you take care of it and keep it nice, you can stay here for half the rent you're paying now."

"Half my rent?"

"Half. I want someone I can trust to keep it up."

"I'm yer man."

"I thought so. Just send the rent to Berenberg Bank every month until I return."

"Yes, sir."

"And I need to borrow your wagon for a day or two."

"My wagon?"

"Yes. I'm going to London. There's a livery near The Globe Theatre. I'm afraid I'll probably have to leave it there."

"I have to go to London to get it back?"

"You're getting my house."

He considered the exchange. "Fair enough."

Arthur handed over the reins and Dan and Freddie boarded the rickety wagon. Arthur walked up the path to the front door, admiring his new acquisition.

As they rode away, Dan was curious. "Do you expect to collect that rent?"

"Eventually."

"Interest compounded for a hundred years."

"Or a thousand."

"Why Berenberg Bank?"

"Because they'll still be around."

Dan took in that helpful bit of information. "How many times have you traveled to?"

"Not so many. A couple hundred."

"That's 'not so many'?"

"Some have traveled to thousands—tens of thousands."

"I would think that would be very difficult. Doesn't it get very tiring when you get to… you know, your age?"

"The timestream keeps you young. When you enter a jump, the timestream begins to reset your age to when you first entered the stream."

"So if you spend 27 years in that village… ?"

"The timestream can bring me back to age 26."

"When you first went in."

"Exactly."

"So when we come out of the time jump, you may be…"

"Younger than you."

"How old are you?"

"A lady never tells her age."

"But you're a man…" He tilted his head and squinted at his companion. "Aren't you?"

"Looks can be deceiving. You've seen how women are treated here."

"Actually, I haven't. Other than a waitress at the tavern and a couple of women in the street..."

By now they were out of the little hamlet and on the open road, as much as you could call a larger rutted dirt path an open road. The Romans constructed long lasting roads in England during their visit in 180 AD, mostly for their soldiers to march round the place as quickly as possible. But some places weren't worth marching around so those roads stunk.

The hamlet had been one of those places.

This road was a rural, less traveled path, with no side ditches or drainage. There were trees on either side to provide shade and many plants that might or might not be poison oak.

But probably were.

"Trust me, being a woman here sucks," Freddie said. "The only way to maintain any independence was to be a man."

"And the beard is... ?"

"False, obviously."

"Obviously."

Dan had a hard time wrapping his mind around Freddie being a woman. He'd only known her a day but had been very confident in her maleness. In fact, there were many times in his life he had been less confident in his own maleness than he was of Freddie's.

– Chapter 7 –
Drunk Shakespeare

The ride had been quiet as Dan digested the change in his companion's status. Traveling through time with a man who looked to be in his seventies was one thing. Traveling with a 26- year-old woman was quite another. This presented all kinds of new complications. Separate sleeping accommodations chief among them. But what if she didn't want separate sleeping accommodations?

Dan's image of Freddie was a 70-year-old man. Turning that into a woman was not easy or pleasant.

Even worse: what if she turned out to be pretty and he was attracted to her? He remembered how difficult it was just traveling to Las Vegas with Jeneane; traveling to the 16th Century would have been a nightmare. Luckily, then Freddie spoke.

"I thought women were supposed to be equals in your age."

"They are."

"Equals or supposed to be?"

"Both."

"The woman thing is freaking you out."

"I'm not freaked out by women."

"Then you'd be the first man who wasn't."

"I just wasn't expecting you to be a female was all."

"I don't think my father was either, hence the name Freddie. You could pretend I'm a man if you want."

"Will you keep the beard?"

"At least while we're here."

Strangely, that comforted Dan immensely. "What do I need to learn to control my jumps?"

"Everything there is to know about jumping."

"Is that a lot?"

"Yes, but mostly it's about learning to relax and stay focused on the jump. You need to learn to be a Zen master of the timestream."

"But, my brain gets shredded in there."

"Thus the reason it takes so long to learn."

The two rode for some time while Dan tried to sort out more questions, many that didn't make much sense. Among the questions were such things as:

Is time really a giant shredder?

Can you go to the beginning of time?

Can you land underwater?

Can you get enough control to do a gastronomical tour of history's fine restaurants?

Is it possible to live forever by time jumping?

Can you go back in time to keep yourself from getting married?

What's David Hasselhoff like?

If you took a martini into the timestream, would it be shaken or stirred?

Before he knew it, they were entering London.

Most people believe The Globe Theatre is in Stratford-upon-Avon, which the locals call Stratty as Stratford-upon-Avon was a bit much to write on a sewage payment check.

If they had checks.

Or much of a sewage system.

But Shakespeare was only born there. They didn't even get a theatre for a couple hundred years and that was to cash in on the Shakespeare connection.

The Globe was in London. And they didn't have much of a sewage system either. It was smelly, crowded, and plague ridden. Dan could see why Freddie chose to live outside of the city.

Suddenly Freddie froze. "Holy mother!!" Quickly she spun around to face Dan.

Dan, of course, recognized the universal reaction of running into someone you have negative history with and thus desperately wish to evade. He experienced this last week, when he spotted Jeneane's parents at the farmer's market.

"What?"

"That's Chantell."

"And Chantell is?"

"Another jumper."

"Another jumper?"

"Remember when I said some jumpers have had tens of thousands of jumps?"

"Yes?"

"Chantell." She peeked over her shoulder, then turned away again. The wagon continued moving forward down the road.

"So why are we avoiding her?"

"Because I've met Chantell—many times—and she told me the story of her jump here."

"And?"

"I'm not in it."

"But you are."

"But I wasn't in the story. This is before she's ever met me."

"Is this one of those time conundrum things?"

"Yes. Best to not get into it."

"Which one is she?"

"The gorgeous one."

Across the way there was a dark, raven-haired beauty that stood out, even at quite a distance. She was surrounded by well-dressed young men.

"Are you sure that's her? She's pretty far away."

"It's Chantell. No matter what time you're in or where in the universe, you'll always know Chantell."

"I wish I could meet her."

"Like every man, but you'll get your chance. Sooner or later every jumper meets Chantell."

Dan watched as the woman strolled around the corner to head another direction. The cluster of men followed in her wake like hypnotized lemmings. "It looks like she's turning off."

"Good. I'd like to find Shakespeare before you jump. We're here." Freddie stopped the wagon in front of a stable and passed the proprietor some instructions and coin.

As they walked along the south bank of the River Thames, Dave spotted the Globe Theatre—one of the larger structures in town, an amphitheater, three stories tall, with a roof over the spectator seating, like a little Coliseum. Above the main entrance was inscribed "Totus mundus agit histrionem."

(That's Latin for "The whole world is a playhouse," but Dan did not know Latin. He barely made it through high school Spanish 101. It pays to know a second language, but not Latin. Unless you're a time traveler.)

Dan automatically started to head toward the theatre, but Freddie veered to the left. This left Dan confused.

"That's the Globe over there, isn't it?"

"Yes, but Shakespeare is this way."

Dan followed. "How do you know where he is?"

"I have learned a thing or two about him while I've been here."

Soon they reached a pub, which was a galleried coaching inn in London. One might say it was The George Inn, because that was a place Shakespeare liked to frequent and they staged his plays in the courtyard, so we'll say that's where they stopped.

Freddie looked sidelong at Dan. "You didn't suppose anyone could whip up 'Midsummer Night's Dream' sober, did you?"

Score one point for the idea Shakespeare wrote his own plays.

Going inside, they spotted the Bard sitting at a corner table with a mug of ale in one hand and a quill in the other. He was hard to miss, surrounded as he was by crumpled sheets of paper on the table and floor.

Dan was nonplussed. "It's actually him."

"That was the plan, wasn't it?"

"Sort of."

"Not sort of. Exactly. Come on."

The first thing Dan noticed was William looked real. Not the bust or painting real, but the blotchy skin, bad hair day kind of real that comes from spending most of the previous night in a tavern.

The second thing he noticed was the distinct lack of the ubiquitous Elizabethan collar. Apparently when he wasn't getting his portrait done, he dressed rather normally.

Freddie spoke. "Mr. Shakespeare."

He did not look up as he replied. "Call me Bill."

"Bill. Firstly, I'm a big fan of your work."

"Everyone is."

"True, but to be fair, you don't have much real competition."

"True."

"I wanted to ask you a question about Francis Bacon."

With that, Bill looked up from his writing, rather cross. "Hell, him again? If he sent you round here to pester me again, tell him to bugger off. I'm not interested in turning his thoughts about science and philosophy into performance."

"No, no, he didn't send us… Wait, he what?"

"He wants me to write a play based on his ideas of science and nature. Can you imagine anything so boring? He even wrote a couple of dramas himself, horrible things, all talky and going nowhere. I told him to burn them. Stick to your damn essays, I told him, but no. He's got the theatre bug and can't cast it off."

"Unbelievable."

"And this is a man they say is on track to direct our country. I wouldn't trust him to direct a revival of 'Oedipus Rex.'"

Shakespeare died in 1616. The Merriam-Webster Collegiate Dictionary says "revival" was first used in 1651. So while

Shakespeare did not say "revival," that's what Dan and Freddie heard.

Dan suddenly became concerned they had broken the creative flow of the greatest writer in history. "Can we buy you a drink?"

Bill grunted. "Someone should."

After a round, or perhaps four, Bill was writing away furiously, perhaps a scathing indictment of the aristocracy in which most of them would die. Dan was using precious battery life to take selfies of himself and Shakespeare.

By the time Freddie and Dan left The George Inn, morning had turned to afternoon and was creeping into evening. Dan felt a little wobbly and sought a place to sit down. He found a small fountain and sat at its edge.

Freddie sat beside him. "You feel all right?"

"How much alcohol is in that ale?"

"More than you're used to."

"Apparently. Does it normally make everything smell blueish?"

"Not normally." Freddie scooted a little closer to him.

"Do you think they serve haddock here?"

She moved closer yet.

"And I hear music."

"What kind?"

"Could be Procol Harum."

"When did you hear that last?"

"When I time jum—"

Suddenly Freddie wrapped her arms around him.

And the world began to lose its hold on them.

– Chapter 8 –
I Smell Cold

Traveling through time was difficult in the best of circumstances. This was not the best of circumstances. When two people enter the timestream together, both are shredded into their component bits. Who you are is mixed into who they are. Dan was now sharing memories with an older female time traveler, who had very peculiar memories.

Freddie found herself sharing memories with a 32-year-old plumber from Pacoima.

As the timestream reintegrated them, Dan lost most of Freddie's memories. For which he was thankful. Retaining the memory of making love to several men might have caused him to question his maleness again.

What he did retain was the impression that Freddie, for everything else she was, was a nice person. For which he was thankful.

As they emerged from the timestream, Dan noticed Freddie's arms wrapped tightly around him and thought she did feel rather feminine. Then they hit the snow.

"Ouuffffff."

They both let out a lungful of air.

Freddie spoke. "Snow. I hate snow landings."

"At least they're soft."

"So's a bear when you land on it." Freddie's voice seemed a little higher than before.

Dan noticed several objects on the ground. "My tools!" He began picking up the tools that he had had in his tool belt before the last jump.

Freddie watched him retrieve the accessories. "They must have fallen into the bog when you landed."

"But why are they here?"

"Whatever you initially take into the timestream generally follows you into the next. Mostly, it's the timestream protecting itself. It's very tidy that way."

"Leave nothing but footprints."

"Something like that."

He tucked the tools into his tool belt. "Where do you think we are?"

"Someplace cold."

"That's it?" Dan tried to sniff out a clue, taking a deep breath through his nose.

Freddie took notice. "Smell anything?"

"I smell cold."

"Let's look around." After looking around for several minutes, Freddie changed her assessment. "Someplace fucking cold."

And Dan agreed with her. He was extremely grateful for the extra clothes and hooded cloak—even if the wind cut right through them.

There was snow. Lots of snow. And ice. Everything was covered in one or both. There were rocks covered in snow, hills covered in snow, and trees covered in snow. There may have been more things as well, but Dan and Freddie could not tell because the potential things were covered in snow. And ice.

"We need to find shelter," she said.

"I'm hungry."

"Of course you are. We'll eat when we're out of the cold."

Seeing a small hill, they headed up the incline to get the lay of the land. Their feet punched into two feet of snow along the way, leaving deep footprints. Tiny shards of ice hung from the tree branches. From the apex they could see no roads or settlements. No buildings or any sign of civilization at all, just trees and rocks…

… and snow.

Deciding the rocky areas would be their best bet, they headed to an outcropping about a half-mile away. The actual journey felt considerably further.

Freddie muttered to herself. "And I wanted out of the Elizabethan age."

Dan noticed the hair sticking out of Freddie's hood was now black with some gray—in contrast to the full gray of her beard. "At least you're younger."

"Am I?"

"Yes."

"How much?"

"I'd have to see you without the beard."

"It's the only thing keeping my face warm." Freddie pulled her hand out of her cloak and stared at it. "Fewer spots. Best guess, my 40's."

"Do you feel younger?"

"Nope, I just feel cold."

Dan looked more closely at her face and noticed that her nose and cheeks were pinker, but that was probably the frostbite setting in.

The outcropping was a bit of a disappointment as it only protected them on two sides. They cleared a camp and ultimately built a snow wall to provide more shelter from the cold. They scavenged wood and used Dan's micro welding torch to start a fire. They were still cold, but no longer freezing. Eating some of the food Freddie packed made Dan feel a little better.

It was evening and starting to get dark.

Dan was thankful the fire was going. "I wonder when we are. Do you think it's the Ice Age?"

"Doesn't feel cold enough to be the Ice Age," said Freddie. "It could be anytime, just someplace cold."

"What should we do?"

"I might be able to get us a location by the stars—if they come out."

"I wonder what brought us here."

"We may never know. Sometimes you're drawn thousands of years to a person or event you never get to see."

"That's depressing."

"Sometimes it's worse."

"Really?"

"Sometimes it's snowing."

"Perfect."

"At least there are no cannibal mutates."

"Yet."

"Point taken."

"So what time are you originally from?" Dan imagined her from some futuristic world.

"I was born in 1908."

"Really?"

"Timewise, we're next door neighbors."

"Give or take a century."

"Which time does."

"What was it like?"

"What was what like?"

"Living then."

"Exciting. The Great War, the Roaring Twenties, women getting the vote. Then it all went to hell with the Depression. Every step toward gender equality went backwards. I'm glad I got out when I did in 1934."

"Were you married?"

"Engaged, but the stock market crash put the whole thing on hold, then it kinda petered out." Freddie paused a moment and looked at Dan. "It's kinda nice talking to someone who knows what I'm talking about. You do know what I'm talking about?"

"Yeah, World War One, the Crash of '29. At least you got out before Harlow and Lombard died."

Her eyes widened in astonishment. "Harlow and Lombard died?? You mean young? When?"

"I assumed you knew."

"I've learned a lot of the big stuff, World Wars Two and Three. Computers, outer space, but I miss a lot of the basic stuff."

"I'll tell you what, you give me an overview of things I need to know from the future and I'll give you details from the 20th Century."

"Deal. It's kinda like finally getting to see how a book you've been waiting a long time to finish turns out."

"Like *Gone with the Wind*?"

"Like what?"

"Sorry. That came out in 1936."

"Was it good?"

"It won a Pulitzer."

"You can give me a synopsis."

"That'll take a while."

"There are a lot of books I haven't got round to."

"Well, all of time has a lot of books."

"And you might want to know about other planets."

"Other planets?"

"Yes, you're not locked into just the Earth. Anywhere mankind has visited could pull you in."

Dan thought about that. "And those other planets, do they have, ummm. Are there… ?"

"Other life forms?"

"Yes."

"Yes."

"So I could just…" He waved a hand.

"Pop in on an alien?"

"Could I?"

"You could."

"My."

"It's pretty rare, though. Space is so vast, most races don't acquire interstellar travel until they are near their civilization's end; and those that do have a lot of universe to cover before they meet anyone else."

"So is it possible tomorrow we could find ourselves on another planet?"

"It could happen."

He shook his head in dismay. "I don't think I'm ready for that."

"Two days ago you weren't ready for time travel."

"I'm not ready for time travel. It's not like I volunteered. I'd rather stick to the Earth for a while."

"Then you're definitely going to need to control your jumps. Getting to where you want to go is great, but being able to stay someplace a little longer or get the hell out of the snow early is even better."

"What do I need to do?"

"First, it's easier to hold off a jump than make one happen. It's hard to reenter the timestream right away. It's like the power has to rebuild. Focus on the sensations you feel when you jump, try to feel anything like them."

Dan tried for several minutes but got nowhere. "I can hardly remember what it feels like."

"The time scramble does that. Didn't expect much. That will come with time. When you start to jump, you can try to stay focused on where you are to stay there longer. We can't really practice that until you jump. For now, we'll focus where you'll land. Think of a place you'd like to go and work on getting the details sharp. Make the picture in your head like the picture on your shelf. Add smells and sensations if you can."

Dan tried for what felt like an hour, but was closer to fifteen minutes. It's hard to think of anything other than frostbite at those temperatures. "I can't focus. Too cold."

"That's okay."

They were silent a moment before Freddie spoke.

"So what happened to Jean Harlow?"

For the next few hours they talked about the 20th Century and the future of the planet while huddling over a fire, before falling asleep.

When Dan awoke the next morning freezing, Freddie was tending the fire. Dan pulled closer to the flames. It didn't help much.

The wind had died down and they could see more clearly. There was no sign of roads or settlements, but they could see a small mountain in the distance that might enable them to get a good lay of the land. Or warmer shelter. Freddie showed Dan how to create makeshift snowshoes from plant material.

The walk was not particularly arduous; however, it was exhausting. They spent most of the morning getting to the mountain. They spent much of the afternoon climbing. The climb was not particularly steep, but it was exhausting.

Looking off in the distance, Dan thought he saw something. "Look, over that way."

"Which way?"

"That way."

"By the trees?"

"No, the dark spot." He pointed northward. Not that Dan had any idea it was northward, but it actually was.

Looking towards the dark spot, Freddie thought it looked out of place—different from the surrounding landscape. It may have been different colored rock, a shadow, or a fuselage of a Boeing 747. There was only a slim chance that it was anything, but it was the only thing that they saw that was potentially something.

Dan looked at the dark spot. "Well what now?"

"I saw what looked like a pretty good place to camp near the bottom of the hill. I think we should climb down and make camp for the night."

"So that's it? We slogged all this way so we can discover a dark spot and then go to sleep."

"Now you're beginning to understand time jumping. We won't have time to do much more than climb down the hill before it gets dark and we need to set up camp."

"I can see why you don't like snow."

"I like swamps even less."

"I'm not too fond of bogs myself."

They didn't talk much during the descent as they were mostly preoccupied with not falling. Once they reached the bottom, they found the place Freddie had spotted on the way up. It was a large indentation that, although not a cave, would afford them shelter on three sides. By then it was starting to get dark so they hastily moved snow and set up camp.

This camp was more protected and warmer than the one they had the previous night. Which is to say they were mildly protected and pretty damn cold.

Dan started thinking about tomorrow's hike to the dark spot. "Do you think we'll find anything tomorrow?"

"Probably not."

"Then why are we walking all the way? Why don't we stay here until we jump?"

"Because we *might* find something. If we don't jump soon, we'll run out of food or freeze."

"Have you gotten any better idea of where we are?"

"A little. From the position of the sun, I say northern hemisphere. I'm thinking Greenland, Alaska, Nova Scotia, Norway, maybe Russia. It's cold but not *really* cold so I'm thinking it's not winter or we'd be in real trouble."

"That's as close as you can get?"

Never mind that Freddie had eliminated 95% of the planet. "And what have you deduced?"

"That I don't like snow."

"Now you sound like a jumper."

"I wonder why we're here?"

"Maybe Man is discovering fire in that little dark spot, or maybe after the robot uprising all that's left of mankind is just over the next hill."

"There's a robot uprising?"

"There's always a robot uprising. Luckily, robots like snow even less than we do."

It is a near universal truth that robots hate snow. On every inhabited planet that has developed artificial life, robots hate snow—even on the planets that don't have snow. Two of the quickest ways to kill a mechanical creature is to get it very cold or very wet.

Snow is both.

This is further proven by the fact that there never has been a successful robot uprising on an ice planet. Generally the robots cease to function before they can kill more than one or two million humanoids. At which point the best they can do is sit under a blanket or beside a warm fire waiting for the humans to hit them with an ax.

It was at about this point Dan recognized he was singing to himself. "One of sixteen vestal virgins who were leaving… "

Freddie interrupted. "Who sings that?"

"Procol Harum."

Freddie turned her head to the side looking at him. Dan turned his head to the side and nearly fell over.

Freddie rushed over and wrapped her arms around him. "Think about where you want to go."

This time Dan realized why Freddie had locked him in a bear hug. He wrapped his arms around her and held on. Swordfish swam in his vision.

They stood there like that for 20 or 30 seconds before it started to get a little weird.

Dan spoke. "Do you think it's a false alarm?"

"Maybe, or maybe you—"

She was interrupted by a lack of false alarm.

- Chapter 9 -
A Forest for the Trees

The couple slipped into the timestream. Dan was not sure if being more prepared was easier or if he was getting accustomed to having his body disassembled. He almost managed to keep his thoughts together and his stomach in one place.

When he and Freddie's minds touched, he could actually make sense of more of her memories and was slightly more able to block out the ones he didn't want to see.

When Dan's bits were back where they belonged, he sheepishly let go of Freddie and immediately noticed her age had once again decreased and her femininity once again increased. Freddie was more interested in the jump itself.

"That was less nauseating than last time. I hope this means you're getting the hang of it." At the sound of her own voice, she paused. Inspecting her hands, she smiled. "How old do I look?"

"About 70."

Freddie pulled at her whiskers and peeled away her beard. "Now?"

Dan knew she was a woman and that she was younger than she first appeared. He was nevertheless quite surprised to see her without the beard. "Wow."

"That's a good answer."

Her hair was now blacker with a little grey and her features fine, yet she looked like she could handle herself. She looked to be in her 40's and was still a knockout. Totally out of Dan's league and he knew it.

"I'd say you're 40ish," he said. He was thinking 48, but knew better than to say it.

"And yet 'wow.'"

"I call them as I see them."

Freddie surveyed their surroundings. "Where are we?"

They appeared to be in a forest—the smell of leaves was the strongest either of them had ever smelled before. Other than that time Dan got stuck in a maple tree.

It was no longer evening. From the chill in the air and the shadows on the ground, Freddie was thinking it was morning and she was quite correct. From the color of the leaves on the trees, she was thinking it was fall and she was quite correct. From the clean smell of the air, she was thinking it was a pre-Industrial period; in this she was quite incorrect.

"Well, it's not snowing." Dan was definitely paying more attention to his environment.

"Let's see if we can find civilization."

"We can't do any worse than last time."

"Unless there are cannibal mutates."

"Agreed."

They set out and walked some way with no sign of anyone. There were birds, squirrels and insects, but no people. They continued on. Dan was disappointed there was nothing time travelly here.

Freddie, on the other hand, was thrilled that they were not in a dead world. Or, perhaps worse, a cloned dinosaur world. A T-Rex can definitely ruin your day.

Dan was starting to pay more attention to his empty belly than cautious navigation when he stumbled upon a path. And when I say stumbled, he physically stumbled. Coming out of the brush, it was a step down to the path, yet Dan took several extra steps so that he could meet the path face first.

"Owww."

"Oh, you've found a path."

"Does that mean people?"

"In this case it means deer."

"So it's not real helpful."

"It could be. If there are people around here and they're looking for deer, we're in the right place."

He picked himself up and dusted his trousers, aiming for a cool demeanor. "That's a lot of ifs."

"Is two a lot?"

"It can be."

"Also, deer tend to travel to water sources on a daily basis. The way I see it, following the deer path increases our chances of finding water which increases our chance of finding people."

"I'm feeling better about my discovery then."

Following the deer path, they seemed to go even deeper into the forest, although they really had no way of knowing, as forest is forest. But for the sake of argument let's say there was more of the forest and normally you would think that is deeper in the forest but in this case density does not equal deepness. They were, in fact, nearly out of the forest.

But not out of the woods.

As the trees grew closer together, the sky filtering through the pines started to disappear and it got darker. Night dark. In order to see, Dan pulled out his phone. That was when he noticed the very odd thing.

"I have signal."

"What?"

"My phone has signal."

Freddie stepped over to look at his phone. "You have signal."

"That's what I said."

"That means we're post-2000 but before cell phones were outlawed in 2163."

"Cell phones were outlawed in 2163?"

"Yeah. It turns out they were more addictive than heroin."

"I can see that."

The addictive properties of cell phones were so severe they came closer to destroying the human race than disease, famine, war, nuclear annihilation, or cannibal mutates. No one wanted to do daily tasks when they could be fighting World War II with laser rifles. Once three-dimensional realism was truly achieved by projecting images directly onto your retina, the real world was less real than the virtual one.

The human race began to degenerate into entertainment addicts and virtually (and nonvirtually) everything was run by computers and robots. If not for the robot rebellion of 2160, mankind would have ceased to exist within two generations.

Thank goodness for the evil robots.

Dan and Freddie continued to push their way through the very thick forest until the trees were so dense they could not pass. Dan decided to climb a tree to see if he could get a better view. It turned out he could. In fact, as he climbed upward, the branches thinned out and he had an unobstructed view for miles—just past the giant plastic dome.

"What do you see?" called Freddie.

"A dome."

"On a building?"

"No, on us." Dan struggled to find his way back down again. "There's a dome on us."

"On the whole forest?"

"Pretty much."

"It must be a biosphere."

"Must be."

"In the 22nd Century biospheres were created to protect the Earth's forests from all the crap mankind had put into the soil and the air over the centuries."

The idea was that after people cleaned up the planet, they could open up the biospheres to repopulate the Earth's flora and fauna. It turned out celebrating Earth Day once a year was not enough to do the job. It was later determined the planet would've needed to celebrate Earth Day 347 days of the year to reverse the environmental damage.

Luckily, this is exactly what our robotic overlords did in 2185 as they preferred the planet the way it was supposed to be.

Freddie was keen on leaving the artificially perfect environment. "We need to find the door."

"It seems pleasant here to me. No rain, no snow, comfortable temperatures…"

"And how do we explain our presence here if someone finds us?'

"Well, we just, uhhh…"

"Right. What are we doing trespassing in a sealed biosphere created to save the planet?"

"Surprise inspection?" Dan was pleased with his answer.

"I'm sure that will go over gangbusters."

"If there are people tending the forest, then there have to be access trails."

"Right. They have to make sure there was no blight or insect problems."

"So if this is a circular dome, then traveling from the wall to the opposite direction should eventually lead us to a central path."

"We've already walked for miles. How big is this place?" Freddie was considering climbing a tree to see for herself, but she couldn't quite remember she was no longer an old man.

"Bigger than most cities."

"What's to keep us from getting lost?"

"There's a compass on my phone."

By using Dan's phone to get a bearing, they were able to move towards the center of the dome. Hours later they located a small path through the forest. From the tire tracks in the soil, it was obvious that it led to civilization or at least an exit.

They might have been less thrilled at finding the path if they'd known someone else had also found them.

Alden was a tall thin man with a world-weary demeanor that was truly justified.

He was in Biodome 16 Central Monitoring, examining soil moisture when he saw the anomaly. Each life form was monitored by the system and suddenly there were twelve more than yesterday. In a unit this size twelve births was not at all unusual, but when he went to add them into the system, he noticed two of them were over 100 pounds. If this were the Indian or African unit, it would be expected, but not in a North American facility.

Stowaways.

Stowaways were outsiders hoping to live off the land. Land that was the valued property of "Lifeinc" and therefore they were living off of "Lifeinc" (a licensed contractor for United Really the Best Guys Governments {formerly United Good Guys Governments}).

"Hey, Abernathy. Looks like the boat has a couple of stowaways."

From down the hall came Abernathy's voice. "Really?"

"Unless the deer are growing really fast."

Abernathy stuck her head in the doorway. Her hair was a bright enough red that even Alden automatically snapped around when he caught a glimpse of it. "Finally some action. I'm getting really sick of watching grass grow."

Watching grass grow was one of Abernathy's listed job duties.

Freddie and Dan were making good time traveling down the pathway. They had just come across an intersection with the main road through the center of the structure. Turning down the main road, they were startled by the sound of a roaring engine behind them. Spinning around, they saw a large frightening vehicle bearing down on them. They dove off the road inches before being plowed down.

Dan yelled the most lucid thing he could think of.

"Hey!"

The vehicle stopped and the roaring stopped. From an opening on top of the vehicle, out popped Abernathy with what looked like a large menacing weapon but was in fact a *very* large menacing weapon. Dan and Freddie scrambled for the trees. Abernathy aimed her weapon and prepared to pull the trigger but then Alden spoke.

"Wait! We can't hurt the trees."

She looked as if she wanted to throw the vehicle over the trees—and probably could. "Oh, right." She brushed the hair out of her eyes and raised her voice to semi-shout. "Could you come out of there for a little bit?"

Freddie responded from the trees. "So you can shoot us?"

"No, so we don't hurt the trees when we shoot you."

"I don't think so."

"Come on out. We are going to have to shoot you anyway so you might as well make it easy on the planet."

"The planet hasn't been making it very easy on me."

"Well that's not the planet's fault, is it? After all, we've been treating the old girl pretty badly."

Dan chimed in from the trees. "We're still not going to let you shoot us."

"Please?"

Seeing this was going nowhere, Alden stepped in. "Pursuant to section 6 of the URBGG/Lifeinc Agreement, all non-authorized personnel will be capitalized and their remains used to sustain the artificial environment."

"But we are authorized." Dan's voice was unexpectedly confident.

Alden blinked. "What?"

"We are authorized. We're here for secret inspection."

"Secret inspection?"

"Yes."

"But those are usually announced."

"Ahh, but this is a *surprise* secret inspection "

"That's never happened before."

"That you know of."

Freddie joined in the game. "There have been 37 surprise secret inspections of this facility. This would have been number 38 if Baker here hadn't gotten lost."

"You were lost as well," responded Dan.

"But I wasn't reading the map."

Abernathy was getting impatient. "So are we shooting them or not?"

"I vote not." Dan did have a sizable stake in the outcome.

Alden was weighing their options. "What about how you're dressed?" He was not ready to give in.

"Undercover. Helps us blend in."

"What are you inspecting?"

"Plumbing."

"No one's looked at the plumbing in decades."

"Then it's about damn time, don't you think?"

"What are you doing way out here?"

Freddie had expected this question. "We came in through the surprise secret inspectors' entrance and got turned around."

"Surprise secret inspectors' entrance?"

"You can't have a surprise secret inspection unless you have a way of getting in that is both surprising and secret."

"Hmmmmm."

"Come on. You might as well take us to base." Freddie climbed up on the humongous vehicle.

Dan followed suit. "Why do you need a vehicle this big?"

Abernathy set aside the weapon. "Because the government paid for it."

"Oh, well then." Dan settled on the edge of the vehicle.

Alden started the engine and it made a tremendous racket.

Dan covered his ears. "It doesn't sound very environmentally friendly."

"What?"

"IT DOESN'T SOUND VERY ENVIRONMENTALLY FRIENDLY."

"OH." Alden pushed a small button and the engine became silent. "That sound's just for effect."

Traveling along in this huge electric vehicle, it only took minutes to get to the other side of the dome. Then again, traffic was light.

They disembarked from the vehicle and entered the control center.

Alden eyed the two suspiciously. "So. Plumbing inspectors, ehh?"

Dan took the lead, pulling out a wrench. "Yes. Show us to your pressure valves."

Alden grunted and gestured to them to follow him. He was not sure of these "inspectors." "This way."

They headed further into the building and then down several flights of stairs before reaching a brightly lit airplane hangar-sized area of pipes, fittings, and valves.

Everything looked pristine, shiny, and new. Dan knew differently.

Following the water flow from the inlet to the shiny new pipes and valves, Dan tracked the water flow from the maze out towards the main habitat. The pipes left the brightly lit airplane hangar-sized area and entered one of several access tunnels that were dimly lit, slightly claustrophobic, and not at all shiny.

The look on Alden's face shifted to less doubt, more concern.

Continuing to follow water flow, Dan led them deep under the forest above. The air became moist and the ground became damp.

"Do you ever come down here?" Dan asked.

"Not if I can help it," said Alden.

"You better get used to it."

As they continued to walk, the ground went from damp to wet. Dan's boots sloshed and the soles began to stick and his feet began to slip inside the leather. Hiking shoes—like Alden and Abernathy wore—were at risk of getting lost in the muck. The suction slowed the two workers. Dan spotted several leaky joints and rusted pipes. He tapped the rusted pipes with his wrench and shook his head. Soon they were trudging through water.

"I've seen enough." With that, Dan reversed and started back out of the tunnel.

The others followed. The ground went from water to muddy muck to wet to damp until they emerged into the brightly lit airplane hangar-sized area of pipes, fittings, and valves.

Alden was most interested in Dan's findings. "What are you going to report?"

Freddie answered. "That depends on you."

"On me?"

"The way I see it, we can submit our report and you'll look negligent for such a monumentally poor maintenance job. What do you think it'll cost to fix this, Baker?"

"Oh, millions, perhaps even billions," Dan said. "That's if they can fix it before it collapses in on itself."

"Oh my, that doesn't sound good," said Freddie. "Of course if we submit that report, you'll probably mention that our surprise secret inspection is not so secret and that makes *us* look bad. It might be easier for everyone if you submit a report detailing this danger you just discovered."

Alden looked pale. "At a cost of billions of dollars, Lifeinc will have my ass."

"Depends," said Freddie. "Who is responsible for the cost of major repairs?"

"The URBBG."

"Then Lifeinc will charge them…"

"Billions of dollars!"

"And who becomes the hero of the bottom line?"

Alden looked less pale. "I do?"

"Now. Where's your crew quarters? We need some rest and some lunch." Freddie nodded. "Definitely lunch."

Alden showed them into the administrative facility, quarters and kitchen as Abernathy went back to work. Alden left the pair alone as he went to compose his plumbing report.

The crew quarters were large and spacious and housed absolutely no crew. Originally the facility had a staff of 25. Cutbacks over the years had shrunk personnel down to Abernathy and Alden, who were staying in private manager suites.

The kitchen was well-stocked, as with no natural predators there was an over surplus of venison and varmint meats. Fruits, vegetables, and meats were processed primarily by robots.

Surly little robots planning their revenge.

As they ate, Freddie recognized a newfound respect for Dan. "So what did you do for a living back in the 21st Century?"

"I'm a plumber."

"That's fantastic."

"Is it?"

"It is."

"I've never noticed."

"It's a great time jumping skill. No matter where or when you go, people need to move water and waste. The technology changes, but the basic process is always the same. That means if we ever need to earn money, you've got a skill that can do that."

"What's your profession? Apothecary?"

She smiled. "It has been. My father was a pharmacist. I wanted to be a surgeon but everyone was pushing me to be a nurse. I compromised and was studying to be a general practitioner for women when I started time jumping."

"I should think that would be more valuable."

"It helps, but in the past I have to hide a lot of what I know and in the future I don't know enough. A plumber, though, *that's* a time jumper's free pass."

"That's not an advantage I ever considered when I learned the trade."

"Well you need to think that way now. The way to stay alive is to learn things that will help you in the future or in the past. Oooooohhh, wireless charging. Put your cell phone on that pad."

Dan picked up the pad and waved it in the air. "It doesn't have a cord."

"That's why it's wireless. It absorbs energy directly out of its environment."

"That would be handy." He set the phone on the pad and watched it hum contentedly.

"If we can only trick time into letting us take this with us."

"Can you trick time?"

"It doesn't do well with riddles; it doesn't have much sense of humor. It is good with conundrums, though. You can take basic items like food and clothing into the timestream as well as anything you had when you first jumped. We just have to convince time that this is food or clothing."

"Is that all?"

"I have an idea." With that, she pulled out a small knife and neatly cut a section from her bag. Removing a needle and thread, she began sewing the charging pad into her bag like a patch.

Dan was impressed with her technique. "You'd have made a good seamstress."

"Or a surgeon."

"Touché. When do you think we'll jump?"

"No idea."

"So isn't it a 'we've done what we came for' kinda deal?"

"No, it's a 'we were here and now we're not' kinda deal."

"But if we're attracted to certain events in history…"

"Don't overthink it. Some things we change, some things we fix, sometimes we wander in the snow for a couple days." She completed the sewing project and stored the kit.

"So it doesn't matter what we do."

"Of course it matters. It matters what we do when we don't time jump. If you live a crappy life, you helped create a crappy world; if you live a good life, you helped create a good world. When you're a time jumper, you have the opportunity to make a crappier or gooder world than most people."

"So if I went back in time and used what I know for personal gain, would I be making the world crappy?"

"Depends on what you did with the personal gain. And if anyone else suffered because you made it. Buying stock or making a bet could make you a lot of money, but that means somebody else lost a lot of money."

"What if I won the money from organized crime bookies?"

"Then they'll find a way to get money from someone else and that someone else's life will be crappy."

"It's very complicated."

"Time is woven very carefully and we get to play with the threads."

"That's profound."

"I'm thinking about having it made into a tee shirt. Now if you'll excuse me, I'm long overdue for modern hygiene." And with that, she stepped into the women's locker room.

Freddie had her clothes robotically cleaned while she scrubbed a couple of decades of Elizabethan England from her body. She'd shed a few more years and was feeling good about herself. She didn't even mind putting her old coarse clothing back on. In general it's good to jump in clothes that don't stand out. Maybe she'd try to snag a Lifeinc jumpsuit for a modern era quick change.

Dan's shower was boring, although he did try to see if he'd aged. Given it had only been a few days since he escaped Pacoima, he was not impressed.

They replenished their supply of food and water, filling their satchels.

The rest of the night passed uneventfully as did the next day. Dan and Freddie walked through the forest, occasionally acting like they were inspecting something, but mostly getting close to the animals. The deer, squirrels, rabbits and other animals were completely unafraid of humans. Processing robots scared the shit out of them.

They spent the second night under the dome and had just started talking about leaving. Alden and Abernathy were beginning to wonder why they were still there. Freddie decided if they hadn't jumped by lunch, they would leave the conventional way.

This was not to be an issue.

At about 10 that morning Dan heard music and, strangely, fins flapping in his head. Paying careful attention, he noticed the smell of pine—no, Pine-Sol the all-purpose cleaner. He knew that all too well. When he was small his mother had washed the floors with it, so her plastic mop bucket absorbed the smell. Whenever he had the flu, she handed him the bucket and soon the sensation of nausea was associated with the odor of Pine-Sol—which meant he now became nauseous from holding the barf bucket.

Swallowing hard, Dan opened up his arms and Freddie reciprocated the gesture. No unexpected leaps, sudden grappling, or mental confusion. The jump was, while not smooth, at least less traumatizing.

– Chapter 10 –
A February 16th Space Lunch

Time is anything but predictable. Except when it is. Most jump locations are driven by the experiences of the person jumping, the racial memory of their planet, or the memory of the universe itself. And given that the universe is infinite, something must be fairly large to get it to notice.

The same way a car accident transforms rational people into looky-loos, any huge event attracts viewers—birth of a galaxy, end of a civilization, or explosion of a star. It always starts out the same way: enterprising scientist wants to study the phenomenon and sends a long-range telescope, which leads to a closer ranged telescope, which leads to an even more enterprising scientist to want to see it first hand, which leads to a space station, which leads to tourists.

Every decent cataclysmic event has a place to watch it.

Or ten.

The explosion of the Earth's sun, while not unique in the universe, is a significant event. It's equally as important as the Earth's birth and way cooler to watch. Besides, people missed being around for the birth by a few billion years so it wasn't widely celebrated.

Just so you know, Earth's birth was on March twenty-third. At the time there was no calendar as there were none of our usual ways to measure time, by earth rotations, moon phases or consistent orbit around the sun as none of these things existed. But trust me.

March twenty-third. I think it was a Thursday.

The end of our sun came on February nineteenth.

When Dan and Freddie reconstituted, they were on a space station. With no view ports or loss of gravity, Dan was not aware of his unearthly location. The wide, long hallway rather resembled the concourse underneath Shea Stadium without the hot dog vendor. Or the music.

What he was aware of was Freddie. Her hair had lost the last of its gray and her shape was definitely more feminine. Dan found himself standing next to the most stunning 26-year-old woman he had ever met. Even with her old baggy clothes. His tongue stopped working.

Freddie's didn't.

Freddie recognized the base immediately as SolWatch 3 or possibly 13 or 6. "This is brilliant!"

"You've been here before?" Dan said.

"A couple of times. It's the most important event in our solar system's history—at least that we can visit."

"What event?"

"The death of our sun."

"Our sun dies?"

"Of course it does."

"And it takes Earth with it?"

"No, that would be silly. Earth died millions of years ago."

"So we got pulled here to watch the Sun die?"

"The whole solar system really."

"Wait, then where are we?"

"In a space station."

"We're in space!!?" He looked around the hall again—and saw solid walls and no view ports. He would at least expect a neon sign proclaiming "Space" somewhere.

"Yes we're in space, but do catch up, we're in a SolWatch station to watch the sun explode."

"I'm in space... To watch the sun explode!"

"But that's not the main thing."

"It isn't?"

"Secondary at best. For us it's all about the Club 6.480..." She grabbed his shoulder and urged him to follow her down the long corridor.

"The Club 6.4 something, something, something?"

"The Club 6 4 for short." Freddie rounded a corner, and they saw a big neon sign. It didn't say "Space" but instead said—

"Club 6.480..." Dan read aloud.

A doorman stood outside holding a scanner. Dan thought the doorman looked like a movie star; this much was true. He also thought the doorman was a living, breathing, human being.

Dan was wrong on all three counts.

Freddie strode confidently to the entrance. "Albert, it is so good to see you."

"Ms. Townes, it is good to see you, but scuttlebutt has it you've lost the timestream."

"Vicious rumor, Albert. Just been visiting distant relatives."

"I am going to have to check you."

"Certainly. We can't have any straight timers inside, can we?"

Albert waved the scanner over her. It beeped mildly. "Hmmmm, that is a very low reading, Ms. Townes. Be careful; you might be on your way out."

"You know me, Albert. Always careful."

"Yes." Albert did not sound fully convinced.

"Dan, this is Albert. Albert, Dan Baker."

"Pleased to meet you," said Dan.

Albert waved the scanner over Dan. The scanner beeped loudly. "Welcome, Mr. Baker. We are always pleased to find new members."

"Thank you, I—"

Freddie yanked him into the room.

Albert watched them enter, then typed a message onto his data pad.

Inside was a luxurious lounge filled with comfy chairs, comfy chairs, comfy chairs (there were a lot of them) and tables.

There was a bar, sandwich platter, and a variety of gaming machines, with everything from pinball to atomic hammer drop. Tucked in a corner was an ATM for the Berenberg Bank.

A handful of patrons idled about. Dan thought the club was having a slow day, but Freddie knew better—it was a surprising number since not many were chosen to jump through time. Depending upon where they had originated, one wore Victorian garb (long-sleeved gingham day dress; narrow-sleeved jacket, vest, tubular trousers, and shirt), another 1940s fashions (square-shouldered jacket, skirt below the knee; tailored suit and Panama hat), but most had changed into more time generic clothing.

Freddie pointed. "The pinball was my idea. Grab a sandwich." Which Freddie did.

Dan snatched up a sandwich.

From a busy table in the back a voice lilted. "Freddie, my girl!!"

Dan recognized her immediately. The raven-haired beauty from the filthy London street.

"Chantell." Freddie sprinted to the table where a large, lovely lady in her 30's was beckoning her.

The six people at the table turned and stood. It looked odd to Dan that they were all wearing or carrying satchels of some sort. Chantell and Freddie embraced wildly, with Chantell spinning Freddie around in her arms. Chantell wore a long-sleeved red blouse and high-waisted wide legged beige pants.

Several other tablemates hugged or waved.

Chantell studied Freddie up and down with a critical eye. "Girl, where have you been? Word was we lost you."

"I was lost and now I am found. Let me introduce you to Dan."

Dan was busy eating a turkey on sourdough, or at least that's what he told himself it was.

"Dan, this is Chantell—and everybody else."

Everybody else laughed. In this group there truly was Chantell and everybody else. Chantell was a jumper who had managed to make obscene amounts of money while doing more good than harm. Knowing that more Earth jumpers were attracted to this spot and time than any other, she bought this place and several others as a refuge for them.

Club 6.4 was a place where a jumper could eat, drink, and socialize with other jumpers, an otherwise rare opportunity, all at no cost—unless you wanted the upgrade. Chantell merely wanted their company. And they wanted hers.

"Freddie, you have got to tell me what happened to you."

"I got stuck in Shakespearian London."

"Haven't we all."

"For 27 years."

"Wow."

This led to much chatter amongst the companions.

"Yeah," said Freddie.

"How'd you get out?" asked Mortimer, a tall thin man with dark hair and a pointed nose and chin.

"Hitched a ride with Dan."

Curtis, a newer member of the group, leaned in. "How'd you get in here?"

"I'm becoming friends with the field again."

"Is that possible?"

Chantell took over. "Of course it is or she wouldn't be here. ALBERT, bring Ms. Townes a Pilsner and a bottle of the best bourbon for the table."

The bartender looked exactly like the doorman, only dressed like a bartender. Dan thought they must be twins.

Freddie leaned in to Chantell. "You'll never guess who I saw there."

"Shakespeare?"

"Better. You!"

"Child, I could have gotten you out of there."

"You didn't know me yet. Besides, I had a ride."

Chantell turned to Dan. "Dan, we thank you for returning Freddie to us. What's your drink?"

"Umm, a dark beer?"

"ALBERT, a Moose Drool for Dan."

Albert the bartender pointed at his pad.

Dan looked uneasy. "Moose Drool?"

Freddie leaned back from greeting her friends. "It's an excellent dark beer."

"Oh."

Club 6.4… had the best liquor cabinet in the galaxy. Imagine a bar with the best that time has to offer. The same wine that Caesar supped on, Napoleon's favorite liqueur, Jack Spice from the year 13432—the original, aged in oak barrels, which had to be replaced every six days.[1]

Albert brought over drinks and he and Chantell shared information. Dan thought it looked a little suspicious, but Freddie was too busy to notice.

Chantell looked at Freddie. "So you hitched a ride and now you're a full-fledged jumper again?"

"Apprentice, anyway."

"What's that mean?"

"I wanted to talk to you about that. It's kinda weird."

"Then step into my office." She put out her arm to usher them towards a door. "Freddie, Dan."

As they walked toward the door, Albert opened it for them. The office was more playroom that workspace. There was a desk, but around it were various music and entertainment devices from throughout time and space.

Dan was quite in awe. "Wow, nice collection."

"When one has visited as many eras as I have, there's a lot to choose from. So, Freddie what weirdness did you wish to discuss?"

"Yeah. I'm pretty sure I was done with the timestream. I mean, I had no connection. When Dan popped in, I thought maybe I could jump with him until I got a few years younger and someplace less archaic, but after a few jumps I was back to baseline. And now I'm storing tachyons."

"We should run some data."

"Data?" Dan sounded concerned. Data was what made the robot revolution possible.

---

[1] After six days the corrosive power of the liquid causes the barrels to detonate.

"To make sure nothing else is going on," Chantell said.

"Like what?"

"I don't know. It might wear off, or it may be happening too fast. Freddie could lose stability."

Dan didn't like the sound of that. "What do you mean 'lose stability'?"

"Time is tricky," said Chantell. "If it moves too quickly, she could end up with altered DNA."

"So like a mutant?"

"More probably like dead."

"I feel great," Freddie said.

"Let's take a look at you." Chantell gestured to Dan.

"What are you going to do?" Dan asked. He'd lately been too close to a colonoscopy to trust anything that hinted at medical procedures.

"It's okay, Dan," said Freddie. "Chantell knows more about time than anybody."

While not completely true, this was certainly mostly true. Being a time traveler who had accumulated thousands of years of adventures in time *and* owned the only resorts for jumpers to share stories in the twelve galaxies meant Chantell knew more about time than anyone in this time/space vicinity. Remembering the universe is infinite, however, means no one can ever be the best at anything as there is always someone better.

And someone better than them.

And them, ad infinitum.

Infinity means there are no absolutes, there is always something more.

Infinity hurts my brain.

Chantell went to a closet and pulled out what looked to Dan to be a radar gun, like the one that caught him doing 72 in a 65 zone last month. Last millennia. Or three. Or a hell of a lot of millennia ago.

"What is that?" Dan said.

"It measures tachyons."

"Those faster than light thingies—particles."

"Yes and no."

"Yes and no?"

"Yes they are particles, no they don't travel faster than light. At least not in our universe."

"Then in whose universe do they?"

"In the time field. The laws of physics keep anything in our universe from traveling faster than light and thereby altering time, but in the time field, tachyons can travel faster than light and thereby affect time."

"And we have them?"

Chantell looked at Freddie's readings. "Well, girlfriend has some, but not quite enough to open the time field." She turned the device to Dan.

He didn't like the looks of the device. "Wait a minute."

"You, on the other hand, have enough to open up your *own shop*."

Freddie glanced at the device. "She's not kidding."

"Can you take them out of me?" said Dan.

Chantell frowned. "Out?"

"I didn't ask for the timestream. It just happened to me and I've been along for the ride."

Freddie was surprised. "You don't like it?"

"I don't know," he said. "I haven't had a choice."

"But it's a great ride."

"Look, I like roller coasters, but I like to get off sometime."

"You just need to learn to control it."

"How?"

"With time and practice you can choose when to jump and sometimes where."

Chantell was doubtful. "I don't think he can."

Both Freddie and Dan turned to her.

"I've never seen readings this high," Chantell said. "He may never have control. All jumpers attract the time field and when it opens, we get sucked into the stream. With practice we can suppress our tachyon emissions and keep the field at bay. Mental focus allows us to shape our destination. Dan's tachyon levels are so high I don't see how he can suppress them."

"So I'm stuck being a pinball in the time field."

"That's what Club 6.4 is about." Chantell tried to offer them some comfort. "It gives us all a chance to recharge. Freddie, why don't you get a full gene reading at the station clinic—my treat? Meanwhile, I can look into Dan's excess tachyons. Nobody has to decide anything yet."

Freddie looked at Dan warily. "I don't know."

"I guarantee you have some time before he jumps."

"Fine." Freddie walked toward the door. "Don't leave without me."

"Wouldn't dream of it." Dan looked at Chantell. "Now what?"

– Chapter 11 –
Less Fun than a Barrel of Monkeys

(Which is actually a barrel of angry claws, teeth, and disease potential)

Dan was set to work detailing his time travel history into an unseen virtual assistant. Chantell and Albert pulled some equipment into the room and plugged in all kinds of devices. Chantell went to a storage area and rolled out a medical table, then had him lie down. Taking the remote control, she instructed Dan: "Hold on."

The table tilted upright until Dan was near standing.

"Why didn't you let me just step into it?"

"It's more fun this way. Now relax."

The machine started to hum. Quite a nice rendition of "Thus Spake Zarathrustra," Dan thought.

Chantell had wheeled out a projection table, and it was now displaying an image of Dan's internal plumbing. Various readings included brainwaves and bio impulses. It seemed to Dan there was too much red.

"Interesting," Chantell said. "It looks almost like you're still connected to the time field … but that doesn't make sense. Let me see if I can absorb some off of you."

"Absorb?"

"I've discovered certain frequencies will attract the tachyons and I can contain them in an interspatial field. Inter space being similar to inter time."

Or, according to Einstein, kinda the same thing.

"Go slow," he said. "No offense, but I really don't want to get stuck here—exploding sun and all."

"I'm not going to let you explode with the sun." Chantell flipped a switch.

Dan felt a tingle. An everywhere kinda tingle. "It's kind of itchy."

"We are getting a small power absorption, but… your levels aren't changing. Let's try a little more."

She increased the power and Dan felt like he was vibrating. His head started to hurt.

"That hurts a little."

"Still no changes in your tachyon levels. They are rebuilding as fast as we can absorb them. Let's turn it up a notch."

"And why would we want to do that?"

"Do you want to see if we change your level of control?"

"… All right, just a little higher."

Chantell adjusted her display and the vibration inside Dan increased. It was like he was on a really good Shiatsu chair while someone poked him between the eyes with an ice pick. Which is not the best way to be Shiatsued.

"Ahhhhhhhh."

Chantell turned down the machine.

"Turn it offffff."

She did. "You okay?"

"I don't know. It… it felt… like… like I was coming apart—without the time field to hold me together."

"Sounds horrible."

"It felt horrible."

"Here, let me…" She reached into a pocket and fumbled through several dime sized objects. "Uh, give you a room key. Lie down and rest. Anything you want, ask for it. It's a premium room package."

Of course Dan didn't know a single night of the premium room package would cost most people a year's salary. "Thanks."

"I'll send Freddie over when she gets back. I'm so sorry about this. Albert, assist Dan to 168."

"Yes, Chantell."

"I'm sorry, Dan. On the plus side, I've collected tons of data that should help you." She smiled at him.

Dan stepped out of the table and his ankles buckled—his knees would have buckled, but the ankles felt his weight first. Albert caught him and mostly carried him, while allowing him the illusion he could walk. Dan thought the room must have been miles away, but it was in fact just down the hall and to the right.

Albert opened a door and sat Dan down on the couch. Albert walked out, closing the door behind him. The premium room package consisted of a spacious salon furnished with a couch, chairs, table, and a separate bedroom with a really nice king-sized bed, but the bed was far away from the couch.

Far being anything that was just out of reach.

Dan lay down on the couch. He would have turned the lights off, but there was no mechanism to do so that Dan recognized. He really wanted an ice pack but couldn't find a phone. In combination frustration and total body trauma, he shouted.

"WHERE THE HELL'S THE PHONE??"

"THERE'S NO NEED TO SHOUT."

"What?"

"There's no need to shout. There is no 'phone,' although I believe Chantell has one in her collection." The voice was Albert's.

"Albert, are you listening in on my room?"

"I respond to my name, cries of strong emotion, physical distress, or offers of free foot massage."

"Can you bring me some ice and turn the lights down?"

The lights dimmed by half.

"Would you like that ice in a glass, with a beverage?"

"No, crushed in a bag for my head. No wait, I would also like it in a glass, with club soda as well."

In 32 seconds a table with an ice bag and club soda, rocks, rolled out of a service closet and stopped beside the couch.

"Thank you, Albert."

"You're welcome, sir."

Dan still didn't know Albert was an android, or in this specific instance an AI.

Which was odd, because at his home he had two virtual assistants—and he loved them both equally.[2]

Chantell was careful with her staff. She didn't trust sentients with knowledge of the jumpers, so that meant employing androids. To further protect the information they held from non-jumpers, she kept the androids in a closed system, a system that eventually became all Alberts, her favorite model.

Over one hundred Alberts, all linked, managed her clubs, rooms, resorts, and other enterprises. Far fewer problems with Space Employees Local 936 that way.

When Dan awoke, Freddie was sitting nearby. She looked worried.

"Hey," he said. "Been here long?"

"You're awake."

"Yeah. First time I've fallen asleep this soon after a jump."

"Chantell said you didn't react well to the scans."

"The scans were fine. When she tried to absorb some of the tachyons was the problem."

"She tried to absorb the tachyons???"

"Just a few, but she said they kept replenishing."

"That doesn't make sense."

"That's what she said."

She stood up. "I'm going to talk to Chantell."

"Can you hang out here a while longer? I think I'll be up to going with you soon."

"Sure." She sat down.

"How were your scans?"

[2] Never let Alexis and Siri know you favor one over the other. Ever.

"Normal—no genetic abnormalities. I'm a healthy 26-year-old woman."

"Give or take a few decades."

"Give or take."

The specifics of Freddie's real age are somewhat of a mystery, even to her. She has spent years wandering through time and like most of us, hasn't kept track of the days as they pass. We keep our age as years passing on a calendar and a calendar is useless for marking the passage of time when you're jumping.

In the future, when medical science makes infirmity a thing of the past, they will measure a person's physical and mental ages based on body deterioration and memory. Our best guess is that Freddie is 26, with 80 years of memories. 26/80 years old.

After about an hour, if time is relevant, Dan was ready to meet with Chantell. They found a fresh change of clothing in the closet, clothing that was nearly timeless. Simple white linen shirts and trousers for Dan and plain dresses for Freddie. She put on a shirt and trousers.

Things had been so hectic Dan hadn't noticed Freddie had lost another decade, but her new wardrobe gave him laser focus.

Until business intruded.

Back at 6.4… they sat down to talk. Well, Dan and Chantell sat. Freddie paced. And Dan and Chantell talked. Freddie yelled—politely.

"WHAT THE HELL, CHANTELL?"

Chantell shrugged. "It was just a test."

"STRIPPING HIM OF HIS TACHYONS?"

"Never enough to damage his connection to the field."

"JUST ENOUGH TO KNOCK HIM OUT FOR THREE HOURS."

Okay that's annoying. I'll skip the caps and you just assume she's mad.

"I didn't know that would happen."

"Then you shouldn't have done it."

"Agreed. I'm sorry."

"Don't tell me. Tell him."

Dan stepped in. "She did… and we talked about taking some tachyons… I said it was all right."

Freddie stared at him. "Do you want to give up jumping that badly?"

"Yes… no. I just would like a little choice. Being able to direct where I might end up sounds nice."

"It is."

"But if I can never have that…"

"Yeah."

Chantell took that moment to break in. "I hate to be the bearer of bad news, but you may have a bigger problem."

Dan was wide eyed. "Problem."

"Freddie, I don't think your tachyon storage is stable. My guess is that they will break down quickly after a jump and may never get high enough to jump on your own."

Freddie was crestfallen. Dan saw the energy drain out of her eyes.

"What?" she said.

"Freddie, you know rejoining the field is impossible."

"But it seemed like…"

"I know, but Dan's levels are so high you can feel them for hours, maybe even days—but they're not enough."

The emotion drained from Freddie's voice. "I see."

"You need to think about what you want to do. You said you planned on getting younger and finding a good place to stop jumping. I can't think of a better place than here."

"But if I'm losing the field, I can't stay here."

"My place, my rules. You can stay until you decide when you'd like to live and I'll take you there."

"But Dan needs me."

And Dan realized he truly did. And not just for her time survival skills.

"He needs someone to show him the ropes," Freddie said.

"And what if you get separated? You'll be stuck who knows when. Tell you what, I'll ride along with Dan. I'll help him learn to jump and keep him safe."

Freddie couldn't argue with the offer. Dan would be in better hands with Chantell, but even so… "Let me think about it."

"You do that. Now if we can talk about the data. I'm learning things even I didn't know were possible. Dan is connected to the timestream in a way I've never seen before. I've tested hundreds of jumpers and everyone has residual tachyons from their last jump, unless they've lost the field—then they're just gone. Freddie, after you lost the field, you should have stopped storing tachyons—you should jump with Dan and minutes later, nothing." She pulled out her scanner.

Dan recoiled from the device. "Hey."

She aimed the device at Freddie. "Look, you've retained a few tachyons hours later. And I drew enough particles from Dan to power a dozen jumps; he had only a tiny loss. Tiny."

"So I can't control when I jump?" said Dan.

"Probably not—or at least you can't prevent a jump for long. You might be able to learn to slow it down."

"And he could jump more often," said Freddie.

"That's true. He could jump as soon as he wanted, at least after his body had refueled."

"Dan, when did you jump for the first time?" said Freddie.

"About a week ago," said Dan.

Chantell didn't take her eyes off the readout as she spoke. "No, dear, time passage that way is useless for tracking jumps."

Told you.

Chantell continued. "No, do you remember the calendar date and time you jumped?"

"September something, about 5:30."

"Gonna need a little more than that."

"How about your phone?" said Freddie.

Dan frowned. "What?"

"Do you keep track of your appointments?"

"I do!!" Dan reached for his phone.

"Bless you, Dan, for not being a Luddite. Give it to me." Chantell's hand shot out and he handed her the phone.

For the first time since Dan jumped, his phone requested an update. "Hey, it can update."

Chantell was searching as she was talking. "I keep frequencies open for most tech here. You can access the universe's knowledge now—at least as long as you're here."

"That could be helpful."

"Here it is. September 27th was your last appointment."

I told you, dear reader, that date might be important. Did you write it down, or at the very least bookmark it?

Freddie watched with keen interest. "So how does that help you?"

Chantell looked at her. "I think I need to go there."

"Oh no you don't. First you drain him, now you want to mess with his prime jump. Do you know the first rule of time travel? Don't mess with the prime jump!"

"Honey, I wrote that rule."

"For good reason."

Dan was getting lost again. "Why don't you mess with the prime jump?" Dan didn't know what the prime jump was, but hoped he'd figure it out if he acquired some context.

Freddie explained. "Because if you mess with someone's first jump and cause them not to jump, you get a time loop."

Dan was so excited he figured out what a prime jump was he almost lost the rest of it.

"Then they never jump, then you never had reason to mess with the jump, so they jump, then you go back and stop it, then they don't jump, so you don't go back… ad infinitum."

Infinitum hurts my brain.

Chantell was insistent. "We need to scan his prime jump if we want to understand his condition."

Freddie shook her head adamantly. "No, it's too dangerous."

"I won't touch a thing."

"No."

"It's not up to you."

They both turned to Dan.

"Ummm, if Freddie says it's too dangerous, I can wait. You said you have lots of data to go over."

"But—"

"You did say that," Freddie reminded her.

Chantell scowled. "Fine. I'll go over data. But if he jumps out before I can figure something out, we'll lose the opportunity."

"We'll take that chance."

Chantell reached into her pocket and took out a key. "Well, here's a room for you."

"That's okay. I'm staying with Dan."

Chantell gave them an inquisitive look. "So you are a couple?"

They both answered. "No, uhhhh."

Freddie continued. "We have to stay close. In case he jumps."

"I see. Then perhaps Dan and I can have dinner sometime."

Freddie eyed her suspiciously. "Really?"

"He fascinates me."

"Okay." Freddie had her doubts. Dan did not seem like Chantell's type.

Chantell's type would have been a Highlander, ready with sword and kilt to defend his clan against invaders. Like "Outlander," only more muscular.

Dan and Freddie headed to their room. The premium suites were along a wide corridor with rich carpeting and oil paintings of pastoral scenes of chubby children frolicking near ponds and Victorian ladies in hats and parasols strolling through lush countryside. Dan hadn't noticed the décor the first time he passed through.

In their room Freddie was trying to play it cool. Not successfully.

"Do you realize what could have happened if Chantell screwed up your connection with the time field!?"

"We'd both be trapped here until someone gave us a lift out?"

"Well… yes. But then neither of us could have jumped again."

"Chantell promised that wouldn't happen."

"Do you know what her promises are worth?"

"Ummm, a lot?"

"Well… yes. Damn it, Dan, if something went wrong, we couldn't have left together. Even if a single jumper had the power to take more than one person into the timestream, two people sharing minds is insanity—three you might not recover from."

"I didn't know that."

"Well now you do!"

"Then I absolutely won't take that chance again."

Freddie softened. "Good."

"What about you. Are you really thinking about staying here?"

"I don't know."

That answer didn't satisfy Dan. "I pulled you out of the 17th century and made you young again and now you're going to just leave?" Hearing it come out of his mouth, it sounded angrier than he'd intended.

"What do you mean you made me young? The time field did that, not you." That came out of Freddie's mouth just as angry as she'd intended.

"But you wouldn't have entered the field without me."

"And you wouldn't have survived your next jump without me."

"Not true."

"Two days in a frozen wasteland wearing a plaid shirt and with no food."

"I'm very resilient."

"What about you? You were ready to abandon me if you could stop jumping."

"I didn't say that."

"It sounded like it to me."

"I'd like to have time to think about it."

"Then start thinking!" Freddie stormed over to the closet and stuffed a spare set of clothing in her satchel.

Dan went into the bedroom and tried to think about what he wanted. He obsessed about everything Freddie said and did. The last woman who made him this angry he'd divorced.

Of course he had married her first.

After an hour or so Dan came out of the bedroom and sat on the couch.

Freddie was finishing up ordering room service. "No, I want a small bottle of whiskey and three pounds of jerky. And a few MREs."

"Are you planning a jump, Ms. Townes?" asked the AI.

"No, Albert, but one never knows."

A great weight lifted from Dan's chest as he saw what she was doing.

Quietly he began to pack some things as well, which turned out to be a good thing a half hour later. Dan thought about trying to stop the jump, but when Freddie grabbed him, he didn't want to stop it.

Down the corridor, Chantell was examining data in her lab when an alarm went off.

"Shit."

Grabbing her tachyon syphon, she sprinted down the hallway and threw open the door just in time to see Dan and Freddie wink away.

"Noooooooooooooooo!!!"

– Chapter 12 –
Dinosaur Attacks and Stuff that Attracts Readers

When they exited the timestream, they found themselves in a wooden storeroom—that seemed to be rocking. The room was full of bales, crates, and barrels stacked on top of each other and lashed to the walls with ropes. The smell of salt water was strong.

Freddie may have well gotten cuter, which Dan found hard to believe, making it hard to survey his new environs.

Freddie pointed toward a set of stairs and they stealthily climbed up through a hatch onto the deck of a wooden seafaring ship. A three-masted sailing ship with a square rig and two decks. Dan expected to see Errol Flynn sweep down from the quarterdeck to confront them. Maybe Olivia de Havilland or Virginia Mayo was in the captain's quarters?

The most disturbing thing was they were completely surrounded by water.

"Mr. Conover, are these the new men?"

Freddie turned away and reached into a pocket for her beard. Dan could feel panic building inside. That old gray beard would never hide Freddie's now 26-year-old, definitely female face. He heard her whisper something unintelligible and when she lifted her head, the beard was now black and fit her chin and cheeks perfectly.

"The Carded 3000" was the ultimate in facial disguise accessories. Three thousand years of theatrical experience begat a self-fitting beard or mustache that was attuned to your natural hair color. It was guaranteed to fit seamlessly and never slip. Most importantly, it could not be removed with a simple tug or yank, but rather needed voice printed instructions.[3]

The end result was that Freddie no longer looked like a very beautiful woman wearing a beard but rather a feminine man with a masculine beard or a very beautiful bearded lady.

While Dan worried about this, it is a historical fact that women entered service disguised as men and remained undetected due to the low frequency of bathing among the crew. Sailors were drenched with seawater so often they normally didn't feel the need to bathe. As long as Freddie did not undertake a thorough cleansing, she could maintain her illusion.

Conover, a stocky middle-aged sailor, glanced their way. "Simpson, are these the men you found in port?"

A tall thin sailor looked their way. "Aye, those are the ones I brought."

In reality, Simpson would've claimed responsibility for two lemurs wearing clown suits as there was a bonus involved for abduc— recruiting new volunteers.

---

[3] Not old enough to score booze? Young face but an old soul? Feeling masculine but looking feminine? The Carded 3000 is the solution to all of your age and testosterone related needs. Go instantly from Jill to Jack. Hide that baby face with a coating of manly fur. You set the length and let the Carded 3000 do the rest.

Not responsible for early alcoholism or gender confusion. Do not use if allergic to Carded 3000. If rash develops, consult your dermatologist. May result in permanent loss of facial hair. THAT INCLUDES EYEBROWS. Not for use on animals.

Try our sister product Make-A-Merkin.

The captain, in need of a full complement, didn't ask any more questions but just barked out orders. "Put 'em to work, Mr. Conover."

Conover pulled the pair to the side. "Do either of you have documents?"

Freddie reached into her satchel. "I've got a letter somewhere." She produced a weathered piece of paper.

Conover skimmed it and handed it back. "Well, what can you do, lads?"

Dan's brain leaped into overtime trying to think of what he might be able to do on the ship. Luckily, Freddie gave him some time as she was well-versed in coming up with instant value. The first rule of being a time jumper is to make yourself very valuable very quickly.

"I've got medic experience."

"Aye, so the letter said, although I could barely make out the signature."

He wasn't supposed to. The date was also meant to be illegible.

"Captain Roosevelt of the *Andrea Doria*," said Freddie.

Dan stifled a giggle.

"We've got a sawbones, but we can use a loblolly boy. What else can you do?"

"I can cook some."

"All right, you are officially cook's helper and loblolly boy. You'll spend your time in the kitchen unless Doc needs you. What's your name, boy?"

"Freddie, and this is Dan."

"How can you serve *The Traveler*, Dan?"

Dan thought of something at last. "I'm good at pumps and keeping the water out."

Freddie winced.

Conover cocked his head. "Oh, a bilge rat, eh?"

That did not sound good.

"Head down to the bilge, lad."

Dan thought keeping the water out might be the kind of thing a plumber could do shipboard. He didn't think about where he'd have to do it.

Freddie was sent to talk to Doc, then to the galley to help Cook prepare food for the next watch. The job interviews were quick and to the point—Doc asked if she could read and Cook asked if she could make oatmeal.

Dan's bilge was in the very bottom of the ship where any water that seeped in had to be pumped out. This was cold, wet, dirty work as all the crud from the upper levels of the ship dripped down to the bilge as a mix of seawater and sludge.

It's not nearly as glamorous as it sounds.

Dan had not even considered that the water needed to be pumped by hand. Wooden ships constantly leaked. Since the bilge was the lowest level of the ship and well below the water line, the bilge pumps were the last defense against sinking in a storm. Sailors also tended to use the bilge as a latrine due to the lack of heads on board.

Again, the worst possible job on ship.

Freddie spent her day trying to hide how much she knew about medicine from the ship's doctor-barber. She wanted to be knowledgeable but not *too* knowledgeable. A good medical practitioner was a rarity on a merchant ship. She played the role of an apprentice surgeon, assisting with procedures and disposing of body parts. Then she chopped onions.

Dan spent the day wallowing in the most unrelenting filth ever.

By the time his watch ended, Dan felt as though he had been dragged through a sewer. His skin and clothes were covered with a black substance he could not quite identify. There wasn't much of a supply of soap and it seemed like much of the crew didn't bother cleaning up anyway.

That seawater drenching thing.

Dan thought he would catch up with Freddie during dinner. Unfortunately, she was too busy serving the rest of the crew. Dan was ravenous. He had never gotten a chance to eat since the jump. Freddie, on the other hand, had been nibbling in the kitchen all afternoon.

After supper Freddie was stuck cleaning the implements and copper kettles. By the time she finished, it was late. Dan had been hanging around on the deck eavesdropping on conversations. When he saw her step up to the deck, he spirited her off to a secluded area he had scouted earlier.

Freddie went right to time jumper business. "What have you learned?"

"That being a plumber isn't always a good thing."

"That's a lesson you shouldn't have to learn twice."

"Well, you smell like onions."

"And you smell like—"

He cut her off. "I know."

"I couldn't get much information from the cook. He mostly wanted to talk about food and his wife and children. From the medical instruments and clothing, I'd guess we're post-Columbus but pre-Civil War. I may get more from Doc after I spend more time with him."

"Most of my time was spent listening to my coworkers complain about the stench." To be fair, Dan did most of the complaining. "I did find out we're on an English merchant ship taking tea to the Americas. You don't think we're on—"

It was Freddie's turn to cut him off. "No, I doubt it. You don't usually jump directly into seminal events, just near them."

"I wonder what we might be drawn to in the middle of the ocean."

"Let's hope it's not a sinking, pirate attack, storm, or spontaneous combustion."

"Let's hope. Wait a minute, besides impending death, what other choices do we have?"

"I can't think of any."

"That's comforting."

"Very little about time travel is."

Dan had noticed that. He felt safe in his old life. Get up, go to work, come home, watch TV, go to sleep. At times he had felt he was missing something, but inertia was comfortably numb. Sometimes the universe saves you from disappearing into your own mediocrity. Other times it just screws with your head.

A look of concern came over Freddie. "We need to find a way to get you out of the bilge."

"That would be nice."

"More than nice. You realize that if something goes wrong, you're in the worst possible place."

He hadn't. Images swept through Dan's mind. He imagined the ship taking on water, him manning the pumps with all of his might. By the time they abandoned ship, the bilge would be filled with water. He imagined *The Traveler* catching fire. It would be simple for an oil lamp to ignite old timber. By the time news of the fire reached the bilge, there would be no exit.

Every scenario he could conceive—from tidal wave to whale attack—did not end well for him.

The one scenario he did not think about was killer bees.

Historically, the bilge on the ship is one of the safest places to be during a killer bee attack.

But there was no imminent assault of avian assassins. Say that three times quickly. Out loud.

Waiting.

. . .

Still waiting.

. . .

Now, people will leave you alone, by god!

Unless you don't want to be left alone.

Sorry. Too late now.

Mindless sheep that you are, you will now be relegated to the bilge—and if you did not speak out loud, shame on you for not following instructions. Hopefully, you will behave more appropriately the next time.

Where was I? Oh yes, Freddie tried to lessen Dan's anxiety.

"You know, Chantell won't rest until she's figured out the deal with your time connection."

"You think so?"

"Oh yeah… Boy, she must be pissed."

"You think so?"

"The girl does not like it when she doesn't get her way."

In the crew's quarters they found anything that resembled a bed had already been taken. As tired as he was, Dan thought the hammocks strung from the cross beams looked inviting. They were not. In fact, they taunted you with a come hither stare and then shattered your dreams—literally. It took considerable time for him to mount the beast and even more to tame it.

Freddie, the veteran time traveler, was fast asleep in her hammock before Dan's feet made it off of the floor.

When, after a fitful night's sleep, Dan awoke the next morning, his back felt like someone had used it for accordion practice. As he tried to get the kinks out by standing upright and moaning, it occurred to him he wasn't seasick. He had tried sailing a few pitiful times, always ending in the voiding of the contents of his stomach, then trying to void his spleen, lungs—anything that could conceivably come out.

This time nothing. As he thought about it, he realized this must be a boon of being a jumper. If you survived the timestream, the ocean was a comfortable meal at a clean table. Definitely not a picnic.

Picnics are not easy. Uneven ground, wind, trips from the car burdened with unwieldy containers of food and supplies. Eating portable foods with unfamiliar utensils. Heat, spoiled mayonnaise, listeria. But not ants. Never have had a problem with them. Perhaps because I leave quickly and just as they arrive, I go.

Freddie was already up working the breakfast shift. Food aboard ship was simple fare for the crew—beef, pork, bread, oatmeal, suet, and raisins. Two hundred pounds of raisins. Raisins to help prevent scurvy. Officers could bring their own more palatable food aboard, but that was separate. Freddie helped prepare the meal. Then served the meal. Then dishes, then a nap, then lunch, then dishes, then a nap, then dinner, and then dishes. Not the most glamorous situation she'd ever jumped into, but definitely not the worst.

Dan pumped and raked out the muck. It didn't take long for him to become an expert mucker. It wasn't an especially impressive skill set.

This routine continued for days, with little opportunity for advancement. The plan to get Dan promoted to anything else was going nowhere. Days turned to weeks and Dan started to wonder how long they'd be stuck there.

The timestream kept its own counsel and Chantell was not the boss of they.

When the crew got ripe enough and the seas were calm, they stripped to their skivvies and bathed in the sea. This presented a problem for Freddie; she had gone from ripe to spoiled. And since her work was below deck, she didn't get the occasional drenching the deckhands did.

Smell would not normally be a concern for the crew, but working with food, especially fish and onions, made her more pungent than most. The blood on her clothes from helping Doc added to the aroma.

Eventually she was smelling worse than the food and a mutiny was in the works.

Sailor Thomas Moon started it. "Freddie, lad, you need a bath."

"Find me a tub."

"Too good to swim with the rest of us?"

With that, they grabbed her and carried her on deck. The winds had calmed and it was a good time for a swim. Luckily, Dan had heard the scuttlebutt about the plot and grabbed her around the middle, artfully blocking hands from going where they should not.

As they hauled her up on deck, they started to pull at her clothing.

She shouted, "Wait!"

Again, luckily, they did.

"I can't swim."

"Time to learn, boy."

She pulled away, with Dan granting a clumsy assist by crashing into her groomers. She jumped on the edge of the ship, ready to climb the rigging. Dan decided to fix the problem himself.

Dan leapt towards her and knocked them both overboard. They fell into the ocean with quite a splash and cheers from the men.

Dan noticed she seemed to keep her head above water just fine. "You learn fast."

"You threw me in the ocean!"

"Better me than them."

"Better no one."

"That wasn't an option."

"There could have been a better one."

"It didn't come to mind. Besides, you were starting to smell like old squid."

She laughed. "I beg your pardon. I am now *young* squid."

"My mistake." Dan suddenly had an additional concern. "Is your beard… ?"

"No, it's good. You can't even tug it off. Try it."

Dan gave it a tug; all he did was pull her chin into the water.[4]

And he noticed her eyes for the first time. Dan wondered if they were always so green or if it was the reflection of the water. Either way they were amazing.

After a good soaking, they climbed up the Jacob's ladder onto the deck. Dan had never climbed a rope ladder with wooden rungs before and it was more difficult than expected. Of course, this was made more difficult by the way Freddie's clothing was clinging to her in a most unmasculine way. Freddie adjusted the situation as she carefully boarded the ship.

The flying tackle into the sea elevated Dan in the men's esteem. He received many a smile and back slap as he scrambled board.

Freddie received derisive laughter.

"You all know I touch your food before you, right?"

---

[4] Early models of the Carded 3000 would short out when immersed in liquid. This led to a series of lawsuits for electrocution.

The laughter quieted considerably.

Freddie did feel much more human after the dunking and resumed work in the galley as they waited for the wind to pick up. When the ship finally did start to make headway, Freddie expected the first mate to come down for dinner and the captain to take control of the no longer becalmed ship, but he didn't. Instead, food was sent up to him.

The captain hadn't sent down for lunch or supper, so Freddie went to his cabin to inquire if he wanted to eat. Before she could ask anything, she heard low moaning from his quarters. She went to fetch the doctor.

The captain denied them access, but they ignored him. He insisted he'd be fine: "It's just a stone. I've had it before. There's nothing wrong with me a good piss won't cure."

Doc checked him over. His groin was tender. "How long since you last went?"

"A couple days."

"And how much then?"

"A trickle."

"Has it ever lasted this long before?"

"No."

"Captain, I don't think that stone is coming out on its own."

Freddie's thoughts zoomed over medical history. Long before ultrasound or catheter suction. That meant surgery. Little anesthesia, few antiseptics—even sutures were new. Cutting a man open on a moving ship. Two hours ago they were listless; why didn't they notice the problem then?

"Freddie, prepare the surgery. And get Luke and Guffer down here."

In the doctor's quarters, she cleared off the operating table and grabbed the instruments. On the way to the galley, she caught the attention of Little Wendell, a 10-year-old page, and told him to fetch Luke and Guffer. Without thinking how odd it would appear, she took the instruments into the galley and placed them in a pot to boil.

Cook was skeptical. "What in the name of Poseidon are ya doin'?"

"Doc has to cut open the Captain and wants the tools washed."

"Why'd ya put 'em in the pot?"

"Hot water cleans better."

Cook had washed enough pans to know a hot pan cleaned up easier than a cold one so it sounded reasonable.

Freddie also dropped some thread in the water along with sewing needles. She rushed back to the makeshift OR and wiped down what she could with rum. She stopped as Doc, Luke, and Guffer carried in the captain. Luke and Guffer looked like they could hold down a steer in a rodeo which was good because what they were about to do was similar.

Doc's nose wrinkled. "It smells like a tavern in here."

"I was getting the rum to help Captain with the pain and spilled it." Freddie held up the bottle.

"Drank it more like. Let me smell your breath."

Freddie complied.

"Not that I'm against rum, but we'll need clear heads for this."

Having passed the test, she poured a small glass of rum and handed it to the doctor to administer. As the glass reached his hands, Freddie tipped the glass, pouring rum on his fingers.

"Nervous, are we?"

"I'm so sorry! Let me help you."

After which she grabbed his hands and rubbed the rum more thoroughly onto them. The Captain took a healthy swig from the bottle.

On deck, Dan was thankful he didn't have the night shift. Not that it made much difference, as it was pitch dark in the bilge if the lamps were not lit. He was gazing up at the stars, quite oblivious to the emergency below, when his own emergency became paramount.

He noticed that quite suddenly the stars vanished.

Well not vanished, but he couldn't see them, and not all of them, only the ones being blocked by that enormous thing in front of him. Luckily, when the enormous thing fell back into the water, the stars came back into view.

If not for the wave that rocked the ship and the obscenities emanating from several sailors, he would have thought he imagined it. The crew were vocal.

"What in the hell was that?"

"It was a whale."

"No, it was a sea monster."

"It was a demon from the bowels of hell."

Dan didn't know it at the time but it was a Mosasaurus, a giant crocodile-like reptile that had been extinct for millions of years. Not that knowing this would have been at all helpful. Dan was too busy looking for a place to hide to engage in anthropology.

Realizing trying to run was useless, he searched for a weapon. He found the fishing gaff and thought that might be the kind of thing to drive this creature away, or to really piss it off.

The beast reared again, lifting its massive body out of the ocean and splashing back down. Looking out at the water, Dan saw multiple fins amongst the waves. He heard the first mate call out.

"Unlock the muskets, men. We'll blow that thing back to Davy Jones."

Dan shouted back. "I think it's hunting sharks."

"I don't care what it's hunting. I don't want that thing striking this ship."

"If we get away from the sharks, we'll get away from it."

While the helmsman was not willing to postpone the creature's trip to the bottom of the sea, he did spin the ship's wheel, changing direction suddenly. Unfortunately, the sharks were using *The Traveler* to protect themselves from the breach attack by the Mosasaurus.

Below decks, the sudden change of direction tilted the ship and jarred the room. By now Freddie had retrieved her sterilized instruments and Luke and Guffer were holding the Captain down on the table in the "lithotomy position" by brute force. Little Wendell stood near the doorway, observing the open surgery with a combination of fascination and horror.

The doctor had made his first incision to search out the offending stone. He was not happy with the ship's movement. He yelled at the crewman. "Whatever they're doing up there, make stop it."

Little Wendell rushed from the cabin.

From Freddie's estimation, Doc was a fair surgeon for his time period, but this type of surgery was in its infancy. Well sure, ancient Hindu, Greek, Roman, and Arab surgeons removed bladder stones, but since they didn't use anesthesia it was more an exercise in pain tolerance than surgery.

I mean, even the Hippocratic Oath says physicians aren't supposed to do this surgery because it's so dangerous, but leaping off of a building due to excruciating kidney pain is even more so.

As the boat rocked, Freddie offered to help steady the wound. "Do you want me to hold the jewels steady?"

"If you can keep your fingers out of my way."

During this period in medicine they had few ways to stop bleeding, so fast surgery was good surgery.

Freddie carefully held the jewels so that Doc would make his incision in the most appropriate place—and not nick anything the captain would want later.

On deck, Dan was trying to convince the crew not to make a hungry dinosaur angry. Although technically the Mosasaurus was not a dinosaur but a carnivorous aquatic squamate, Dan could not appreciate the difference. "We need to drive the sharks away."

"We need to kill that thing."

The men argued about the best way to achieve that unlikely goal. A fully equipped whaling ship would have difficulty with such a large aggressive beast.

Suddenly Dan had an idea. No matter how much the sharks were threatened by the Mosasaurus, there was something that could get them to leave the relative safety of the ship. While the men bickered, he rushed to the galley. He was surprised he didn't see Freddie, but that didn't stop him from rummaging through the stores.

"Where's Freddie?" he asked.

"Doc needed him to help with the captain," said the Cook.

"With what?"

"Cut him open for somethin' or other. What're you doing there?"

"I need fish."

"The salted fish is tomorrow night's dinner."

"I need to make sure we're not tonight's dinner."

"Aye?"

"There's a monster out there and I want to feed it shark."

The cook didn't always seem to be the brightest bulb—or perhaps candle—but in this case he caught on quickly. "Then take that fish cleaning barrel over there. It's chum you want."

Dan grabbed the small barrel and lugged it upstairs.

Doc had successfully made a small incision and removed the blockage. The little stone *clunked* into the small bowl.

Freddie offered to suture the wound. "I do excellent needlework. I've been told I could've been a tailor."

"Show me."

Freddie's deft work with a needle and thread quickly convinced the doctor of her skill.

"You're using thread. Will it hold?"

"It will," she said. "They use it in Paris. You can pull it as tight as you want and it's easy to remove."

"I've heard about it. You better hope it holds."

"If it can hold what I'm packing in my pants, thread can hold anything."

Freddie was overcompensating for her lack of maleness.

Luke and Guffer craned their necks to watch her work with the needle. Freddie briefly considered embroidering her initials, then decided against it.

Meanwhile, Dan had managed to haul the barrel on the deck of the rapidly moving ship. Dragging it aft, he poured it into the sea. Dan watched as the spot where he dumped the chum disappeared into the darkness.

Sharks have long been thought to be dumb killing machines, but you don't get to be an apex predator by being stupid. Well, unless you have a rifle.

Sharks have survived for millions of years without rifles and even use some of the more complicated hunting strategies dolphins favor. At least that's what they say during Shark Week. That being said, drive them into a primitive brain frenzy by, say, chumming the water, and they really want to eat something.

The number of sharks around the ship decreased as the sharks' brains screamed "Dinnertime!!" It was just not specific as to whose dinnertime it was. The reptile breached and Dan could see thrashing tails in its mouth silhouetted by moonlight.

As the ship pulled away, there continued to be quite a bit of activity behind them.

Then Dan heard music and smelled an odor of fish—the latter was quite understandable as he was fairly coated in chum. Dan dashed down the steps towards the doctor's cabin. As Freddie came out, hands covered in blood, he grabbed her and held on tight.

Doc seemed surprised by the suddenness of this affectionate gesture. Not that he hadn't seen plenty of men hugging during his years at sea, but generally it was behind closed doors and not in the main passageway. He continued out of the cabin to wash up.

Realizing what was occurring, Freddie reciprocated the hug and waited. And waited. And nothing happened.

Soon they disengaged.

Dan was perplexed. "Nothing happened."

"Are you sure you were jumping?"

"I heard music and smelled fish."

"How did it feel?"

"Like I was jumping."

They began walking up towards the ladder to reach the deck so Freddie could clean up.

"What were you doing when it started?" she asked.

"I was fighting a sea monster."

"Fighting a sea monster?"

"Well, making it go away."

"Was it a whale?"

"I said a sea monster. It was a gigantic alligator thingie."

"Hmmmm. Sounds like it could've been a wild jumper."

"Wild jumper?"

"Yeah, sometimes a wild animal gets caught in the timestream. It jumps from place to place until it dies, which usually doesn't take long."

"So that thing… ?"

"Was probably a dinosaur."

Carnivorous aquatic squamate. My new favorite animal name.

"So dinosaurs are merrily roaming about the timestream?"

"Not really. They're mostly bound to their own time, but sometimes an idiot builds one from DNA and that puts any Jurassic jumper in mankind's time frame. That's where most tall tales about sea monsters and giant beasts come from. Dragons, griffins, Grendel—all time-displaced dinosaurs."

"They come, make a fuss, and leave again."

She nodded. "Pretty much."

"You said they don't last long."

"They're not real adaptable. Anything that can't survive extreme environmental changes can't handle jumping."

"I can see that. Still, why did I feel like I was jumping?"

"The dino must have jumped. Sometimes if you're near a jump, you can feel it."

"So I felt her jump."

"Yeah. We need to stay close. One jump will often lead to another. Kind of like time dominoes falling."

He noticed her messy hands. "What were you doing?"

"Cutting open the Captain."

"On purpose?"

"Kidney stone. Had to get it out." She stared at her hands. "Let's go up on deck and I'll clean up."

The pair stood on the deck side by side for a good two hours—or a bad 20 minutes—before they jumped. This time they both smelled an aroma of fish.

Spinning into tiny little time pieces, Dan became more aware of his own mind. There were thoughts, impulses, memories, and primitive instincts swirling together. He could feel his animal/reptile brain wanting to kill his enemies and defeat his friends who were competition for resources, jobs, and women, but mostly women.

Then he could feel the call of his more enlightened self, the self that was civilized to the point where he lost virtually every battle, but could consider it a win when he washed his oily hands in the victor's sink. When even your aggression is passive, the only way to win is to refuse to engage.

Dan also noticed loneliness. He wasn't sure if it was his or Freddie's.

– Chapter 13 –
Space with a Bang

When they finally or quickly exited the timestream, Dan didn't realize he had finished the jump. This was because normally the first thing he noticed was gravity pulling him firmly to the earth. This time there was neither gravity nor earth.

Dan was floating in a hallway. And he was holding a dongle. He put it in his pocket because he might need it later.

Everything was white. When you jump, you are normally assailed by sensations—like stepping into a movie halfway through the first reel. Here there was no sensation. No feel, no smell, and little to see.

"You gotta love those zero-G landings." Freddie looked quite comfortable floating above the floor. The only thing distinguishing up from down were the lights in the ceiling.

Assuming the lights belonged in the ceiling.

For Dan it was disconcerting. He attempted to reorient himself but was having all of the success of Napoleon at Waterloo. To make matters worse, not touching a surface meant he had no means of propulsion.

This was not strictly true as this was an oxygen atmosphere; waving his arms would create thrust against the oxygen and propel him forward—at an almost negligible rate.

Also the micro torch on his tool belt would make an excellent source of propulsion—but in an oxygen atmosphere, an even better source of combustion.

"Where are we?" he asked, hoping she'd have more information than him.

"Space?"

"Again? At the club?"

"I don't think it's Club 6.4 this time."

"There's *another* club in space?"

"Well, yes and I don't know. I mean, Chantell has multiple Club 6.4's to reduce the odds of you meeting yourself. But there may be more clubs than hers. Space is infinite and I suppose so are clubs."[5]

"But we're floating."

"Usually that's what happens in space."

"I don't think I like it."

"You've barely gotten to know it. Give it time, buy it a couple of drinks. Perhaps it will grow on you."

"I don't want it to grow on me."

She surveyed the cylindrical area in which they floated. "Feels like a big structure."

"You can feel a structure?"

"You can't hear the engines so they're either quite a ways away or we're in orbit. Either way, given the amount of empty corridor around us, it would suggest this thing is pretty big."

"Is that a good thing or a bad thing?"

"Good. The more people that are here, the less likely we'll have to explain what we're doing here. The less likely we have to explain ourselves, the less likely you will be working in the bilge."

"Yay for big corridors."

"Come on, this way." Freddie propelled herself along the wall.

Dan, while not immobile, was quite stationary. "How?"

"Say S. T. R. A. P."

"Strap?"

---

[5] There are an infinite number of clubs, all of which are extremely popular once space travel becomes open for tourists, but after a short time they close due to space being boring much of the time (i.e., "space ennui"). Therefore, there are also an infinite number of shuttered clubs in space.

And with that, a strap rolled out from above him.

Space vehicles had people getting stranded in mid corridor all the time. It was ridiculous how much time was spent trying to get anywhere. It was relatively easy when the vehicles were small and cramped, but once they gained some volume it became harder to get somewhere. Many solutions were tried: personal propulsion systems, telescoping pushrods, cowboy robots with lassos. Most of these solutions ended in rope burns, high-speed personnel collisions, or putting someone's eye out.

Ultimately the simple solution of soft straps to allow passengers to direct their travel seemed to be best. Although some chose to keep their personal propulsion systems as collision was their preferred form of human contact.

Soon Freddie and Dan were careening down the hallway searching for life. Dan couldn't resist doing a somersault or two—well, four—and some aerials, salchows, and X-Outs like an Olympian. Without the constraints of gravity, he could execute a mid-air dive with a Degree of Difficulty factor of 3.8—a reverse 2.5 somersaults with 2.5 twists in pike—which was a measure of vindication after his unpleasant experience on the high school diving team.

Freddie was right: this was a large structure, a very large structure. When they finally found a viewport, they discovered how large. They were in the inner ring of a space station that spanned more than a mile.

That bit of knowledge informed Freddie of their approximate time period. Before the development of the elemental reorganizer in 2411, there were not enough resources to build a station so large.

By 2437, no one could understand the value of building a station so large.

The big "TT" over the viewport told her this was a TellTom ship. TellTom was one of the top three builders of space vehicles on the planet and this was the largest thing they had ever built—other than enormous wealth.

Freddie looked over at Dan. "I know what you're feeling."

"You do?"

"Looking out at space, everyone feels small. Even this ungodly gargantuan space station feels small compared to the vastness of space."

"No."

"No?"

"No."

"You don't feel small?"

"Well now I feel as though I should."

"What do you feel?"

"Mostly an increasingly desperate need to find a bathroom and a kitchen."

Psychological theorist Abraham Maslow would have said this was a perfect explanation of his needs hierarchy theory, excretion and food being two of the seven primary human needs and feeling small in the vastness of space not even cracking the top 100.

Still, to be fair, in the absence of a more immediate need, feeling small in space is a pretty common reaction.

In fact, Freddie was spot on about the way the space station felt being in space. She looked down the corridor for any suggestion of a facility. "This way."

They propelled themselves down the corridor until they reached a sign that appeared to display waves.

Freddie translated. "It's a room with gravity."

"Gravity is not what I need."

"I think it is. Gravity rooms on the space station use a lot of power, so there aren't many of them. Anything that needs gravity is built in the same spot. Showers, exercise equipment, kitchens, bathrooms, they all work better with gravity."

Although Dan had never really thought about this, it seemed that gravity would be a boon in his immediate situation.

Opening the door, lights powered on and Dan heard a quiet humming sound and as he floated into the room, he quickly became acquainted with the floor. "You could've warned me that would happen."

Freddie glided down gently to the Berber carpet. "It was more fun this way."

"Not for me."

"You'll laugh about it later."

"I seriously doubt that."

But he would. Tragedy plus time equals comedy. Except when someone's eating orphans. The equation tends to go a bit south in that situation.

The room was a large common area, with metallic tables and chairs on one side and comfortable overstuffed chairs on the other. In a corner was a Berenberg ATM. Several doors led to other areas of interest.

Dan found the room he needed and took care of his needs. When he came out, Freddie was sitting at a table, having found a kitchen and prepared them a meal.

Even though time reset her to nearly clean, she still felt the need to scrub her hands thoroughly.

"Nothing fancy, no fresh foods, only basic rations," she said. "I don't think this station is ready for humans yet."

He sat opposite her. "What are we?"

"Two very out of place beings." She looked down at her clothes.

"There's a locker room attached to the bathroom."

"We'll look for clothes after breakfast."

"Is it breakfast?"

"I think these are eggs."

"Why don't you think this station is ready for people? Besides the food."

"First, there's no sign of people. Even on a station this large there should be someone."

"They may all be working somewhere else."

"That would be because the station's not ready for people yet."

"Anything else?"

"Most of the systems are turned on. Doors should open automatically, we shouldn't have to open them."

"It seems functional."

"Yes but it's not lived in. People leave stuff everywhere they go. Dirt, food, candy wrappers, but there's nothing."

"Maybe they're all in cryostasis."[6]

She shook her head. "No such thing."

"Suspended animation?"

"No."

"Hibernation?"

"Animals hibernate, not people."

"Cryostasis would save on supplies on a spaceship."

"Everyone on these ships grew up watching movies with cryostasis. Did it ever work right? Engineers could meet and get the systems perfect, but no one was about to put their lives in the hands of technology they'd seen fail over and over."

"I would."

"I doubt it."

"Still, there's got to be some reason for the ship being empty."

"True. I just don't know what it is yet."

They finished their breakfast and headed to the locker room. There were several jumpsuits hanging in the closet. They both grabbed one as the garments were an upgrade on the Lifeinc suits. There was also a shower. The first real shower either of them had in centuries.

Dan finished his shower in a leisurely half an hour. Freddie took considerably longer. When she came out of the bathroom, she was wearing a robe and drying her hair on a towel. The beard was off and she looked every bit a 26-year-old woman.

"I needed that," she said.

Dan suddenly realized he was staring. "Me, too."

"Salt water is not good for my hair."

"I can see that."

"Can you?"

"Well I mean I can see salt water is bad for the hair, not just your hair, but hair in general, and you never really feel clean. Not you specifically, but me as well. And even if you weren't particularly clean before, I'm sure you're very clean now… as am I… clean."

---

[6] Cryostasis is a leading cause of freezer burn.

Freddie let out a small laugh. "Spoken like a man who used to be married."

"Well…"

"Single guys never backtrack that quickly. Must be PTSD."

Dan tilted his head sideways, in a "got me" nod.

She gazed away thoughtfully as she spoke. "Funny, you've gotten more nervous around me the longer we've been together."

Been together? Dan's brain spun on this like a dreidel in graphite (it's funny, trust me). In microseconds he imagined them dating, engaged, married, and divorced.

"This is the first time you looked like that," he said.

"You saw me in the biosphere."

"You made me nervous then."

"And at Club 6.4?"

"I was too busy being tested, prodded, and recovering from tachyon removal."

"Okay then, on *The Traveler*."

"You were a bearded sailor."

"I think I made a very pretty sailor."

"I know the other sailors thought so."

"Really?" Freddie hadn't noticed this aboard the collier.

"If they didn't think we were a couple, you would have had callers."

"They thought we were gay?"

"Those who think about such things."

"I'm having a hard time imagining you gay."

"My friend Ambrose says I don't have a gay bone in my body."

"Do you?"

"I haven't found it."

Dan, in fact, did have not one, but two gay bones in his body. His third right side rib and a femur we will not single out as it's still in the closet, which is surprising as Dan's skeletal structure is a very accepting environment.

"So it's my being younger that's making you act weird."

"Partly." Dan regretted saying this as soon as it came out of his mouth.

"What else then?" Freddie regretted saying this as soon as it came out of her mouth. She knew it would not end well.

The answer was, "*Because you're beautiful,*" but both Freddie and Dan knew that response would likely make things awkward in a platonic friendship kind of way.

The dreidel began spinning until smoke started to waft out of Dan's ears. Dan was now fighting Maslow's hierarchy again. He had food, air, water, and an empty bladder—next on the list is sex. The reptilian[7] part of his brain was trying desperately to get laid, but the higher functions were screaming, "*NO, NOT NOW, YOU IDIOT!!*" This resulted in a very unpleasant form of brain lock that only occurs between a man and a woman.

"You were an old man, then an old woman—well not old, but certainly middle aged—then a younger woman, then a bearded sailor, and now a wet young woman in a robe. I don't know what you'll be next."

This rant, while not technically the answer, provided them an out.

It is a long-established fact that the reptile brain and the rational brain don't like each other very much, or in most cases loathe each other and want to see the other die a long painful death. Dan's and Freddie's reptile brains wanted to abandon all protocol and give in to their primitive instincts.

Their higher functions realized, "These two have to be together for some time and better to not dive in that can of worms."

"I don't mind the worms if I can fulfill my urges," the reptile argued.

---

[7] Interestingly, at least to me, the reptile brain theory was at least partially based on the evolutionary theory that the dinosaurs existed long before mammals, so obviously we evolved from them. As most paleontologists now believe land dinosaurs are actually the ancestors of birds, this theory may be invalid. Instead of our primitive brain being a reptile brain it may, in fact, be a bird brain.

"I, too, want to fulfill my urges, but I want to avoid the misery of being trapped in time with an ex-lover," the higher brain countered.

"We have to be lovers before we can be Ex."

The reptile brain is a stickler for Maslow.

Ultimately, the higher functions enlisted shame, doubt, and fear to suck the strength from the reptiles' passions.

Those of you without higher function might not recognize this process. Don't worry about it. Just go back to skimming this book for the dirty or violent bits.

The Mosasaurus with a mouthful of sharks was included for your benefit and there is likely to be some nudity later.

All thought was distracted by a loud booming sound, echoing down the corridor.

BOOM!

– Chapter 14 –
Boom

BOOM, BOOM, BOOM, BOOM, boom!

That sound means the same thing everywhere, except one small backwater planet where it's part of the mating ritual.

In this case, though, immediately the reptile brain and higher functions got on the same page post haste.

"What in the hell was that?" Dan had been repeating this phrase more often than he wanted to lately.

Freddie was already moving to get dressed. If she was going to die in space, it would be with her pants on, not floating about space for generations naked. She dropped her robe reaching for her clothes.

Dan, ever chivalrous, turned his head. His reptile brain let out a series of swear words and suggestions concerning his virility. Dan headed toward the corridor to find out if he could see anything. There seemed to be light coming in from the viewport.

Freddie caught up to him just as she zipped up her jumpsuit. Dan's reptile brain smiled.

She handed him their satchels and the two sprinted toward the viewport, becoming airborne under the gravity loss in the corridor. They saw flickering to the left side. Leaning into the window, they saw floating objects coming from the side of the station not too far away.

"Crap!" Freddie said it for both of them. "Come on." She propelled herself towards the flickering.

"Shouldn't we be going the other way?"

"We should, but if the seals don't hold, this whole station will turn into a pyrotechnic show like no other."

They hurtled down the corridor to the next section. The auto-close on the door had triggered, but the door opened for them. Flying through the next section, they found the next door closed and not willing to open.

Freddie touched the wall. "It's hot."

"But if it exploded, shouldn't the other side be open to space?"

"It should. We saw the flame so we know the hull ruptured."

"Then why is it hot?"

"Because something is very wrong."

That was an accurate assessment.

Freddie pulled at an access panel near the door. The acrid smell of burning rubber made her eyes sting before the plate was off. As she removed the panel, sparks began spraying through the opening. She pushed the cover back into place.

"Run."

Hard to do without gravity, but yelling "Float!" did not seem appropriate.

She turned and propelled herself the way they had just come. Dan followed close behind.

When they reached the next door, they closed it from the other side and Freddie carefully removed the access panel in the wall. No sparking and the wiring was only warm. She traced the electrical circuits with her finger. Dan began to automatically trace the pipes and plumbing. Finding nothing obvious, Freddie looked around for a computer terminal and found nothing.

Station terminals were limited to secure areas so that random visitors could not access the system. Things were not at all like you see in the movies—probably because the architects had also watched those movies.

But if Freddie had found a terminal and hacked in (not that that was in her skill set), she would have found nothing.

Dan felt the pipes. One was very cold. "Hold on. What's this? It's freezing."

"Compressed gas."

"But what kind?"

"It could be carbon dioxide."

"That would be ideal. What are the other choices?"

"Oxygen, hydrogen, methane—pick one."

"Those are all explosive!"

"Two out of three."

"What?"

"Oxygen isn't explosive."

"It is."

"No, it oxidizes other material, making that material extremely explosive at a lower temperature than normal."

Freddie said it with enough authority Dan automatically accepted what he knew to be ridiculous.

Ridiculous, but true.

Freddie extrapolated the situation forward. "The pressurized gas flows through the access panel to the ceiling and is distributed to the corridor. The electronics go to the access panel and on to the various controls. The wiring is bad or overloaded, causing it to overheat…"

"Plus we've got oxygen, hydrogen, and methane waiting to explode."

"Right."

"Why?"

"Because they can't run away." Freddie was particularly proud of this retort.

"Why are those gasses here? I mean, oxygen I get, but methane, hydrogen, and the other one?"

"Carbon dioxide. They convert carbon dioxide and hydrogen into water and the methane is left over in the process. Honestly, the pipe we saw was probably oxygen; the oxygen supply goes everywhere. The others are just in the air scrubbers and the converters."

Even as they were speaking, technicians from TellTom (Your Way Into Space) were examining schematics trying to diagnose the problem. The ship was abandoned four days before its grand opening after sections began to spontaneously combust.

They had been testing the air recycling system to verify each section's scrubbers could handle processing and reclaiming carbon dioxide when the explosions began. In order to do this, they had to release enough carbon dioxide to simulate a densely populated space station.

They guessed something went wrong, allowing methane and/or hydrogen to mix with the oxygen in the cabins.

What they knew for sure was that when the first section blew, it caused an overload, which fried the circuitry that would have allowed them to vent the atmosphere, eliminating further explosions.

Most of their efforts since that discovery were dedicated to trying to figure out who to blame for the debacle. The techies had grabbed a shuttle and left.

Dan and Freddie didn't have that option.

Freddie had a horrific thought.

"No, no, no." Freddie rushed to the nearest viewport and scanned the ship. She saw what she was afraid of. "Look, there." She pointed. "And there, and there."

Dan looked over and saw nothing but darkness—where there should have been lights. When he stared harder, he could see flickers in some of the pockets of darkness.

Freddie continued. "Other sections have blown."

"And the wiring is failing everywhere." Dan tried to think like a plumber. It was not that difficult for him. "We need to stop the flow of oxygen."

"We'll need that to breathe."

"Not if we blow up."

Suddenly another BOOM! And the compartment next to them exploded. Freddie and Dan grabbed each other and held on. (That was for those of you waiting for violence and sex.)

They propelled themselves into the next section and closed the door.

Dan opened the nearest wall panel to take a look. "How long can we keep this up?"

"Only until we hit a collapsed section."

It suddenly struck Dan since they couldn't see the section closest to them when looking out the viewport, that may not be long in coming. Dan thought of *The Traveler* and how he spent all of his time keeping water out and air in—now it was the air that would kill them.

"Wait," he said. "Is there a way to vent this section?"

"Into space?"

"Yes."

"Not really something people usually want to do."

"If we could release the oxygen—"

"There'd be no explosion. But how do we do it?"

"I could burn a hole with my torch. Never mind. Saying it out loud showed me the flaw there."

"How about puncturing a hole?" Freddie countered.

"How long will that take to drain the air?"

"A big hole. No, we'd get sucked into that. Saying it out loud, you know."

"Maybe several small holes."

"That would take days. There's actually little pressure in these things."

"Damn. Can we pull out the wiring?" Dan did not like messing with electricity.

"Not without electrocuting ourselves. We know it's all live."

"Then the question is: why is it getting hot?"

"Faulty wiring."

"Yes, but why now?"

"Too much current?" Freddie looked down the corridor. "Why are all the lights on?"

"To see."

"Yes, but why are they *all* on? Why are all the systems on? They completed this entire station with no problem and when it's done, it turns into a string of firecrackers. Why?"

"Because they turned all the lights on."

"Because they turned *everything* on. Until it was ready to go, they tested systems individually and moved on."

"You don't test the disposal until everything's finished."

"We need to turn everything off."

"What draws the most power?"

"Gravity generators."

"Those first."

They propelled themselves forward, searching for this section's common area. A sign with a plate and crossed forks made that easy for them. Dropping to the floor upon crossing the threshold, they searched for a control board. Freddie was stymied. Dan hunted for an out of the way closet; he'd had vast experience finding breaker panels—water and electricity don't mix. Well they do, but it's not pretty.

"Here," he said.

"I'll shut it off, you check the wiring."

Dan ran to the door—which he reached as Freddie switched off the gravity. He had planned to very coolly leap into the corridor Superman style using his momentum to fly to the overheating area.

Instead, as he started to leap, his feet floated off the ground and he was unable to control his direction. He ended up spinning into the opposing corridor wall very unlike Superman. "Story of my life."

Flashbacks of belly flops on the diving team emerged.

Pushing off of the wall, he floated to the panel and checked the wiring. "It's hot."

Turning off the other systems one by one, Freddie shut down all but emergency lighting and air filtration systems. She didn't have access to those systems anyway; those functions were on the bridge.

Slowly the wiring began to cool.

Dan breathed a sigh of relief. Freddie was still holding her breath.

"We're missing something," she said.

"Getting killed?"

"No. Well I hope so, but that's not all. We eliminated the primary source of ignition, but there's something in the air."

"Is that like a premonition?"

"No, in the actual air. To be safe we need to figure out what's igniting."

"We need to find the maintenance room."

Dan spent more time than he liked in maintenance rooms. They were the modern version of the bilge—the place you send the stuff you don't want around people.

They floated to the back end of the section and located an employees' only door. Inside was a bewildering conjunction of machinery, pipe, and wiring.

Freddie began looking past the wiring. "There should be an air reclamation system. If there's a leak we can find it from there."

"Because?"

"Carbon dioxide from the air circulation system will be scrubbed out and sent to the water reclamation system to be mixed with hydrogen to make water and the leftover methane will be directed to a storage tank."

"And methane or hydrogen is what's blowing up."

"Probably."

Dan spotted something that looked like a hot water tank. "Over here."

Rushing over (which looks odd in zero-G), they inspected the tank. The label said, "Caution methane storage." Along with a host of MDSS warnings. Strangely, there was no line or hose attached to the tank.

Following from where the intake hose should have been, they found a hose on the floor and, near the opposite end, the water reclamation unit.

They didn't know that the water unit installer thought installing the hose was the storage tank installer's job and the tank installer thought it was the water unit installer's job.

Dan carefully secured the line. "Why doesn't it smell?"

"Methane is odorless."

"But…"

"No buts. Methane is odorless, it's the stuff that usually comes with it that smells."

Freddie said it with enough authority Dan automatically accepted what he knew to be ridiculous.

Ridiculous, but true.

Then they had to hurry to the next sector. And the next.

They repeated this process a dozen times before they encountered a locked door.

Dan was stuck. "I guess that's it."

"I don't think so."

"Our sections should be safe."

"Don't count on it." Freddie was looking out of the viewport. Having moved a quarter of the way around the wheel, the view was different. First, you could now see the edge of a blue planet, which could have been Earth. Second, you could see different sections of the ship that, although they were not on fire, were obviously damaged. "I think those sections were hit with shrapnel from the explosions."

Dan didn't pick up on what she meant.

So she continued. "If more sections explode—?"

Dan caught on. "We might get punctured."

Freddie nodded.

Luckily, they had just concluded a lightning tour of a dozen sections and knew what resources were available.

"This way. I think there were Triple S suits two sections back." She pushed off.

Dan followed, wondering what a Triple S suit was.

What it was, was redundant. It stood for the Space Safety Suit by Lifeinc, so when you say Triple S suit, it's like saying Space Safety Suit suit. Like Sat. Nav. Navigation.

The marketers at Lifeinc were aware of this most human penchant, and were going to call it the S. S. suit, but a burrito farmer from Iowa happened to mention in a focus group the initials sounded vaguely Hitlerian. With that realization, they quickly slapped an extra S onto the ten thousand finished suits.

Better redundant than offensive.

This only mattered because even after hundreds of years the Jewish people never forgot—mainly because memory implantation technology allowed them to share the trauma with subsequent generations.

Two sections down they found a staff area with Triple S's.

Freddie turned on the lights. "The lights should be okay. I doubt they caused the overheating."

"You *doubt* they caused the problem."

"We'll turn them off before we go."

As a general rule, one should always turn out the lights upon leaving a room. It's just good manners. And not doing so can make your space station explode.

Dan started to put his Triple S suit[8] on over his clothes. Freddie moved into another room.

"Aren't you going to put it on over your jumpsuit?" he said.

"I need to put on underwear. I didn't have time before. Although it is pretty freeing in zero-G."

Dan's reptile brain had a stroke. But not before dilating his pupils and sending saliva to his mouth. It would have sent it everywhere if it could have, so it settled for extra sweat.

As Dan donned his suit, he began thinking about what he was about to do: go on a space walk without training. As this was never something he had expected to ever do, he had never decided he would never do it. This was a lot of nevers for something he was about to do.

The good news was that with death staring him straight in the face, Maslow came to his aid and his impending doom drove the thought of Freddie putting on her underwear from his mind. His reptile brain made a note to save that thought for later.

---

[8] See? Even narrators make the mistake.

"Have you ever done this before?" he called to the next room.

"A couple of times."

"Is it hard?"

"No harder than falling off a log."

Dan had fallen off a log twice before. Although he recalled the falling as fairly simple to accomplish, the landing was decidedly hard.

Freddie came out with her Triple S on. She definitely had more practice changing in zero gravity than Dan, as his total experience in that area was zero.

"How are we going to bypass the door lock?"

"We're not. Since there are suits here, this is also where the exterior maintenance hatch should be." Carrying a helmet, Freddie headed to a door labeled **"Do not enter"** and promptly entered.

Dan followed.

Inside was another maintenance room with wiring, pipes, and a "guys of the month" calendar all three exposed. At the far end was a heavy door labeled, **"Danger! Do not enter!"** which Freddie promptly entered.

They were now in an airlock. It was a utilitarian room with an abundant lack of furnishing. As Freddie locked the door behind them, Dan studied the suit controls in the back of his right glove.

"How do the suits work?"

"Simple arrow control. Left, right, up and down. If you get off track, hit the red button."

Dan had been well trained by cartoons to never under any circumstances hit the red button. "What will that do?"

"Magnetize the boots to pull you to the hull."

"So to the nearest ton of metal."

"Better than being adrift."

"Not by much." Dan tried the control and was sent careening around the small room. "A little help!"

"Use small taps, just little bursts of compressed gas."

Dan's reptile brain thought of a joke and was very disappointed Dan did not repeat it.

Soon Dan was able to attain some control And Freddie was unlocking the very small hatch, which was labeled:

Extreme Danger **Do Not Enter.**

We're not kidding. Really. And when we say Enter we really mean Exit. Do not Exit! Sorry for the small print, but as this message has gotten rather wordy there's really not room. Did you remember to put your helmet on? Put it off to the last minute, didn't you? Do it now… Did you? Good, now don't go out! Space is one of the most inhospi…

Here the author ran out of room. It's a good thing Dan didn't read the warning. As he maneuvered down, Freddie double checked both of their helmet seals and clipped the suits' tethers to a loop on the wall.

"That's so you don't fly off when I open the hatch."

It was entirely possible to build an airlock that gently let the oxygen vent, slowly exposing the occupant to the vacuum. But that's expensive; save that for the paying customer. Besides, what's the fun in that?

Freddie hit a big red button. The door swung open and the air whooshed out—only the sound of the whoosh was quickly suffocated by the void of space. Dan heard a voice on his comm. unit.

"Whooo, that'll wake you up."

"I was quite awakened by the exploding space station, thank you very much."

"Best if you use your tether to move about." Freddie maneuvered herself out of the hatch and hooked her tether to a ring on the outside.

Dan followed suit. From outside of the ship he could clearly see a planet that could only be Earth. Well, it actually could have been any number of Earth-like planets. It was, in fact, Earth, but it could have been some other planet.

They moved slowly over the back of the ring to stand on top. From there they could see all around the huge structure. It looked like seven of the three and a half dozen sections had exploded and at least two more had taken damage.

Suddenly Dan had a nagging feeling he had left the lights on.

They headed to the next undamaged section.

What would have taken five minutes inside took thirty outside. And it was tiring. Entering through a rererecalcitrant hatch, they repeated the airlock procedure backwards.

Shutting down the next fifteen sections proceeded relatively smoothly. And when I say relatively I don't mean comparably—it was like dealing with your relatives. You hope it will go smoothly, but it invariably goes sideways and you have to manage things quickly and delicately or face an inevitable explosion.

They exited that section from another hatch. As they opened it, Freddie noticed a different message:

Extreme Danger **Do Not Enter.**

That's it. You've been warned.
I wouldn't go out there.
Then again I'm just a painter, but it seems scary. Just take a look at a photo of someone left unprotected in space—it's not pretty.
In summary: inside, good; space bad.

It was a good thing Dan didn't see the message.

The process of shutting down the various sections took all day. They did stop for a meal, but ended up eating while they worked.

In section thirty-three, Dan was struck by a thought. "How come we're not sleepy?"

"What?"

"How come we're not sleepy? We finished a twelve-hour shift on a sailing ship, came here, almost got blown up, and have be working all day. I mean I'm tired, but I should be exhausted and falling asleep."

"It's the timestream resetting things. It not only resets your age, it kinda resets your brain. I think being in the timestream is like sleeping for a week. It drains the fatigue poisons from your body."

"I'm glad the corporations never figured out time travel—they'd never let you sleep. Your shift's over; jump into the time machine and start the next shift."

The last section Freddie wanted to work on was one damaged by shrapnel. "It will probably be all right, but why risk it?"

They entered through a rather sensible hatch, who had decided she'd had enough problems lately, what with the section damage and depressurization and everything. On the inside of the hatch Dan noticed a simple warning:

ABANDON ALL HOPE YE WHO

EXIT HERE.

"That's rather odd," he mused.

They went about the business of shutting down the power to the section. Freddie found some repair panes and wanted to see if they could fix the hull fractures. Normally this would have been quite the undertaking, but these were self-sealing panels. If they could repair this section, one contiguous third of the ring would be viable.

Given they had no idea how long they would be here, it seemed like a good idea.

They put the sheets in place and activated them. Each panel molded itself into place fitting the contours of the damaged section and adhering to the surface of the inner wall. They worked like a charm. This was now another section that would not be venting atmosphere into space. They noticed the air pressure returning, then went to see if they could open the doors to the other sections.

The first opened easily and more air whooshed into the room. The door on the other end was more calcitrant.

They unlocked the system, but the door had been slightly warped by the decompression. They pushed until it began to creak open. When it opened enough, Dan slipped through to pull from the other side.

That's when it all went to hell.

One of the repair sheets slipped a little and air began leaking. To be fair, they were not installed by factory-trained technicians as recommended on the packaging. To be more fair, the factory never actually trained technicians.

With that, the door started to close and Freddie could not fit through. Freddie pushed and Dan pulled, and by the time they figured out the full situation, Freddie was on one side and Dan on the other. Freddie would have to reseal the panel to halt the decompression and open the door. Simple.

Then Dan heard music. "Please tell me the sound system is on."

"What?"

"I SMELL TRONA." (He meant sulfur—but it's kind of the same thing.)

"Hell!"

Dan could feel it coming and the calcitrant door just became recalcitrant. Dan's reptile brain took over, the sex was about to get away, and Dan began hitting the door with his wrench.

Freddie's reptile brain took over and she began hitting the door with her fists.

The hitting did not improve the situation in any way, except it did lower the door's self-esteem as it was already slightly warped and now needed a new paint job to cover up the blemishes.

As Dan edged closer to the jump, he stopped hitting and put both hands on the door. When Dan stopped banging, Freddie in turn put her hands on the door. Dan tried with every inch of his being to focus on the space station He was rooted to this spot and could not be moved. For an eternity he was half in and half out of the stream.

Cuttlefish.

And Dan jumped.

On the planet below the station, the TellTom techies had noticed there were no more explosions—hell, half of the planet noticed as people were staying up all night to watch the pretty pyrotechnic show. Everyone but the folks at TellTom were saddened the party was over earlier than expected.

– Chapter 15 –
Time Travel for Fun and Profit

As Dan hit the timestream, he could feel Freddie on the other side of the door. He could feel her panic and loss, as well as his own. He could swear he even heard her saying "Goodbye."

Then his brain unraveled and things got muddled up.

When he popped back into time, he was in a familiar environment—a public bathroom. And not just any time's public bathroom, a real one with tile floors and metal/porcelain fixtures. He was overjoyed that he was near his own time—unless he was in a bathroom museum, displaying the primitive ways people used to relieve themselves.

Or worse, a robot museum displaying the primitive ways humans used to relieve themselves.

He looked around for Freddie as she could usually shed light on such things—then he remembered. In a second he went from overjoyed to fear to grief. The reptile was proud of him.

His vision narrowed and he began to sweat as fear raced through him. How would he survive without her? He was surprised at how afraid he was—and that it was less about his physical survival than losing *her*.

Dan believed she'd be fine. They stopped the space station from exploding and she'd take care of herself, but how in all of time could he find her again?

Dan pushed aside those thoughts; he had to assess his situation like she had taught him.

Examining the fixtures, Dan guessed this was the 1940s or 50s. Nothing newer than that. Cerulean blue sinks and toilets—a popular 1950s color—and soldered copper pipe—an improvement over galvanized iron pipe. Dan knew his plumbing.

Dan looked into the mirror. He was no longer wearing the Triple S, but just the TellTom jumpsuit, and he had his plumber overalls underneath.

"The timestream resetting my clothing." It was barely a mumble.

Dan peeled off the jumpsuit and stuffed it in his satchel. He wondered if he would lose the satchel sometime as it wasn't part of his original equipment. In the mirror he could see some of the oil and grime he'd smeared on the hedge fund manager's sink.

"Perfect. I guess filth is something the timestream resets."

Peeking out of the bathroom, he saw neither futuristic voyeurs nor victorious robots, but a busy lobby of an old hotel—although at this time it was still relatively new. The cavernous lobby was filled with guests coming and going. Many were sitting reading a paper or talking with friends. Large green plants gave it a relaxed ambiance.

Dan walked through the lobby toward the elegant entrance/exit. He would need money for breakfast—or lunch or whatever. Absentmindedly he pulled out his wallet and found his money had been restored. It was no good, with its futuristic anti-counterfeiting measures and odd look, but it was restored.

"Hey you!"

Dan ignored the call, as he knew no one here.

He was wrong about that. His grandparents and a plethora of other relatives were alive in this era, but since they were nowhere near him, he was functionally correct.

"The Plumber!"

He turned and saw the manager coming toward him. Dan assumed he was the manager as he had that "better-than-you stick" inserted up his exit. The manager assumed Dan was the plumber since he had a tool belt around his waist.

The manager was tall and skinny, with a pencil thin mustache. His fine features were stuck in a stuck-up position. "The leak is this way." The man began walking away, expecting him to follow, which he did.

"I need to be paid in cash."

"You can bill us."

Dan stopped. "You can find someone else."

The manager stopped and stared at him. "Fine."

"One hundred per hour."

"One hun… Are you out of your mind???"

"Just kidding… Ten?"

"This isn't a holiday."

"Okay. Five."

"That's more than most."

"I'm better that most."

"Fine."

The manager took Dan to the kitchen and pointed out a faucet under a sink that was leaking badly, then started to walk away.

"Wait a sec, let me see what we've got." Dan studied the pipe and turned his wrench on the nut. "Okay. That's five bucks."

"You're done?"

"Yes, sir. And you still have 55 minutes on the clock. If I can get…" He noticed the sandwiches being prepared by white-gowned chefs. "… a sandwich, I'll give you an extra half hour."

The manager handed Dan a sandwich.[9] "Follow me."

As they bustled toward the lobby, Dan had a thought. And a sandwich. "Don't you have a maintenance man?"

"He quit yesterday."

"At least it hasn't been long."

---

[9] Turkey on sourdough.

"Turns out he quit because he wasn't very good." The manager buttonholed a bellhop. "Take him to every leaky fixture in the building."

The bellboy was short and getting old for the gig—there was a little gray in his hair. He was also the friendly type—a plus in his business. "I'm Tyrone. So you're a plumber, huh?"

"When I'm not a time traveler."

"Like H. G. Wells, huh? Do you like those kinda shows?"

"Some."

"I like all the television shows, especially the westerns. Wanna see my quick draw?"

"Knock yourself out."

Tyrone drew his hand from his pocket. "Fast, huh?"

Dan didn't think so. "Yeah, pretty quick."

"I'll bet I coulda beat Billy the Kid."

Dan thought if he grabbed Tyrone's hand the next time he thought of fish, the bellboy might have a chance to try.

"Plumber's a union job, right?"

"Pretty much." Dan realized his union card was invalid as it was dated over sixty years in the future.

The first stop was another faucet in an empty room—easy fix.

The second was a bad trap in a public bathroom that had been repaired with duct tape. Duct tape is great for repairing many things.

Plumbing isn't one of them.

Dan made a note he'd need a new trap and went on.

In the next hour and a half he fixed six sinks, two toilets, and made four notes for parts.

"How many more plumbing problems you got?" he asked.

"At least a dozen."

Given the nature of the "repairs" he'd seen, Dan guessed it was at least double that.

At the front desk, he collected his five dollars.

The manager consulted quietly with Tyrone, then turned to Dan. "Tyrone says you got a lot done."

"I think so."

"So you work for your pay."

"I haven't figured out another fair way to get it."

"You want a job?"

"Not really, but I could use work."

"Three dollars an hour."

"I'm better than that."

"Three twenty-five."

"Plus room and board."

"Deal."

"I'll fix whatever plumbing that needs it. After that, we'll see."

"Tyrone, show..." The manager gave an inquiring look.

"Dan."

"... Dan to a staff residence, then get him to work."

Tyrone resisted. "Mr. Gaurtier, *I* need to get back to work."

"Just get him started. I'll give you the fifteenth floor tonight."

Tyrone caved. "All right, but I don't like it."

Tyrone walked away with Dan in tow.

"What's the fifteenth floor?" Dan asked.

"That's where the rich play. Separate elevator, with separate staff. The best of everything."

"So it's a whole floor dedicated to making the rest of us feel bad."

"Pretty much."

"And you want the fifteenth floor for the tips?"

"Yes and no. The money's good, but the people aren't."

"Where should I start?"

"After you put your stuff in your room, I'll show you supplies so you can see what you're dealing with. Fill out the order form for whatever we don't have and drop it off at the front desk for Gaurtier to review. You should get what you need in a few hours."

"How about today I check the public and staff plumbing and tomorrow I follow housekeeping in?"

"Perfect."

Dan suddenly realized he had no idea where he was. He could see big buildings, but beyond that… "So what's fun to do near here?"

"Are you kidding? You got Broadway a few blocks away and you're asking what's fun?"

"Let me rephrase that: fun if you're broke."

"You got five dollars."

"That's my whole bundle."

"What kind of a poker player are you?"

"Decent."

"Staff run a game most nights, just nickel and dime, but you can win a few bucks."

"I'm in."

"At seven. I'll look for ya."

Dan spent the rest of the day fixing leaks and requesting parts. The supply room contained a good supply of replacement fixtures, but fewer parts to repair them. He had what he needed to replace a whole toilet, but not a leaky valve. In five hundred years, cloning science would make the same true of heart surgery.

Yes, I just compared hearts to toilets—both function by moving liquid from one place to the other. Admittedly, hearts do recycle the liquid and toilets wouldn't do that for a few more hundred years, but you get the point.

After Dan finished work, he counted off the time to seven o'clock. He'd been able to marginally function while being up to his elbows (sometimes further) in plumbing, but now it was quiet. His brain was twisting, missing Freddie and wondering what happened to her. Was she marooned in the sealed-off section? Did someone ever come to rescue her? What would she look like in a bikini?

Reptile brain missed her as well.

He felt guilty he couldn't get to her in time—or in space.

Since according to Einstein time is a location point in space, they are part of the same thing. They are both relative, so they change depending on dimension and situation, which sounds like a recipe for shady billing practices if you ask me. For instance:

"How much will it cost?"

"That depends."

"On what?"

"What dimension you're in, where in space you are, and whether you're sitting on a hot stove."

"What?"

"I'll charge you whatever the universe tells me to charge you."

But Dan knew precisely none of this.

The room assigned to him was a bottom-of-the-line guest room, which meant it had a bed, a dresser, a tiny bathroom and no window. Nothing more elaborate like Pay Per View or a wet bar. While it gave him a place to lie down to relax, it wasn't all that relaxing. By the time seven o'clock came, he was thrilled to escape his room.

The other players were members of the staff. He expected it to be all men, but there were some women there; and two looked like sharks. There were two tables going and that shrank to one as the evening progressed.

Dan was holding his own pretty well until he introduced them to a new game—Texas hold 'em. At first they were wary (as no gambler wants to be caught in a game of Tegwar or fizzbin), but soon they learned the rules and the game caught on. Dan did have an advantage here as he was the only one with experience with the game.

By night's end he doubled his money. Maybe not a good way to start out with his coworkers, but he didn't intend on staying here long.

Dan also collected gossip along the way.

One woman, whose name he could not remember (Elsa), told another woman, whose name he could not remember (Margaritha) that Gaurtier had a girlfriend he was keeping at another hotel. She had a sister who worked there and sis saw him visiting this girl daily during his lunch hour.

She was right about everything but the word "girl."

Another man (whose name Dan could remember, but I can't) had noticed Dan's satchel. "Is that a purse?"

"No, it's a satchel."

"What's the difference?"

"This is manly."

"Do you take it everywhere?"

"Yeah, I use it to carry spare parts."

"Then why do you have it here?"

"To carry home my winnings."

Tyrone insisted the famous blonde on the fifteenth floor was coming on to him. Two other bellboys, whose names Dan could not remember (Earnest, the tall one, and Tommy, the squat one), claimed the same story.

The second one looked at Dan. "She's complaining about the plumbing."

"What's wrong with it?" Dan asked.

"Probably nothing. My guess is she's just lonely."

The first one looked at Tyrone. "You didn't take care of that."

"I don't have that kinda time."

Elsa snorted.

Tyrone continued. "Now if I was a plumber who could conceivably stay in a guest's room for an hour or two, I might consider it."

Dan realized they were prompting him to bring a story to tell tomorrow night. Dan had his doubts.

Since Dan's divorce, he had dated, but with less than spectacular success. Most of the women he met were divorcées, or college age, or really weird. Each had her own baggage. The former either caused their divorce or had lost all faith in men, the mid group were too young and he couldn't relate to them, the latter had never married due to odd nature (usually involving numerous cats, the numbers of which increased exponentially with their age) or a strong independent streak, which while not a negative, did tend to inhibit long term relationships.

Dan's night was fitful. He had dreams of Freddie trapped in the decompressing space station or lost in the timestream.

He awoke covered in sweat—which gave him an excuse for another shower. After weeks at sea, the two he'd had since then didn't seem nearly enough. In addition, since the timestream kept resetting him to after work grungy, it was hard to feel clean.

Dan had left his coveralls to be cleaned last night and found them folded and pressed in the hall, as well as a hotel coverall emblazoned with a stylized RR. He put his clean coveralls in his satchel and wore the hotel brand.

Dan went downstairs with the intent of having breakfast, but Gaurtier intercepted him first.

"I need you to go to Fifteen C now."

"Sure, right after breakfast."

"I said now."

"What's the emergency?"

"Did you not hear? *Fifteen* C?"

"So it's a rich person, non-emergency emergency?"

"Yes."

"After breakfast then."

"People on the fifteenth floor pay extra for our best service."

"She's not paying *me* extra."

"If you tell her you're missing breakfast, she'll tip you well."

"How well?"

"Could be as much as ten dollars."

It didn't sound like much, but if his hourly wage was an indicator, it could be worth around a hundred bucks.

"Breakfast can wait," he decided.

Dan headed to the private elevator. He'd wanted to see the fifteenth floor anyway. The walls of the car were cushioned in a silver damask pattern and buttoned into a diamond formation.

The elevator operator gave him the stink eye; he was a small man slight of build, who was too young to be losing his hair but was managing to do it anyway. It was his job to guard the fifteenth floor and give its occupants whatever they wanted with the utmost discretion. His name tag said "Richard."

"What do you want?" he demanded.

"Fifteenth floor."

"Obviously. Why."

"Is that any of your business?"

"Anyone going to the fifteenth floor is my business."

"Then take it up with Gaurtier, he sent me to Fifteen C."

"Hmmmph." Richard pulled the handle and the elevator ascended. As they reached the floor, Richard stopped the elevator but didn't open the door. He gave Dan a frozen stare. "Do not do anything in there that makes my life more difficult or I will absolutely make *your* life more difficult."

Dan was having a hard time imagining what "Little Richard" could do to him. "I'm shaking."

"You should be. One word from anyone on this floor and you're history. One word from me and they'll give that word." With that, he opened the door.

Dan stepped out and the elevator left. "Good Golly."

Dan cracked himself up.

The wide hallway featured the same diamond tucked wall pattern as the elevator, with an ivory carpet decorated with flowers and the aroma of lavender. Down the hall, he knocked on Fifteen C.

No answer.

He knocked again. No answer. He wasn't sure what the protocol for opening the door of a fifteenth floor guest was. He called out, "Maintenance," while knocking and heard the sound of stirring.

After a bit, the door slowly opened. There stood a beautiful blonde draped in a white robe. She looked at Dan, puzzled. "You're not Bob."

"I'm the new plumber." He pointed to the badge clipped to his coveralls. "Dan."

"What happened to Bob?"

"No idea. He must have left."

"Story of my life."

"So what's the problem, Ms.... ?"

"Miss... Armage, but you can call me Elinore."

"And the problem is?"

"Oh... The commode is making a funny noise." She motioned for Dan to follow her into the suite.

The living area was about as big as Dan's entire apartment. The master bedroom was furnished with a queen size bed, night tables, an armchair, and a balcony with a view of the city. She continued into the bathroom and stood beside the sink.

Dan admired the bathroom. A sunken bathtub with gold mosaic tiling and gold fixtures. A separate room for the shower. Tiny bottles of RR toiletries, shampoos and skin care products on the white tiled sink.

She pointed at the toilet. "It does this from time to time, it will just start squeaking very loudly."

"All the time?"

"No, just when... I... utilize it."

Dan promptly flushed and he was surprised that it did make a god-awful squeak.

"See, I told you."

"You did."

"I'm glad you believed me. Bob always believed me. My father never believed me about anything. That's why I moved here."

"To New York?" He lifted off the lid—there was no obvious problem there.

"No, to the hotel. After the breakup with Montrose, the newspaper people just hounded me everywhere and Daddy was no help at all, so I came here to lay low for a while."

Dan adjusted the water flow and voilà, no squeak. "There you go."

"Already?" She sounded disappointed.

"Easy fix."

She sighed. "It won't last long."

"It should."

"No, Bob would fix it, but it would always come back right after he left."

"It should last this time."

"I don't think so. Bob said I'd have to change rooms so he could rip up the floor if I wanted to fix it right."

"Well let's keep an eye on it then." He flushed again and no squeak.

The woman stuck out her hand. There was a ten-dollar bill in it.

"That's a lot."

"I don't like squeaks."

He took the bill. "Tell you what: why don't I look at all your plumbing?"

She nodded eagerly.

Dan inspected under the sink—the plumbing was new, shiny and perfect, as was the sunken tub. Dan could imagine it filled with bubble bath bubbles and Freddie.

"I told my friend Joyce this is the best hotel in New York, but she doesn't believe me. You know why it's the best? The service. People like you and Bob, who go the extra mile."

The second bath was on the other side of the suite. This one had a claw foot tub with gold mosaic tile and gold fixtures. Gold sink fixtures. Freddie would easily fit into this tub, too.

"Joyce never believes me about anything, either. She thinks I'm dumb or something, but I'm not. I've been tested."

Dan wondered if rich people could buy an IQ. He began examining the pipes and fixtures.

"I could have gone to college, but what's the point? It's not like I'm going get a job as a nurse or teacher or something. I can do whatever I want without going to school."

"What do you want?"

She tossed up her hands. "That's the problem! I can't figure out what I want to do."

"That's why I went to college."

"You went to college?"

"Yeah, it helped me figure out what I didn't want to do."

"What you didn't want to do?"

"Absolutely. I tried all kinds of things and found most of them bored me to death."

"Me, too. Everything bores me. Why, I told my friend Joyce the other day, 'Everything bores me to death,' and she said she was bored too and we probably needed to go to more parties."

"Sounds boring."

"That's what I said."

The second bath was perfect. Dan was beginning to suspect Bob wasn't a bad plumber after all—he simply didn't give a shit.

Unless there was a big tip involved.

Her suite had a pristine kitchen that looked never used. Dan checked faucets, sinks, and the dishwasher—which still had packing material inside. A perk of the rich that they would never use.

She leaned against the doorjamb and watched him inspect things. "I go to parties and it's always the same old faces, with the same old problems. I can't stand it."

"Maybe you need to find real people."

"Are you real?"

"Most of the time."

"I'll bet you're always real."

Dan smiled, thinking of where he'd started the day yesterday.

Although since yesterday was five hundred years in the future, it really wasn't yesterday as even tomorrow was closer to it than yesterday. Dan's concept of his own personal timestream did not allow him to think of where he was previously in his own experience as anything other than yesterday, or last week—as opposed to thinking of where he started the day five hundred years from now in his future/past experience.

But we'll talk more about this later—or maybe earlier.

"Well, everything checks out, looks great."

"I told you Bob was a good plumber."

"How often was he here to check your plumbing?" Dan didn't like the way that sounded.

"Every day. Sometimes twice a day."

"Every day?"

"He was great. You don't have to take my word for it, all the people here love him."

All the people on the fifteenth floor.

That was the reason the rest of the plumbing in the building stunk: Bob was spending all his time with the rich, so he could spend all their money later.

"Well, Elinore, I better be on my way."

"You've done so much, let me tip you again." And she turned to find her purse.

"No, that's fine. One tip per visit is plenty."

"Are you sure?"

"Yes."

"What time will you be by tomorrow?"

"Tomorrow?"

"To fix the commode noise."

"Call the front desk when it starts squeaking."

"Why don't you come by at eleven? It's usually bad by then."

"When it squeaks."

"It might start when you leave."

"It might. Goodbye, Elinore."

"Good day, Dan."

Dan walked down the carpeted hallway toward the elevator and stopped. No need to deal with Richard or let him know when he left. Dan walked to the stairs. He checked the door and found he could enter the stairwell, but his key would not grant him access to the fifteenth floor. Pity.

Dan walked down a flight to the fourteenth floor and took the public elevator from there. Stepping out into the lobby, he headed for breakfast. As he passed the private elevator, Richard spotted him and headed his way. Dan picked up his pace.

Richard (with his tiny legs) was torn between chasing Dan and continuing to man his post. In the end, he knew Dan would be back.

– Chapter 16 –
Time Travel for Fun and Prophet

Breakfast was wonderful. It had bacon.

Dan followed the housekeepers around all morning. Nearly every room he entered had some plumbing or maintenance problem. He didn't like electrical work, so he wrote notes for the next guy.

Not that it did the next guy much good.

On his second day at work, the next guy was working on the laundry's 220 socket when he spontaneously combusted. Was it coincidence or darker forces at work? All we know is the list went up with him.

Bwaah hahahahaha.

Dan, of course, had no idea his careful notations were all for naught. He would be long gone into the timestream by the time (or space) this occurred.

Or he could be dead. I'm not ruling out his imminent demise. Don't lose interest. Awww, who am I kidding? If he didn't die in space or by carnivorous aquatic squamate, he'll probably survive New York.

Wait, survive New York? He probably *is* in real mortal danger!

Jump, Dan, jump!!

I can't look!!

……..

……..

Now I can't type.

Perhaps if I look a little through my fingers.

……..

Nope, still can't type. Need my hands for that.

Dan's day proceeded without much drama until about three o'clock, when he was paged to the front desk by Gaurtier.

"You're needed in Fifteen C."

"I did all the work."

"I didn't say there was work, I said you're needed."

"I've got real work."

"Just check the pipes for her."

"Fine. I'll swing by."

Dan headed toward the elevator. Seeing Richard standing by the open door filled him with dread. Dan stopped and reached into his pocket for his jar of grease.

Then Dan walked over and boarded the elevator.

Richard closed the door, but made no move to get it going. "You didn't come down by the elevator."

"Nope."

"What did you do for Miss Armage?"

"Are you going to get this thing moving?"

"No."

"Forget the way?"

"This elevator moves when I move it."

Dan splayed his fingers, revealing the grease and began moving his hand toward the back wall.

Richard stiffened in outrage. "You will not put that hand on my elevator."

"I get claustrophobic. Who knows what could happen if this thing doesn't get moving."

"I'll get you fired."

"Yeah, but my unemployment won't last long, unlike a grease stain on your fabric wall. Or your uniform."

The elevator started moving.

"This isn't over."

"Maybe not, but I do know Miss Armage will not be happy if anything happens to me." Stalemate.

The door opened and Dan walked out.

Elinore was quick to open the door. Well, quick for someone with a bloodstream containing roughly equal parts blood and alcohol. "It's squeaking again."

"It shouldn't be."

"Well, it is. Look."

Dan walked to the bathroom.

"You would not believe the day I've had. I called up Conover College and they said they'd accept me if I got my father's blessing."

Dan assumed by blessing, they meant cash.

"And I owe it all to you. If you hadn't told me about how you went to college, I never would have called."

Was she really that easily led?

Dan flushed the toilet.

It squealed.

Dan adjusted the water flow and the strangled noise stopped.

"I'm so ex… You are a miracle worker! It always took Bob a half hour." She went on about college.

Dan took out a piece of chalk and marked the handle and wall opposite it.

"My friend Joyce—you remember Joyce?—she says I'll never actually go."

"Do you need anything else?"

"Maybe you need to look at the kitchen again."

Dan doubted she'd even been in the kitchen—unless she needed ice. "It's fine."

"Can you stay a little longer? Maybe have dinner with me?"

"I'm not allowed to have dinner with the guests."

"Bob did it all the time."

He did.

"I'm not Bob."

She moved in closer. "No, you're much younger."

"And better looking?"

"Yes."

"Yeah, you've had too much to drink."

She moved inside his space. Dan felt excitement at the invasion. Reptile brain did a little jig.

"Not so much," she claimed.

For some strange reason Dan reacted with guilt. Freddie wasn't his girlfriend, but rational brain asserted he owed her something. Reptile brain called him a moron.

Elinore touched his chest.

And started to pull down the zipper on his coverall.

She stopped at the sight of a jump suit. "Kinky."

Dan had decided if he wore the jumpsuit, it would be more likely to stay with him the next time he came out of the timestream. He thought it might be handy in trips to the future.

Jumpsuits were overrepresented in movies about the future. He never considered the old movies that were futuristic versions of his timeline were all wrong. Flying cars, jumpsuits, and shiny foil clothing never really became popular.

However, jumpsuits did continue to be a sign of corporate ownership for a millennia.

As Elinore began to pull his zipper down even further, he stopped her. "No."

Reptile brain started beating on his frontal cortex.

Elinore looked puzzled. "No?"

"No, I don't think you want this."

"I do."

"You want to talk."

"I did, now I want this."

"It won't make me stay."

"But it might make you come back."

"I might do that anyway."

"I don't want to be alone."

"Who does?"

"You're not married? No girlfriend or anything?"

"Not married, no girlfriend, but sort of an anything."

"What kind of anything?"

"I was traveling with a woman and I lost her."

"Think you'll find her again."

"I doubt it. She's a long way away."

"I'm not."

"Look, I may not be here long and I don't wanna be some guy who just disappears on you—like Bob."

"Then don't be."

"I won't be able to help it."

"What, are you a spy or something?"

"If I'm here tomorrow, I'll tell you."

"Oooooh, something to look forward to."

Dan opened the door. "I gotta go."

"So you're coming back tomorrow?"

"If you need me and if you're sober."

"I'm friendlier with a few drinks."

"So I've noticed." Dan left the room and heard a noise down the hall.

Another guest was entering Fifteen E. The man looked up and saw Dan. "You there, are you the new Bob?"

"I like to think Bob was the old me."

"I need help with my sink."

Dan spent the rest of the day being passed around the fifteenth floor, from one wealthy guest to another. They were all used to personal service from Bob.

Dan made double his day's wages in tips.

Poker that night was good to Dan as well. Not as good as the first night, but good. The squat one was wearing his name badge, so Dan could remember his name, Tommy. And he remembered Tyrone—he had doubled his name memory.

Mid-game the less not pretty of the maids (Margaretha) threw out the question: "How'd it go in Fifteen C?"

The other less not pretty of the maids (Elsa) snorted.

The tall man he couldn't remember chimed in. "Did she come on to you?"

"No."

Tommy didn't buy it. "Come on, she hits on all the guys."

Elsa smiled. "And some of the women."

Guffaws and giggles chorused the room.

"She's just lonely," said Dan.

Tyrone glanced up from his hand. "Two lonely people looking for love."

Most of the other players were in reptile brain, two were not. Those two players were in shark brain—card shark (or sharp). Pressuring someone over the details of their love life would either embarrass them or make them brag; neither was generally good for their card play.

Dan lost the hand.

Tomorrow night was the big game—the payday game. It was a chance for everyone to get even—or be broke for another week.

That night Dan slept in his jumpsuit with his satchel and money nearby. Not that the money would be likely to be worth anything if he jumped.

Dan hadn't really thought about how light he had to travel. Anything he wanted to keep had to stay on his person, or at least nearby. He might get to reclaim his tools and original clothes, but not anything else he wasn't wearing.

The next day Dan followed housekeeping again and was making good progress at cleaning up the mess Bob left behind. He realized he was cheating himself out of tips by fixing things before they were called in, but he didn't figure he'd be here for long.

Still, he couldn't figure out why he was here. Maybe there was a person or key event he was drawn to, but New York in 1954 covered a lot of ground. He tried reading the paper to get an idea, but too much was happening. Also, he figured just because jumpers were drawn to certain events, it didn't mean he was this time.

Maybe he was only here to fix the plumbing.

At about two Dan got a work order for Fifteen C and headed over to the elevator. Richard was waiting. As the elevator started moving, Dan noticed Richard was quiet and smiling. Obviously his twisted little brain was up to no good.

Dan thought about asking what was going on, but knew he wouldn't get a straight answer. Richard didn't want retaliation on his precious elevator. Dan assumed, quite correctly, he would soon be called on the carpet and maybe fired for some trumped up offense.

No big deal; between a few days' pay, tips, and poker winnings he would have over $100 in his pocket—a nice stake in 1954. He figured that would be close to $1,000 in his time.

If he got to keep it. Freddie would have thrown it in the fire.

Dan stepped out of the elevator and headed to Fifteen C. Inside, Elinore was sober and excited.

"You'd be so proud of me: I haven't had a drop all day. I talked to Daddy and he's agreed I should go to college. I'm enrolled next semester!! Daddy liked the college so much he's building them a new wing or something. I can't wait to tell Joyce. She's coming by for drinks this afternoon, with a friend, and I can't wait to rub her nose in it."

"Drinks?" Dan started moving to the bathroom.

"For someone I've only known a few days, you're such a mother hen. You should come. I'd like you to meet Joyce. She knows all the most fun people. She travels everywhere, like I used to before Montrose and I broke up. We used to have so much fun."

Dan wondered if she drank to reduce ADHD. There weren't many ways to cope with this much energy in 1954. Every generation has its own way of dealing with the brain and is fully convinced they are so much more humane than the last.

Putting someone in an orphanage was better than leaving them on the ice. An asylum was better than an orphanage. Lobotomy was better than an asylum. Shock treatment and hydrotherapy better than a lobotomy. Thorazine better than shock, and so on.

I much prefer the endorphin jumpstart of 3215. You may be nuts on roller-skates, but you're so fun to be around, no one minds.

Dan flushed the john. It squeaked.

"Don't you drink, Dan? I'll bet you used to, in college maybe."

Dan checked his chalk marks. Strangely, someone had turned the handle until the valve water pressure made the squeak. Almost as if someone did it on purpose.

Dan could replace the valve, or restrict the water flow, but then something else would go wrong. It was like Munchausen Syndrome by proxy only instead of making a human being ill to get attention, Elinore was making her plumbing sick.

The plumbing was biding its time for revenge.

It is an accepted fact that most "so-called" inanimate objects will seek revenge on humans (and non-humans) that have wronged them. It is also a fact that inanimate objects don't perceive time as we do. A music system's individual parts age very slowly and so it believes it has all the time in the world to make you pay.

It will invariably choose the most inopportune time to carry out its revenge. Your stereo dies during a party, your disposal clogs when it's full of rotting fish, or your horn honks mysteriously and unceasingly when you are behind an enormous pack of leather-clad bikers.

Fortunately for us, the appliances usually misjudge their own obsolescence. Your computer believes it has decades to pick the right time to burn out its processor, sending your nearly finished novel into digital nonexistence. It doesn't realize it will be obsolete in only four years—it feels good, full of life, never realizing it lives in an era of planned obsolescence.

Can you imagine how often our stuff would break if appliances knew how little time they had?

Dan adjusted the handle and stood up. He wasn't sure Elinore had stopped for a breath.

"I'm leaving to visit Conover tomorrow. What are you doing this weekend?"

"I may be leaving."

"What?"

"I'm usually not anywhere for more than a couple days."

"You can't go."

"I won't have a choice."

"You told me you'd tell me why."

"I will, but you won't believe me."

"I always believe everyone. I know what it's like when people don't believe you."

"Fine, but I did warn you." Dan sat down on a couch. "I'm a time jumper."

"What??" It was almost as if the comment didn't register.

"A time traveler. I move from place to place in time."

"Uhh uh."

"See? You don't believe me."

"I do, but how does that work?"

"I'm just going about my day and suddenly I'm popping up someplace else."

"Are you sure you're not blacking out?"

"If I am, I'm waking up hundreds of years later... Or earlier."

"Show me something from some other time."

"Well. This satchel came from Shakespeare's time." He showed her the manly purse.

"It looks like hand stitched leather, made by craftsmen."

"In Shakespeare's time."

"Do you have something from the future?"

"I don't have much. It's hard to take things through the timestream, other than what I'm wearing. Oh, I know." Dan unzipped his coverall.

"You didn't like it when I did that."

"I didn't want you to see this; I never said I didn't like it." Dan revealed his TellTom jumpsuit.

Elinore approached him and touched the material—and maybe not coincidentally his chest. "What is this fabric?"

"No idea, but it's lightweight and comfortable."

"I need to inspect it. You better take it off."

"Nice try. You have friends coming."

Elinore smiled. "Can't you control when you leave?"

"Nope. I'm still pretty new at this."

"This is not fair. I finally find an attractive man who's truly interesting and leaving for the Middle Ages."

"Possibly."

"Shit."

"So you believe me?"

"I believe everybody. Tell me, what's the world going to be like?"

"Mostly like this, only with cooler stuff."

"Like what?"

"Computers, phones, music."

"We have all those things."

"In your pocket?"

"No."

"Yeah... Oh, I should have shown you this first." Dan pulled out his phone. Strangely, it was fully charged.

"What is it?"

"A phone, computer, music player, encyclopedia. It's kind of a Swiss army knife of gadgets." Dan turned it on.

Elinore sat next to him. Dan turned on his music player and played "Heartbreak Hotel."

She was fascinated. "What is this?"

"It's a music player."

"No, the music."

"Elvis Presley. This hasn't come out yet?"

"No."

"'Heartbreak Hotel' was the song that really made Elvis. He'll be the biggest star out there until the Beatles."

"The Beatles?"

"Yeah, and the Stones. You are going to hear some of the greatest music of all time."

"What else?"

"What else?"

"Do we have flying cars?"

Damnit, we do not have flying cars. Three-dimensional flight in a city environment is a recipe for disaster, unless all vehicles are computer controlled and that inevitably leads to the robot revolution.

And robots do not need flying cars.

Dan and Elinore spent the next hour talking about the cool things coming. When Dan left, she was jazzed about the future only she knew; she wanted to experience the world like never before.

Dan took the elevator down. All the while Richard was grinning.

Dan went into the kitchen and the staff was prepping dinner. Friday night was fish. Fresh fish. Dan slipped away a sandwich which he stowed in his satchel. He scooped a heaping portion of heads and entrails, wrapping them tightly in foil. With no sharks around, he would have to find another use for it. He cleaned up and headed back into the lobby.

He pulled a drain trap from his bag and headed into the elevator. Holding the trap, he rode up with the cheerful Richard. Getting out, he walked down the hall. When he heard the elevator door close, he promptly marched back to the elevator.

Pulling out his screwdriver, he pried the elevator doors open and proceeded to distribute the fish into the shaft, being careful to coat the walls with the guts. He then took the stairs down. He felt a little bad for the guests who would ride that elevator in the coming weeks; they'd have a minute of olfactory assault.

Richard would have to endure it all day long.

Every day.

Dan finished his work, picked up his check, and cashed it in the bar. In his room he changed out of his RR work gear and into his generic street clothes with his TellTom jumpsuit underneath.

He wondered what he should do with his stash. Maybe he would convert it into gold or platinum or something, so he could trade it in other times. Perhaps if he accumulated more than pocket money, he could see if there was a branch of the Berenberg Bank nearby. Tomorrow would be his day off and he could see New York. "Silk Stockings" and "Damn Yankees" were playing on Broadway.

Or maybe he'd discover why he was here.

As he came into the lobby, he saw two shapely blondes crossing to the express elevator to the fifteenth floor. One stood out: she was wearing sunglasses and a scarf, but all eyes turned toward her.

Marilyn Monroe was going to the fifteenth floor.

As it turned out, it was a good thing all eyes were on her. Dan could barely hear the music over the Muzak, and everything felt like fish right now. Narwhal.

When he started to unravel, he moved behind a plant—only partial cover.

As his mind began to jumble, he had one thought that came out clearly.

"Crap, I never left the hotel."

– Chapter 17 –
The Apocalypse or Worldwide Vacation?

When the time coaster finally finished its corkscrew, Dan was in an alley in a large, hazy city. The buildings stretched up until it hurt his neck to look up that high. The air smelled of ozone and exhaust.

Walking out to the main street, he saw no one. Cars were parked, the lights were off, and the streets were empty. He walked for blocks and couldn't tell where he was.

Entering an office building, the lobby was empty. In a market there was still produce on the shelf—it was a little wilty, but not yet moldy.

The skyscrapers were dusty and the streets were numbered and lettered. The wind blew advertisements down the glass canyons. Dan chased a couple down, hoping they would give him a clue as to what had happened here.

BIG MATTRESS BLOWOUT SALE.

Dresses 30% off.

HUGE DISCOUNTS ON FLYING CARS!!

No, there were/are no discounts on flying cars because there were/are no flying cars and if this were after the robot revolution, where are the robots, huh? Flying cars = robot revolution = more damn robots!!

The abandoned city left Dan feeling creeped out.

Then a thought hit. The question wasn't so much *where* was everyone, as *why* wasn't everyone.

Why were the people gone? Surely not for no reason. People don't abandon a perfectly good city for no reason. Well sure, maybe the city wasn't *perfectly* good. The height of the buildings compared to the width of the streets suggested traffic was a nightmare—unless there were flying cars.

And there were not!!

Did they all contract a disease? Undergo sudden decay or disintegration? Flee the planet to avoid alien invasion?

Dan could not conceive they might leave the city, and in fact the whole planet, to go somewhere better—which was what they did. Or, to be exact, was what they were doing.

Dan heard a roaring sound and looked off into the distance to find the source of his imminent death. Surely alien murderers or nuclear annihilation was heading his way. Unfortunately, all he saw was skyscrapers.

Then a bright light appeared to his right and Dan saw a spacecraft passing over the city. Only instead of vaporizing him, the ship continued into orbit and out of sight.

After thousands of years of continual abuse, humans were finally leaving the blue planet—although at this point it was more brownish than blue.

Dan was now the last man on Earth.

He sat down on the curb and ate the sandwich he had stashed in his satchel. He took a minute to relax and listen to the music. It was funny, Dan thought, the meat was ham, but it tasted a little like tuna.

And with that, he was back in the timestream.

- Chapter 18 -
A Romantic Interlude
(and a great deal of blood)

The timestream is a very confusing place. Thought and concepts are turned inside out. The very idea of who and what you are is flipped over on its head. Many a being has thought itself to be a vegetable in the ebb of time, and many a vegetable has thought itself to be human.

Some have postulated there are probably ten times the number of vegetables floating through time as there are people—after all, there are more of them. Luckily, the timestream is infinite or Dan would face constant Tomato Tornado.

And don't get me started on the spiders.

Dan emerged from the timestream hard. He found himself in the dark, rolling underneath something. He knew he was underneath something as he banged his head on it.

Feeling around, he determined that "something" was the underside of a bench. He crawled out and discovered he was in a small park. He sat on the bench to get his bearings. What would Freddie do?

It was evening—the sun was almost down. It was cool, but not cold. That meant Fall or Spring. The bench was wood and steel, he would guess 20th century construction. A nearby streetlight was electric and the road was asphalt—all suggesting that time period.

It dawned on him he didn't know what RR stood for. Did he not know the name of the hotel or did the timestream not reassemble him properly? For that matter, why didn't he miss Freddie as much? He was too addled by the jump to remember jumping causes one to be addled.

What were his assets? He had money, but once again it was no good—probably. He could work, but needed food and a place to sleep. He pulled out some jerky and biscuits he had left. Since the sandwich he'd just eaten was used up in the timestream, he would be down to the rations from the space station next.

While scarfing down the food, he wondered if he could find a place to work tonight. He got up and headed down the street. As he approached the tall buildings, he realized this was another big city. He saw a newspaper in the trash. Looking around and seeing no one, he snagged it.

The *Chicago Tribune*, 1929.

October 28th.

He had been brought to the time of America's darkest financial hour.[10] One day before the stock market Crash. One day before the beginning of the Great Depression. When Freddie said everything went to hell.

Freddie. Didn't she tell him she lived in Chicago?

Don't worry, you didn't miss it. This is something I didn't bother to tell you, along with: "Please pass the toast" and "What kind of a day do you think we'll have today?" and "Does this jumpsuit make my butt look big?" You'd be bored out of your mind if you heard everything. And the conversation where this came up was *extremely* boring, so just say "Thank you" and we'll move on.

Dan thought he should try to find her, warn her they would be separated, but that would make him sound crazy. Better to not see her. He remembered how Freddie avoided Chantell in Elizabethan England. Freddie had talked about what happened to her at this time.

---

[10] Well, one of the darkest. There's that thing in 2008, of course 2020, and then the aftermath of the robot rebellion.

"I'm not in it," he thought.

Reptile brain chimed in. "You idiot, she's 21 years old and Flaming Youth, have you seen videos of the clothes in this era? Thin fabric and frequently braless."

Dan forced the thought back into his head. It was a hard visual to ignore.

No, he was determined to avoid her.

Unless she was the reason he was here.

Damn it.

Skimming the paper, he saw mention of the Union Stock Yards. *There* was a place that ran all night. He'd take a chance.

The stock yards were a long way away. He got directions twice but ultimately it was his nose that told him he was on the right track. The ammonia of 2,300 livestock pens containing hogs, cattle, and sheep was hard to miss.

The Union Stock Yards was 475 acres of pens, slaughterhouses, and processing plants crisscrossed with roads and railroads. Around 45,000 employees worked round the clock. It was a medium sized city dedicated to hamburgers and pot roast.

He found some men at work and asked if they were hiring.

"Come back tomorrow."

"Naw, don't bother. We got a full crew." The voice of authority.

"There's gotta be something," Dan said.

"Not unless you wanna be up to your waist in blood."

"In blood?"

"We got a clogged drain."

Dan wondered if time had a plan. He pulled out his wrench. "I happen to be a plumber."

"Then we happen to be hiring."

Dan put on a company uniform and fixed the drain—which was every bit as gross as it sounds, but not as bad as working the bilge. After that he hauled meat on the dock. He arranged to get paid the next morning as a day laborer. The income was enough for a couple meals and a room. He washed up, dumped his company clothes in a bin, and put on his own clothes.

He still wasn't sure if the TellTom jumpsuit made his butt look big, and Freddie wasn't there to reassure him it didn't.

Dan found a diner for breakfast and a fresh newspaper. He read the paper cover to cover, hoping to find some clue as to what he might be here to witness—if anything. The date was a good start, but was there anything specific about the Crash in Chicago? He would have thought he'd be in New York for the Crash.

There was an announcement in the society column that Fredericka Townes and Evan Preston had set a date for their wedding in the spring. Dan realized he'd never asked her last name. Time jumping seemed mysterious, like they had no past, so he'd never bothered.

He also realized why he had trouble with women.

Could this be her?

Then he remembered Albert calling her "Ms. Townes."

There was no address, but it did have a street name.

Before he could make a decision, he was getting on a bus. He had thought if he could navigate in time, he could find the right bus.

He was wrong.

Five hours later he found the street. It was a nice street. A very nice street. Along the way he picked up a loaf of bread and a tin of Peter Pan peanut butter. (We won't get into the ethical debate about E. K. Pond Company hijacking author J. M. Barrie's character without permission. Barrie never complained and neither will I.)

Dan found a comfortable bench to sit and wait. He wasn't sure why, he just wanted to get a glimpse of her. He was supposed to return to the stock yards to talk to the personnel manager about working another shift, but he didn't care.

Six hours later he saw her. She wore a blue chemise dress that displayed her calves, with a matching light jacket and a cloche hat with the brim turned up. Despite the shapeless shift dress, her figure was unmistakable to Dan.

He moved quickly to get a better look. She was leaving a house in tears.

A sleek beige Duesenberg J Dual Cowl Phaeton pulled to the curb and she climbed in before the driver could get there to open the door. Even with her eyes swollen and hair mussed, the feminine knee-length dress made her even more appealing than before.

He thought about trying to follow her, but with no cab in sight that was impossible. He copied down her address and wandered back toward the city proper, just thinking. On impulse he stopped at a store advertising greeting cards.

He purchased one with a simple flower design, yellow roses, with no sentiment, along with a stamp. He stared at it for some time before pulling out his ballpoint pen (which Freddie would have thrown out the day she met him, had he remembered he had it).

"Times are hard and they may get harder. When you feel like you've lost everything, you have to find something more. When you feel like love has been taken from you, find something you love even more.
Hold on to hope.
You will survive."

They say the timestream scrambles your brain and reorganizes it again. Sometimes that process works out for the better. Other times you get people who "moo" a lot.

Dan sealed the envelope and dropped it into a mailbox. He had a couple hours to look for plumbing work before finding a hotel, so he decided to head downtown.

Dan found a bus and climbed on—he never got off. He noticed the smell of melting steel or would have if he knew what melting steel smelled like. The bus felt like a leviathan swimming through the city and ultimately coughing Dan up into infinity.

– Chapter 19 –
The Short Chapter

Chantell ran her hand across a huge console in a room full of machinery and other huge consoles. She adjusted some numbers, typed in more data, then stepped into a chamber—and disappeared, only to reappear seconds later.

"Well that was interesting."

Chantell checked herself in the mirror. Even dressed in a simple smock, with no makeup, she looked ten years younger and twenty pounds lighter.

"Nice."

She went to change clothes and reapply her makeup.

– Chapter 20 –
Reunited and it Feels so Wood

Upon reintegration, Dan appeared in a sunny forest meadow or perhaps a glade, he really didn't know the difference.

It wasn't a thicket.

Dan stood up, as jumping had, so far, created landings more horizontal than vertical. The air was pure and smelled of pine. Feeling exposed, Dan moved to the edge of the meadow/glen/hollow into the forest.

If he hadn't felt exposed, perhaps he would have taken more time to check his surroundings and noticed the footprints in the grass traveling the same way he was going.

Dan entered about thirty or so feet into the woods, hoping to scout out the clearing from there.

He was surprised to come across a makeshift camp with lunch set out on a rock. He saw movement in the corner of his eye.

Freddie stepped out from behind a tree. She rushed into his arms and hugged him. "I have never been so glad to see someone in my life."

"Freddie!"

"Dan! Thank God. I thought I was stuck here." She pushed away. "Where the hell have you been?"

"Where have I been?"

"Yeah. I've been waiting at least a half hour."

"Half hour? But you've been gone for days."

"No, we jumped from the station and ended up here."

"No, I've been to New York, and Chicago, and someplace that has no people."

"Maybe you time dreamed it."

"Time dreamed?"

"It's where the timestream picks up on events and places them in your mind. It's pretty weird when that happens."

"No, I think I was there." He slipped off his satchel and pulled out the tin of peanut butter. "I bought this in Chicago."

She took the can from him and opened it. "A taste of home."

"I've got so much to tell you."

"First let's figure out where we are."

"And when we are. Have you eaten?"

"I was looking for you."

"I'm glad you found me."

The couple feasted on peanut butter sandwiches while looking out into the glade. There was no sign of people. They saw little beyond the trees. Had they been able to see beyond the dense trees or looked up, they would have noticed the second daytime (children's) moon.

Dan was a little—strike that—a lot confused. "I don't understand what happened. We weren't touching, but you jumped."

"I don't know. Maybe I'm starting to get my jump back."

"So you think you were close enough my jump triggered your jump."

"Could be."

"But we ended up in the same place."

"Eventually."

"So even though we were in the timestream separately, we were still connected."

"Yeah… Kinda cool."

Dan was happy she thought so. "Very cool. Has this happened to you before?"

"I don't think this has happened to anybody before. So you saw New York?" Freddie seemed anxious to hear what Dan did without her.

"Not really."

"You weren't there long?"

"A couple days, but I never left my hotel."

"Never?"

"I was busy… working."

"You found a job?"

"It found me."

"Didn't you get time off?"

"I did, but I was busy. I was going to see the town on Saturday."

"And you weren't there Saturday."

"Exactly."

"First rule of time jumping: never put off anything."

"How many first rules of time jumping are there?"

"As many as time wants. What about Chicago; when were you there?"

"1929."

It was at that moment Freddie glanced up between the trees to see a larger than normal moon. "Holy shit." She sprinted for the meadow.

"What?" Dan saw only trees, but followed her anyway.

"That's not our moon."

Dan reached the clearing. "You mean those aren't our moons."

"Moons."

"Holy shit."

"This is bad."

"We're on another planet."

"Yes, it's bad."

"But you said we could only go where mankind has visited."

"Yeah, but that usually means cities or protected environments. This is the wilderness."

"It's kinda nice."

"That's because it hasn't killed you yet. You don't know what kind of poisonous trees and killer animals or poisonous animals and killer trees are lurking about."

"Trees lurk?"

"You never see them coming."

"These seem like normal trees."

"They're not."

They were.

"That's a redwood, there's a cottonwood." He started pointing. "I think that's a larch, birch, maple, fir." Dan was wrong as often as he was right; however, they were all normal trees, except for three or four who had mental health problems but were taking their meds religiously.

Freddie stopped. "You're right. Something's wrong."

"No, the trees are all right."

"And that's what's wrong."

"That they're right?"

"Right."

"And that's wrong?"

"If we're on an alien world, these should be alien trees."

"Yessss?"

"But they're not."

"So someone put them here?"

"Must have." Freddie checked the ground. "The dirt looks normal, too."

"Can dirt look abnormal?"

"Is this invasive colonization or something more?" she wondered aloud.

It was then they heard the sound—the increasing roar. At first Dan thought it was a creature, but it soon became evident it was an engine. A big engine.

Looking up, they saw a huge spaceship descending on the clearing, its rocket boosters scorching the grass. Dan and Freddie looked at each other and hightailed it into the trees. They could feel the heat behind them, so they ran until they couldn't.

When the roaring stopped, they turned. The outer trees were smoldering and wilted, what was left of the grass was burning. Freddie knew those in the ship would have to run a series of tests before disembarking, so until then she and Dan stomped out grassfires and stripped the trees of some of the more smoldery branches.

Then Freddie peered toward the spaceship. "Let's go meet the ship."

"We just ran away from the ship."

"Yes, that's because its engines were trying to kill us. We can either spend our time here avoiding them, or meet them and get it over with. Most importantly, they'll have more food than we do."

"How do we know what they eat?"

"Given the design of the ship and the likelihood that this area has been terraformed into an earth environment, I'd say they eat biscuits."

"I like biscuits."

After that Dan had just enough time to strip off his outer clothes, revealing his TellTom jumpsuit underneath. Freddie, not having gone anywhere, never changed out of hers.

And while Dan didn't have time to ask if the jumpsuit made his butt look big, he felt confident Freddie would have answered politely if he had.

As the captain opened the hatch (they assumed it was the captain; after all, the reason you become the captain is for moments like these), Freddie and Dan hustled toward the ship.

Freddie called out. "Hello, up there."

Dan chimed in. "Captain, good to see you."

The second in command behind him drew a weapon (they assumed he was second in command; after all, the reason you become the second in command is hoping the captain is too drunk to make it to moments like these). "Halt! Identify yourselves."

The captain gave him a sharp look. "Stop. Tell us who you are. No, no! Okay… Freeze. Who the hell are you?" The captain paused to examine the words. "You there, was my demand stronger than his? My second demand, not the first one. I was kind of thrown on that one as he stole my idea before I said it."

"Captain Hightower, you shouldn't talk to the spies."

"And you shouldn't have taken my captainly response, but here we are, aren't we?"

"You, spies, don't move."

"I already told them to freeze."

"Just reiterating it, sir."

"Well stop it. Once I've iterated something I don't need you to come up behind me to reiterate."

Dan spoke again. "Gentlemen, welcome to the planet."

"Oh, thank you, thank you very much," said the captain. "Ummm, who are you?"

Freddie moved forward. Dan thought he detected more movement in her hips.

"We're the advance crew, here to prepare for your arrival," she said.

The second was not satisfied and, in fact, seemed quite suspicious. "We were not told of any advance crew."

"Isn't that the way things work? One division has no idea what the other is doing? We were sent here to scout out the best places to start colonization."

The captain smiled. "See, Smith, just the company giving us more support."

"But Captain—"

"Ah, ah, it's fine, but if you want, you can search the man."

Dan noticed while this exchange was happening, Freddie cinched the waist belt of her jumpsuit three notches tighter.

"But what about the woman?" said the second.

"Smith, look at her. It's pretty obvious she has no weapons."

Interestingly, both men were in reptile brain, only one was set to fight and the other was set to mate. The closeness of these two functions is what leads to a great deal of spanking.

Freddie eased forward. "Can we help you set up, sirs?"

"That would be marvelous."

"But sir—"

"No, Smith."

"But they're—"

"Smith, do I need to send you to your room again?"

"No, sir."

"Do you want to lose dessert?"

"No, sir."

"Good. Assemble the team."

"Yes, sir."

"You down there, come on up."

The hatch was thirty feet up on the ship and Dan felt obliged to point this out. "Ummm, how?"

"Ohh, forgive me. Someone extend the ladder."

Dan expected a futuristic ladder to slide out.

Someone kicked out a rope ladder. Freddie scrambled up quickly, but Dan experienced a great deal of swinging in his attempt to ascend the unruly hemp. Flashbacks to *The Traveler*.

Inside the ship they found the colonists standing around impatient to get started. They had flown across the galaxy for the chance to start anew; they faced the hardships and rigors of deep space, feeling the loneliness of being billions of light years from home.

It was the toughest ten days of their lives.

The captain called a meeting to make final plans for disembarkation. There were a hundred colonists and a few soldiers present.

The Captain spoke. "We have opened the hatch and the air is pure. Plant life is plentiful, although the grass here is black and the trees look a little wilty. I'm sure it's nothing we can't handle."

A balding man spoke up. "Who are these two?"

"Hmmmm?"

"This man and woman. I don't recognize them."

"Oh they were an advance crew sent to scout the terrain, prep the area, that sort of thing."

"What can you tell us?"

Freddie poured on the charm. "After an exhaustive survey, we have found the plant life is very Earthlike and thriving. Except the wilty bits."

A woman raised her hand. "What else can you tell us?"

"Well… that's it really."

"That's all?"

"Pretty much."

"How long have you been here?"

"Oh, what would you say, Dan?"

"Oh, I'd say, a good… hour maybe?"

"An hour???" The woman was outraged.

The colonists broke into umbrage over the incompetent job that was being done completing a job that no one had expected anyone to do.

Freddie tried to quiet them. "We had some trouble with our ship and ended up behind schedule."

"Behind schedule? If you had arrived any later, we'd be prepping for you," said the woman.

"Kinda."

At this point someone suggested Dan and Freddie knew no more than they did and were not needed for the discussion. Dan and Freddie agreed whole-heartedly.

The Captain tried to make a case for having Freddie stay, but was not able to voice a reason beyond, "She seems nice."

Dan and Freddie walked the halls of the ship, followed not so discreetly by a security detail assigned by Smith. Freddie made a bathroom stop and returned looking even more voluptuous.

Reptile brain made Dan stare longer than he intended to. "Did you just… ummm." He quietly made a hand gesture. "Make additions to your, aahhh, assets?"

"No, I just set the girls free."

He gave her a quizzical look.

"I strap them down in case I need to be a man. Here they might be useful."

Reptile brain was apoplectic. That was an affront to God. At the same time He injected images into Dan's thoughts he tried desperately to avoid. "That must be uncomfortable."

"No more than four-inch heels."

Again with the images.

"It's something I learned from fashion in the 1920s. Flat chests were very fashionable then."

More reptile uprisings.

Luckily, Freddie changed the topic. "So Chi town 1929… Anything happen there?"

"I got covered in blood."

"Blood."

"Cow blood, I think."

"The stock yards?"

"Oh yeah."

"Anything… else?"

"I went to see an old friend."

"Did you find him?"

"Her, and yeah."

"Ummm was it…"

"Yeah."

She frowned, scavenging her brain for memories. "But I don't…"

"You didn't see me. I figured time might get freaky."

"Yeah."

"Besides, you were having a bad day."

"What day?"

"Black Thursday."

"Black…" She became overwhelmed with emotion.

They were quiet for a moment, then she got a small tear in her eye. "Times are hard and they may get harder. When you feel like you've lost everything, you have to find something more."

Dan joined in. "When you feel like love has been taken from you, find something you love even more. Hold on to hope. You will survive."

Freddie grabbed Dan's hands and let the tears flow. "You don't know what that meant to me."

"You don't know what seeing you meant to me. I was lost and alone."

"So was I."

The reptile whispered, "Kiss her, you idiot."

The frontal lobe said, "DON'T FUCK THIS UP!"

Strangely, Freddie's brain said the same thing.

They both smiled sheepishly as they pulled back, still holding hands.

Smith's voice boomed over the comm. system. "Attention, all colonists, pre—"

"Smith, what are you doing?"

"Captain, I was just—"

"Give me that microphone… Listen up, passengers. Now see what you've done? You've taken all the good words. Prepare for disembarkation."

No one moved. They had been prepared since reaching orbit.

"All colonists move to disembarkation stations."

A few people moved a little.

"Disembark."

Someone pushed a button and a large door closed. Dan and Freddie watched as the room nearby swung outside and lowered like an elevator. The elevator took groups down and out until Dan and Freddie were the last people left on the ship.

From outside they could hear the captain over a loudspeaker. "I hereby proclaim this planet Terra Two."

"No, sir, just Terra."

"What did I say?"

"Terra Two."

"That's right."

"No, sir, this is the first Terra."

"Are you sure there's not another one?"

"Yes, sir."

"Yes, there's another one or?"

"Yes, there's not another one."

"Oh well, water over the bridge. I've already proclaimed it Terra Two."

"Under, sir."

"Under what?"

"Water, sir, under the bridge."

Sitting holding hands, both Freddie and Dan noticed they felt a bit flounderish.

And they slipped into the timestream.

– Chapter 21 –
Ambrose Time

The timestream had led Dan to a bewildering number of new experiences in a very short time. His mental, emotional and physical being had been tested in ways it had never been tested before.

This was not one of those times. As Dan hit the stream, he was overwhelmed with happy. He couldn't remember the last time he had been this happy.

Of course his mind was slightly shredded, but happy he was. Can you smile in timelessness?

As Dan landed in time, he could feel a grin on his face. Freddie had one as well, which made him grin even more.

Freddie focused in on the present. "Okay, we're in a city, in an alcove."

As a protective mechanism, jumpers normally jump to a place they won't be seen. It's like that don't jump underwater thing. There is endless jumper debate over whether this is a time controlled occurrence or created subconsciously by the jumper.

This time where they landed was indeed subconsciously controlled by the jumper.

Dan looked out of the alcove. "This looks familiar."

"It should. Twentieth century streets, sidewalks, and buildings."

"No, I mean very familiar."

"How very?"

"I had lunch around here before I left." Dan sprang from the alcove and bustled down the street with the most determination Freddie had seen in him when he wasn't facing impending doom.

"Wait, wait, is this your timeline?"

Dan didn't stop, forcing Freddie to chase after him.

There are rules about such things. Under normal circumstances, there is no possibility the timestream will let you jump into your own lifetime. In your own lifetime, being able to conceivably meet yourself never could happen. Your own lifetime to where and when you were having lunch would be infinitely unlikely.

And yet, here he was.

Freddie caught him as he rounded the corner, grabbing his arm. "Is *this* your timeline?"

Dan pointed down the block. "I ate at that restaurant with Ambrose the day I jumped." He ran a few yards and pointed. "I parked right here."

Looking at the oxidized Mustang, Freddie grabbed him by the arm—firmly this time. "This isn't your car, is it?"

Dan couldn't tell if she was concerned about prime jump rules or the implications of owning an oxidized Mustang.

"No." Dan scanned further down the sidewalk and got noticeably louder. "There's Ambrose!!"

With that, Dan broke free and sprinted toward the café.

In case you're wondering, Dan had indeed discussed Ambrose with Freddie, as well as his parents, other friends, and why Little League sucked. She responded by telling him about the primitive conditions in 1920, her friends, and why being a Flapper is less fun than it looks.

It was another mostly boring conversation and if any part of it becomes important, you will be apprised.

Freddie had almost caught Dan when he shouted, "Ambrose!"

Ambrose looked up at the sight of Dan being pursued by a very attractive woman. This was not a situation he expected to see Dan in.

Ambrose grabbed a fork. "Stand back, harpy."

The alleged harpy stopped.

Dan was oblivious to this part of the drama. "Ambrose, I am so glad to see you. I was worried I might never get to see you again."

Ambrose turned the fork toward Dan. "What are you talking about? You just left. And what are you wearing?" He was now shifting his assumptions from crazy lady to crazy friend.

"This is my jumpsuit. I've got so much to tell you."

"Like who the lady chasing you is?"

"Top of the list. Ambrose, this is Freddie." Dan said this like Ambrose should already have known about this very important person. "Freddie, this is Ambrose, my best friend."

The waiter was no longer flirting but looking rather irritated.

"I thought you were heading to work," said Ambrose.

"I did, but that was weeks ago."

"Did you bump your head?"

"I don't think so, but I might have lost track."

"Dan, you need to sit down."

Freddie took Dan's hand and pulled him toward a chair. "Yes, you don't want to attract attention."

"He never does." Ambrose turned his attention to Freddie. "And how do you know Dan?"

"We're traveling companions," she said.

"Dan doesn't travel."

"You'd be surprised."

"I'm surprised he comes over the hill to Hollywood."

Dan stepped in. He was now eating the remainder of the ravioli he had left on his plate a few weeks/minutes ago. "I'll have you know I am now very well-traveled."

"Since five minutes ago?"

"And five weeks ago."

"Give or take," said Freddie who was helping Dan with the ravioli.

"What?"

Dan tried to calm himself. "Ambrose, you won't believe it."

Freddie touched Dan's arm to get his attention. "That's not a good idea."

"Why not?"

"If people knew about it, they would hunt us down for what we can do."

"Plumbing?" Ambrose looked bemused.

"Time jumping," said Dan.

Freddie had not expected Dan to blurt it out.

Neither had Dan.

And Ambrose wasn't even in the same ballpark. "*Time* jumping?"

Freddie scanned the area, but no one was paying attention. "Ixnay on the Imetay Umpjay."

Dan and Ambrose had watched enough Three Stooges as kids to know pig latin.

Dan quieted. "I've been all over the timestream."

"In five minutes?" Ambrose was looking closely for that head injury. Failing to find anything, he switched to what drug Freddie may have slipped him.

"To you. For me it's been weeks."

"Uh huh. Where have you gone?" Ambrose noted Dan's skin was neither flushed nor clammy.

"London. I met Shakespeare."

"Shakespeare?" Dan's pupils looked normal.

"And I went to New York… Twice!"

"Twice." Dan's rapid speech was slowing, meth was still a possibility, but the level of psychosis made it unlikely. Molly?

"And this is going to sound crazy—"

"More so?"

"I've been to space."

"Maybe you should come back."

"I am back." Dan noticed he was wondering if the menu had fish. "But I don't think I'll be here for long."

"You barely left."

"I just want you to know I'm okay."

Ambrose started to stand. "Then come with me and I'll help you through this."

"There's no time."

"But you said you're a time traveler."

"I'm not very good at it."

Freddie chimed in. "He's not."

"Look," said Dan, "tonight I'm going to disappear from my car without a trace. At about 5:30, my car is going to roll off the freeway, still running, near Henry's. I won't be in it."

"Where will you be?"

"Someplace with rolling green hills."

"So not Pacoima."

"The important thing is to not worry about me. And pick up my car if it's not totaled."

"At 5:30? I'm surprised you were moving at all."

"Maybe 8 miles per hour."

"The car's fine."

"Crap—my parents." Dan pulled out his phone and dialed. He smelled chocolate custard. A jump was imminent, but he was trying to stall it. "Ugh, voice mail. Mom, I'm going traveling. I've decided I need a break and am going to Europe. And Tibet. And lots of places with no cell reception. I'll call when I'm back. Love you guys, bye." Dan looked at Freddie. "We've gotta go."

The two turned and ran down the sidewalk toward the little alcove. Hiding is better—who wants to be tabloid fodder?

Ambrose followed them as soon as he could untangle himself from his chair. As he reached the alcove, they faded into time, leaving him to try to convince the waiter he wasn't running out on his bill.

– Chapter 22 –
The Living Dreidel

Time travel has never been easy. The energy needed to pass through time and space is incredible, the forces at play vast and turbulent. Yet with all this, for the first time, Dan felt comfortable jumping. They were floating in a peaceful pool. Neither felt the unraveling, just a melding with the universe and each other. It felt normal, natural.

That might have been shattered if they had noticed the small device in the timestream that was flashing red, having been alerted to their presence.

Instead, the peace was shattered the moment they landed.

Explosions rocked the stone walls around them, buffeting their bodies with shock waves. Noise echoed and overwhelmed their ears. Boulders began tumbling from above. The stone walls turned out to be cliffs and a mountain was attempting to fall onto them.

Dan saw a figure (we'll call him Doug) running a direction Dan could only assume was "away." Grabbing Freddie's hand as he scrabbled to his feet, he pulled her in that direction. She was still trying to figure out the best course of action, but ultimately anywhere was better than here.

The figure (Doug) rounded a corner and Dan lost sight of her, him, they, it. Rounding the corner seemed like a good idea, but when they did, there was no sign of the figure. Freddie noticed a small opening in the rock, near the ground, and towed Dan to it.

Crawling in on their bellies, they saw the crack expanded into a cave, which enlarged into a cavern, but instead of rock formations, there was machinery; machinery of every description.

Well most descriptions. Not every. I doubt you could call anything there "soupy" or "autumnal," but many, many descriptors would be applicable. Bright, brilliant, loud, scary, and unrecognizable come to mind. Between the noise in the cave and the noise outside, things were positively booming.

Dan spotted the person he had seen before and pointed him out to Freddie.

Freddie again opted for the direct approach "Hello, there."

Doug spun around, pointing a death ray at them. The weapon was brightly colored and elegant, but nevertheless a death ray. Due to the fact that Doug was pointing this surely hostile device at him, it took Dan three full seconds to realize Doug was not human.

Doug was basically humanoid, with arms and legs, but grayish skin and no discernable neck. His voice was also fairly high, which is odd for a no-neck being. "What are you?"

Freddie answered. "Humans. What are you?"

"In a hurry."

"I noticed that. What exactly is trying to blow us up?"

"Tekkore, and they're trying to blow me up."

"So if we surrender?"

"They'll blow you up."

"So how do we get away?"

"I don't know about you, I'm teleporting."

Dan, hearing the explosions get closer, was feeling the pressure. "Do you think you could take us?"

"Why?"

"So we don't die."

"Hmmmph. All right."

Dan was thrilled that not dying was considered a valid justification.

Freddie had one more concern. "Is it replacement or sidestepping?"

Doug snorted derisively. "Sidestepping."

"Let's go."

These are the two basic transporter technologies. Scientists love the mathematical symmetry of replacement, breaking down your component atoms to energy, storing the data, using the energy to power the teleport, then rebuilding the matter in the new location.

Thinking, feeling beings love that sidestepping does not involve breaking down your component atoms to energy, storing the data, using the energy to power the teleport, then recreating the matter in the new location.

Sidestepping is the process of stepping through the fabric of space and coming out somewhere else. It's less precise than replacement as you can only exit the fabric of space at natural conjunctions of the folds of space. Then you may have to take several short hops to other locations to reach the closest conjunction to your destination.

It's like getting a bus transfer.

Doug worked a control board and a blue light appeared.

The biggest argument about teleportation is whether replacers still had a soul. The proponents of replacement claimed, "If you did have a soul, it would be stored as data and reform with you. Of course," they continued, "data analysis shows no data for a soul."

Sidesteppers claimed, "Just because we can't measure that which gives us the spark of life does not mean it does not exist, only that we haven't yet discovered how to identify it. All enlightened beings spent millennia before being able to see germ, atom, subatomic particles and cheese receptors—yet these things all existed before we could prove they did. And if you don't know how to measure it yet, how do you know you can capture it as data?"

"Well, we don't see how you can miss something you don't even know for sure you have."

"That is a good point as I'm not sure you have a brain, and I don't believe I'd miss it if it were gone."

This debate has raged for centuries.

Dan just wanted to know one thing— "Is it safe?"

"Safer than staying here." Freddie's answer was punctuated by Doug jumping into the blue light.

Freddie pushed Dan in and followed a second later. The sensation of traveling through inner space was similar to time jumping, only Dan didn't unravel. It wasn't the vacuum of space, simply a lack of space, a non-place kind of place, just as time jumping was a timeless kind of time.

They popped out in a deep space terminal.

Freddie grabbed Doug. "Why were they trying to kill you?"

"Because I'm Rielle and they are Tekkore."

"And?"

"Don't you know anything about the Great Debate?"

"Let's say we don't."

"We are at one with the universe, we preach the gospel of nature and spirituality. Tekkore know only bending the universe to their will regardless of the cost. Soulless monsters, who corrupt the weak and impatient."

"How so?"

"They are Replacers."

"And you're Sidesteppers."

"We are the masters of interspatial navigation."

"Nice job of that, by the way."

"We pride ourselves on smooth transit."

Dan understood none of this. He only knew someone was shooting at him and now they weren't. "Where are we?"

"Outer spatial coordinate 3,042.179."

Freddie blinked. "Which is?"

"Tergun Galaxy, a stone's throw from Pletus."

"Uh oh."

Dan didn't like the sound of that. "Uh oh, what uh oh?"

"We've never been this far out before," said Freddie.

"We'll *I've* only been off planet three times before, and I'm pretty sure the first two were only in orbit." Dan thought that sounded strange, given a month ago a day trip to the beach was too much trouble.

"When I say 'we,' I don't mean we, you and me, I mean we the human race."

"So we are further out than anyone has ever gone."

Doug gave him a look.

"Sorry," Dan said. "I mean any human has ever gone."

Doug nodded and went to a control panel in the wall. He fiddled with controls.

Freddie grabbed Dan's arm. "This is going to have repercussions."

"I think it's pretty cool," he said.

"Okay, that's a given." Freddie quieted. "But the destination for jumpers just got wider."

"What?"

"Earth jumpers only jump to places Earth beings have gone."

"And we've gone further than anyone."

"So we've created new jump territory—in the middle of an interspatial war."

"Not a good thing."

"So not."

"And if we teleport out…"

"We create a new jump destination each time, until we're in normal human territory. Best not to go anywhere." Freddie approached the alien. "Sir, I want to thank you for getting us out of there. I'm Freddie and this is Dan."

Dan waved.

"I am Douge of the Rielle."

I was so close to guessing his name right. Give me some slack though; he pronounces it "Doug."

Douge opened the control panel in the wall and drew out a canister of something. It could have been spray cheese.

"Douge, why is this war happening with the Tekkore?" said Freddie.

"Because they are murdering millions—billions—of beings."

"By knocking mountains over on them?"

"No, by turning people into energy and then making a false copy of them across the galaxy."

"Does the copy know it's false?"

"No, the soulless thing thinks it is real."

Dan couldn't resist. "They should become politicians."

"Most of them do."

Most of them do not. However, a much larger percentage of soulless humanoids do go into politics than those having soul. This is true for the spiritual state as well as the music.

"But how did the war start?" said Freddie.

Douge opened the canister and took a squirt of something orangish. It could have been spray cheese. "They started murdering the Rielle."

"Why?"

"Because we called them a bunch of murderers."

"Nice."

"People had to know what they were doing."

"And they reacted with violence."

"Predictably."

"How so?"

"They are a terribly grumpy lot. We believe it's because they have no soul."

"Or because they don't like being called murderers."

"But they are."

"Are they forcing anyone into the teleporter?"

"No, but they are playing on the ignorance of the people for profit."

The phrase "Playing on the ignorance of the people for profit" should be the slogan of all major corporations, governments, and religions. Several more enlightened societies have required it to be included in all advertising. It hasn't changed anything, but at least people have warning of what's coming.

It's like the commercials for medications on Earth. After listening to the side effects, one would think that not only would no one buy the product, but that they would dip the manufacturers in chum and toss them in with the Mosasaurus. Yet the companies persist.

I mean, sure they tell you there's only a small chance, but sudden death or anal leakage are not things to play around with. And although Bruce Lee's "Game of Death" is a great movie, I don't recommend playing it. No one recommends "The Game of Anal Leakage."

"How many jumps would it take to get to 28,242.096?" Freddie asked.

Douge pondered a moment. "At least seven."

Freddie turned to Dan. "That's it. We need to stay here. We don't want to open seven new locations."

Douge walked towards a doorway. "Suit yourself. I'm taking the shuttle to the 2,647.279 port entry."

It was at that point the Tekkore intervened. A sudden silent blast hit the station. Although the blast was silent in space, the sound it made inside the station was very significant.

Douge was rattled even more than Dan. "No, no, no!" He sprinted to the console. "Where can I go? Where can I go?"

Noises were coming from down the hall, so Dan leaned down to look. Something was coming down the hall—Tekkore.

The Tekkore were large and squarish—well, cubeish. Large meaning the size of an SUV. Cubeish is not a good shape for living things—you have high wind resistance and trouble fitting through doorways, which they compensated for by blowing the doorways apart.

Nature would never have invented such an odd creature if the universe were not infinite. If the odds were ten billion to one that on a distant planet unlikely circumstances would allow a cube being to evolve and thrive—or at least survive—the whole infinity thing meant it would happen.

Having tiny legs and arms, locomotion was difficult for Tekkore until they evolved to spin. The Tekkore travelled any distance more than a few feet by spinning very rapidly. They could cover a lot of ground very quickly if they got up enough speed.

The only problem with this form of transit was the Tekkore are six-sided cubes, which is not the optimum shape for spinning. Unlike, say, a diamond, a cube is not balanced when placed on one corner, leading to an unwieldy spin.

The end result is that Tekkores spin in a wild wobbly fashion, which even with their best efforts causes them to careen into objects, walls, and nearby humanoids.

Some have said this is what makes them grumpy.

Dan closed the door and yelled at Douge. "Just find somewhere for us to go."

"You think I'm not trying?"

The door started shaking and making a grinding noise.

"Do you have any weapons?" asked Freddie.

"We are a peaceful race."

"You have a death ray."

"It's for monsters and beasts and it doesn't work on Tekkore. Mostly we just teleport away from them."

"Is that all?"

"We blow up one of their receiver stations and they blow up one of ours."[11]

Freddie saw the door beginning to buckle from the Tekkore battering away at it. "Looks like they're upping their game."

With that, the door burst open and a lone Tekkore rocketed in—and crashed into the opposite wall. When she stopped spinning, she sprawled onto her back. She called to them. "Oh dear, a little help."

Small legs and arms made getting up difficult half of the time and impossible the other half. Some said this was the reason they were so grumpy.

"You're trying to kill us!" cried Dan. "Why would we want to help you?"

"I can get up, but that would require spinning again, which might kill you and only works half the time anyway. Or you could help me up and we'll talk before I kill you."

---

[11] Tekkore don't actually need a receiver station, but opening a hole in space in someone's den scares the hell out of them.

"What if we don't want to die?"

"You could let me teleport you."

Douge screamed, "NEVER! I will not be turned into an empty husk devoid of Rielleity."

"Suit yourself."

Dan jumped in. "Wait, I don't mind being an empty husk."

"Help me up."

Dan and Freddie helped her to her feet, which she ignored, preferring to sit flat on the floor.[12]

"The reason I didn't blow up the station is I wanted to try to understand why you started this war," said the Tekkore.

Douge was incensed. "We didn't start the war."

"Yes, you did."

"No, we didn't."

"You did."

"Your people started blowing up our stations and killing us."

"Because you accused us of genocide."

"Because you're guilty of genocide."

"Are not."

"Are so."

"You're guilty of putting the universe at risk."

"You're crazy."

"Are we the ones who send matter through inner space when it's fundamentally dangerous to send anything but energy though the fabric of space?"

"Is not."

"Is so."

"Our scientists assure us it's perfectly safe, other than mild anal leakage."

"And ours have assured us it is not."

Freddie motioned Dan to the doorway. "Come get us when you've sorted it all out."

---

[12] The Tekkore love sitting and sleeping on their flat underside, which has led some to think they are lazy—they are not. They love sports and even have Olympic style games. The most loved event is the spinning in graphite competition.

"Your scientists are biased by a desire for fame and glory."

"And yours are in the pocket of big teleportation."

Down the corridor Dan looked back. "Does this happen a lot out in the universe?"

"More than one would hope," said Freddie.

"Do you think Replacement makes you lose your soul?"

"Maybe, but I don't think we have to worry about it."

"No?"

She shook her head. "Remember the timestream resets you back to entry default, so whatever you had when you went in you should regain."

"But you sounded like you didn't want to be replaced."

"I don't like the idea of my energy being harvested to ship my data across the universe."

"It does sound a bit final."

"It's bad enough we get split into our component parts in the timestream. At least we're not consumed like we're halibut or something."

"Did you say halibut?"

They reached for one another and entered the timestream hand in hand.

– Chapter 23 –
Prime Time Crime

For the first time while jumping, Dan noticed a distinct lack of time. He and she were at peace as they entered the stream. He really couldn't tell how long the jump lasted. A few seconds or millennia. In the timestream you exist outside of time. A few seconds is millennia and millennia is a few seconds.

He could see calmly into her and she into him. Both liked what they saw.

Then things got weird. Well, weirder. They heard a voice—Chantell, calling to them from everywhere. Well, calling through a small blinking device that sounded like it came from everywhere.

"Guys? It's Chantell. I've made some progress and need you back at Club 6.4. I want you to both focus on the club and this device should help you get here. Dan may not be able to control when he jumps, but maybe we can help him choose where."

Being in the timestream, Dan could barely comprehend what was being said, what with staring into Freddie and everything. Freddie, on the other hand, being an experienced jumper and superior multitasker, began to focus on the club, which since Dan was focusing on her, led him to focus on the club.

Expert jumpers are more capable of getting to a specific time or destination than newbies, but the mind shredding can sidetrack even the best of them, so reaching your destination is always a crapshoot.

Chantell's time device could be tossed anywhere or anytime into the timestream to seek out jumpers whose DNA it was programmed to locate, helping to keep them on track. This made Chantell the most accurate jumper in the universe—except for the person who would always be better in an infinite universe.

Dan and Freddie popped into linear existence inside Chantell's office. As they landed, Chantell was sweeping a device at them. A screen to the side reflected the data she was collecting. "Welcome back."

"Thanks." Freddie's voice was on edge. "When are we?"

"A few days after you left."

Dan was nonplussed. "That's weird."

Albert came forward with a plate of food, which both jumpers devoured.

"While you eat, let me tell you what I've been working on."

"Like that Time Channeler?" Freddie reined in her irritation. She didn't appreciate being summoned as if they were Chantell's lapdogs no matter how good the food.

Chantell dismissed the irritation. "That's the biggie. Right now it's set to help you to return to Club 6.4, but I hope it will eventually help you go anywhere."

"Awesome." Dan was thrilled he might get some kind of control over his life.

"What have you two been up to?"

Freddie answered, being between bites. "Well, we went for a sail, I jumped with Dan from the other side of a door, and we may have added a couple of billion miles to humanity's jump range."

"I haven't gone sailing in forever," said Chantell.

Freddie nodded. "That would work for me."

"What kind of a door?"

"An exploding space station pressure kinda door."

"My."

"I know. That shouldn't happen, right?"

Chantell tapped into her handheld device. "Was that in Earth orbit?"

"I think so."

An exploding space station in orbit—that told Chantell it was the TellTom station, in 2436. "I should be able to pull some data on that jump."

"You're not…"

"No, there's a lot of data on that station. I guess I know the answer to the mystery of how the station survived."

"That would be us." Dan was still surprised they were able to pull that one off.

"So that business about expanding the jump range…"

Freddie interrupted Chantell. "We've been through a lot. Can we rest a little?"

Dan thought that was odd as he didn't feel tired.

Chantell waved them down the hall. "Of course. I held your room for you. Come back when you're rested."

"Thank you."

Freddie and Dan headed to their room. Dan was amazed at how short the journey was this time.

When they shut the door, Dan started to speak but Freddie silenced him with a raised finger.

"Albert."

"Yes, Ms. Townes?"

"Albert, I want you to shut down all room monitoring functions."

"But how will I respond to your needs?"

"We will activate you manually if we need anything."

"Even my emergency sensors?"

"Yes, Albert."

"Do you agree to this as well, Dan?"

He looked at Freddie for confirmation. "Yes."

"Then I cannot guarantee your safety."

"I hereby indemnify you from any damage we may suffer during this time," said Freddie.

"And you, Dan?"

"Yes, I hereby—whatever that thing she said."

"Very well. Shutting down monitoring. I'll miss you."

"Will he?" Dan asked Freddie.

"Probably," she said.

Lights on all the monitors blinked out one by one. They couldn't see that a tiny hidden light in the ceiling continued glowing.

Dan crossed to the wide window and gazed out at a scene of black sky and scattered stars. Most prominent among them was the sun, greatly distended as it prepared for its demise. "So you know, I was thinking about it and I've been with you almost constantly for weeks."

She stood beside him. "Even more for me. I didn't get to go to New York or Chicago."

"True. And I know you better than I've ever known anyone. I've had my brain shredded with yours."

"I've seen your thoughts."

"And you didn't run away."

"Nope."

"So are we?"

"What?"

"What Chantell asked us last time we were here."

"And that was?"

"A couple."

"Kinda."

"Sorta."

"It's complicated." Freddie looked at him, searching for understanding. "I still need you to jump, so I *have* to stay with you."

"And I don't know what I'm doing, so I have to stay with you."

"I'll bet Chantell would go with you, and she's more experienced than I am."

"You work just fine for me."

"Yeah, but I need you more than you need me."

"So?"

"So, the relationship is too one-sided. I need to be your equal."

"You're more than that." Dan's reptile brain was very proud of that line.

"So we're a couple, but not really a couple."

"So a couple, with no coupling."

"For now."

They both smiled, while two reptile brains tore up their brain furnishings.

Dan had a thought. "Can Chantell really travel back right to the time of my jumps?"

"She's been doing this for centuries, so if anyone can…"

"That's kinda scary."

"Yep."

"Does something seem a little off to you?"

"That's why I turned off Albert."

Dan wasn't sure how she meant that.

After a bit, Freddie wanted to return to the club lounge, but Dan was being recalcitrant.

"We'll never learn anything here."

"We also won't feel like we're being stabbed in the eye with an icepick."

"Come on," said Freddie. "You'll have fun."

"I'll have fun here."

"You'll have more fun there."

"I was going to try to find out more about history."

"Or you could come with me."

"I'd like to stay here."

"Yeah, but I'll be there."

"That is a powerful argument."

"You wouldn't want to leave me on my own."

She didn't mean like that, but Dan realized there was a danger. If he jumped, she needed to be there. It didn't feel like she was ready to jump on her own. Every time they separated she was at risk of being stranded again. He was an anchor for her. That meant doing things for her, even if he didn't want to.

They were a couple. And that meant Dan was going with her.

When they entered Club 6.4, Chantell was oddly absent. Freddie's friends were thrilled to see her. They didn't get much time with her earlier. They talked of adventures since they last saw her. Freddie hadn't seen them in over 27 years; some of them had seen her a few days ago.

One old friend at the table hadn't even met her yet.

Dan recognized a few guests from the previous visit, but others were new.

Dan reluctantly both had a good time and learned a lot about time travel's dangers and joys. Freddie drew him in to help tell about their time aboard *The Traveler*. His story of the wild jumper was quite entertaining.

Dinosaurs were rare.

Betsy, an older jumper, was amazed by the story. "I don't know anyone who's seen one."

Chantell's voice dropped in. "No, you know three, honey: Dan, Freddie, and me."

Freddie looked toward her. "I never saw it."

"Then it's just me and Dan in our own little club."

Something about Chantell looked odd, but Freddie could not put her finger on it.

Dan was busy avoiding the flirtyness of Chantell's last comment and didn't look directly at her. His reptile brain was screaming, "She's better looking now!!", but Dan wasn't listening.

Chantell squeezed in beside Dan at the table. "I'm glad I got here in time for that story. I knew Dan was a stud, but saving a sailing ship from a Mosasaurus? Nice job, my man."

There's a weird dynamic when a woman flirts with a man in the presence of a woman she knows is interested in him. And despite their protestations, Chantell knew they were a couple.

The flirter feels powerful enough to make a play for the other's man. She has to self-identify as alpha. She attempts to intimidate the other female through chutzpa and brazen innuendo. Comments she would normally never say escape her mouth in Costco-sized proportions. If the other female self-identifies as weaker, she will sit quietly or try to convince the man it's time to go.

Freddie was not weak. "You should have seen him save me from an angry group of sailors."

"I wish I had." Chantell upped her game by licking her upper lip.

Dan tried to place the incident."You mean when I threw—"

"He tackled me into the ocean thirty feet above the water."

"I doubt it was thir—"

"Maybe higher."

In this dynamic the man is both flattered and frightened as this could so easily go terribly wrong no matter what he does or doesn't do. This is frequently followed by guilt and shame over what he did or didn't do.

Although top tier alpha males don't really experience the fear, guilt or shame; they just assume it will end in a threesome.

That was not Dan. "Well, it's getting late…"

"Well, we did want some time alone."

Point Freddie.

Realizing if they left she would lose this round, Chantell changed tactics. "Oh, I'm just messing with you, girlfriend. Stay."

"We've had a rough day."

"I wasn't going to say anything tonight, but I do need to talk to you about my test results."

Dan looked at her directly for the first time tonight. Something looked a bit off. "Did you find something?"

"It's what I didn't find."

"Didn't?"

"All right, gang, I'm gonna need the bar for a couple hours, but after that it's burger barbeque!!!"

An actual barbeque in space was a rare occurrence. A closed environment with high oxygen content does not mix well with charcoal briquettes. It takes precision to balance medium rare against spontaneous combustion.

If you're lucky, you just end up with singed eyebrows and very well-done steaks.

Obviously, Chantell loves her some barbeque.

The patrons filed out, disappointed they had to miss the contest but excited about barbeque.

As the door closed, Freddie turned to Chantell. "All right. What did you find?"

"I was able to pull my satellite data and cross reference it with Dan's approximate jump dates to measure the tachyons present for most of his Earth-based jumps."

Dan had missed a step. "Satellite data?"

"I placed a satellite in Earth orbit millions of years ago to better understand the time jumps."

"How could you send a… ?"

"Satellite back in time? I didn't, but I know a guy."

"You know a guy?"

"An alien jumper who could get the technology in the time period."

"Didn't anyone notice it?"

"Not for millions of years, and when they finally did, they thought it was the other guys."

"We thought it was Russian?"

"And they thought it was—"

"American."

"Right."

Alien technology really scares the crap out of people.

"Anyway," Chantell said, "looking at the data, his prime jump looks normal on exit; the second, I couldn't find. Do you have any idea where or when you were?"

"Green rolling hills—and sheep."

"Third jump looks normal enough, maybe a little tachyon increase. The fourth looked normal, but without knowing where you two landed…"

"For all we know it wasn't even Earth," said Freddie. "Snow, ice, and cold. Pick anyplace."

"Hmmmph." Not what Chantell wanted to hear. "So no data on the fifth jump. The sixth jump had a 23 percent tachyon increase and the seventh, 52 percent. Something happened the fourth or fifth jump. I need to see that fifth jump to get clear data."

Freddie held up a hand. "Wait. *See* the jump?"

"Just a figure of speech. I mean see the data."

"I don't think you did."

"I'm running tests from the satellite."

"I've never seen satellites give more than general information—there are or there are not tachyons. How come you know exact percentages?"

"I'm running an algorithm that gives a more precise—"

"Precise, my ass. You went there."

The accusation startled Dan. "To my prime jump? What about the first rule of time travel?" He was a little proud of using the phrase "prime jump."

"I didn't."

"Now I know why you look different." Freddie grabbed Chantell's shoulder. "Uh huh. Padding. You lost 40 pounds in a week. And you're wearing make-up to look older, not younger."

"All right. I went to his prime jump. I had to."

You never, ever, ever screw with the prime jump. Creating a time loop is like putting a period on that reality.

Not something you want to do.

Chantell found a reason to risk it.

– Chapter 24 –
Can Entropy Happen to Entropy?

Freddie was livid. "YOU WENT TO HIS PRIME JUMP?"

"Let me explain."

"EXPLAIN THAT YOU COULD HAVE ENDED THIS TIMELINE?"

"I know the risk, but this is too big. Dan could be the key to saving the universe."

"From what?"

"From entropy, from decay, from catastrophe. From the inevitable collapse of the whole thing."

(Although if you could save it from the inevitable, that would make it evitable.)

Dan and Freddie looked at Chantell with jaws dropped, heads tilted to the side. Time jumpers know crazy.

Chantell continued. "What if you could send a planet, or a star, or even a galaxy into the timestream and bring it out brand new, where it resided billions of years ago?"

"Are you talking about resetting the expansion of the universe?" said Freddie.

"Yes."

"That's nuts."

"That's what I would have said before today."

"Albert, how long has Chantell been locked out of the time field?"

"I am not—"

"Chantell is not locked out of the time field," said Albert.

"See," said Chantell.

"Albert, when did she last jump before today?"

"Twenty-one years f—"

"Albert, enough."

Freddie glared. "You used the tachyons you took from Dan."

"Yes, I did. I had to see if I could use them to open the timestream, and it worked."

"You didn't give a crap about Dan or the universe, you just wanted to get your hands in his time field."

"Of course I did. It's not every day a man can give you what Dan's got, and he does not disappoint." Chantell drew a small device from her pocket. "I made jumps to eight different time periods and have hardly touched what I extracted from Dan." She spread her arms wide. "Imagine opening up a hole big enough for a spaceship, or this station. Imagine taking a young planet, bursting with life, and time jumping it ahead a minute. Then going to the end of its life and time jumping it ahead a minute, then another, each resetting the years to its original jump as a new planet—that would double its lifespan. The time field is infinite; why not use it to reset galaxies? The universe may not have to end in a whimper, freezing in the farthest outreaches of space. It could be born again."

"That's a lot of responsibility for a plumber." The idea sounded nuts to Dan.

And to Freddie. However, she had to admit: nearly anything is possible with the infinite.

Actually, everything is probable with the infinite.

Infinity hurts my brain.

"Don't forget just collecting your little stash of particles nearly took him apart," Freddie said.

"Yes, yes, obviously Dan can't produce enough particles, no matter what we do. But if I can study him closely enough, I might be able to replicate the process on a larger scale."

"Wait a minute," said Dan. "What are you proposing to do to me?"

"I need to stimulate your field and study its mechanics."

"How long will that take?"

"Years. Maybe even decades."

"That's a long time."

"Not to us. Not to the universe."

Freddie tried to dissuade her. "How are you going to do that if he jumps tomorrow? You have to think of something else."

"I think the jump he just did today should stop him for a while."

"How long could it stop him from jumping?"

"Half a day."

"So, what, you want to drain him for tachyons twice a day?"

"Not *want* to…"

Dan was not happy with this. "Wait, you plan to do that to me twice a day for decades?"

"Only until I come up with something better."

"Strangulation would be better."

"But what if your pain could save untold billions of lives?"

"I don't know if I can do it."

"You have to try."

"No, he doesn't," said Freddie.

"We have the chance to save the universe!"

Freddie looked incredulous. "Or destroy it. You're talking about changing the way the universe works on a fundamental level. Where in God's name did you get the idea the universe was broken?"

"From us! Do you think we were meant to slip through time? To live forever? We are such an aberration we have to make rules to keep our meddling from locking the universe in an eternal loop. Why should we get to play around with time?"

"Because the timestream chose us."

"Bullshit! The timestream doesn't choose anything, it just is."

"Because it rejected you after centuries doesn't mean it doesn't act deliberately."

"The time field works in mysterious ways." Chantell was mocking a jumper axiom that was lost on Dan.

Freddie's eyes narrowed in suspicion. "And how about you?"

"I'm not so mysterious."

"No, you just want to trick Dan into making you young, into restoring your connection to the time field. Maybe you want to be savior to the whole damn universe."

"There are worse things to be."

No there are not.

It's a horrible job, long hours, people resent you. "Who did you save today? The Romans? Why did you save them? They hold slaves and treat the people unfairly. Why haven't you saved the Egyptians yet?"

And it's really, really easy for the universe's savior to become its master.

Freddie looked her directly in the eye. "No one should have that kind of power."

"It's out there, someone is going to use it," said Chantell.

"And you're the one?"

"Who better? I've been alive thousands of years, seen a hundred thousand times. I can make things better."

"Or really fuck them up."

Dan had been listening, wrestling with himself. "If we can save people, maybe I should try."

Chantell brightened 100 watts. "Atta boy, Dan."

He turned to Freddie. "But if you don't want me to, I won't."

"Maybe after you learn more control over the jumps we can try to figure some things out," said Freddie.

Dan turned to Chantell. "After I learn more about jumping I might be able to give you what you need."

"What if you die tomorrow?" Chantell said. "Jumping's a dangerous game. What happens if while you're out learning the ins and outs of jumping, you get killed? BAM! I lose my one chance."

"Your chance."

"Our chance."

Dan stood up. "Come on, Freddie. Let's go."

Freddie rose to accompany him to the door.

"Where do you plan on going?" Chantell was more threatening than curious.

"Anywhere but here," he said.

"That's too bad, because here is all you got."

The doors made an audible click.

Freddie didn't stop moving toward the doors. "Albert, unlock the doors."

Click.

She had just reached the door when:

"Albert, lock the doors, command code 13."

Click.

"Albert, unlock the doors," said Freddie.

Silence.

Freddie looked at Chantell. "Make him unlock the door."

"Albert, please put Dan in the medical restraint harness."

Albert took Dan by the arm and led him, despite Dan's attempt not to be led, to the upright medical table in the other room.

Freddie ran over to free him but Albert continued strapping him in. Freddie ran at Chantell, who elegantly slid aside and guided Freddie into a wall.

"Darling, I've had a thousand years to learn self-defense from the great masters. I could kill you without touching you, but that would be evil."

Freddie crawled up into a comfy chair, staring at Chantell. "Stop this."

Chantell turned to Dan. "I'm sorry this hurts so much, Danny, but there's no other way to keep you here. Gotta drain the tachyons."

As she carefully turned up the power from itch to vibrate, she didn't notice Freddie fiddling with something in her hand.

Chantell turned up the drain even higher and Dan began to moan. She had her eyes glued on the display. Freddie got up and eased toward Dan. She was almost there when Chantell put her hand out.

"Whatcha doin' there, girlfriend?"

"I was going to hold his hand."

"Hmm, sweet. I'll allow it."

Freddie took Dan's hand as the moans progressed to a scream.

"AHHHHH!"

With a tear, Freddie whispered. "I'm getting you out."

Chantell was watching the screen when something changed. "Oh my God, this is fantastic! Tachyons are pouring in. We've opened some sort of floodgate. We can do this."

She looked over to see Freddie defiant, holding the device (which they will later name Timmy) to access the interspatial field, which held Dan's tachyons.

"Yes, we can."

"Noo!!" Chantell dived toward Freddie, grabbing at the device.

Through the pain, Dan saw minnows flitting everywhere.

Freddie was holding onto the device with one hand and Dan with the other as Chantell clawed, hit, and heaved to loosen her grip. Freddie held firm.

Dan felt the pain subside as tachyons flowed from Freddie to him, to the interspatial field and back to Freddie. This loop gave him an indescribable feeling of peace and euphoria, like a really good heroin trip—only better.

And without all the withdrawal, sweating, cramping, panic, and potential for death.

Freddie wondered if there was/were a world out there with seahorses big enough to ride.

There were at least seven such worlds. And in two of them the seahorses might not eat you.

As they entered the field, Freddie managed to kick the desperate Chantell loose, and watched her drift away.

Freddie held the device in the "on" position as she was shredded; the influx of tachyons into a saturated environment seemed to increase the amount of timelessness they were in the stream.

– Chapter 25 –
Jurassic Hijinks
(Man, those tittles look funny)

When they came out, they were energized. And in a forest. With Dan strapped to a table.

Dan hopped to his feet. Well, he would have had he not been strapped to a table.

Freddie jumped up and began to unstrap him. "That was amazing. Did you see how I tricked Chantell? Bitch tried to stop me, but no! I kicked her and she ended up spinning into time knows where. Are you okay? That sounded painful. And then we were jumping and you were better and now we're here and you're all tied up and you're so quiet, are you okay?"

"I am fine."

Freddie stopped. "Are you?"

"I will be if you get these straps off."

In a period of nearly no time at all, Dan had experienced the most pain he had ever suffered and the most joy. He had touched time in a way he could not conceive of—yet he conceived. His thoughts were on overdrive processing new information into theories, into conclusions. He understood time in a new and fundamental way.

Too bad he wouldn't remember most of it.

"It wasn't me," he said.

"What wasn't you?"

"Not all me anyway. It was you."

"What was me?"

"The excess tachyons."

"Yeah, I released them from the interspatial field where Chantell was keeping them. See, she thought I was attacking her, but I wasn't. I was steal—"

"No, the excess tachyons in me. It was you."

"Me?"

"Yeah. My first jump was normal. On the fourth or fifth jump they started to spike. What was different on those jumps?"

"Me."

"Right." By now Dan was free and grabbed her by the waist. "Your jumping with me did something."

Suddenly it made perfect sense to her as well.

When the pair jumped this time they were filled with time particles, Freddie had been fighting and holding on tight, so all of her energy went towards physical activity. Dan had been strapped down so his mental processes opened and increased.

Now Freddie's were doing the same. "Right, right, something about the two of us together, since I had lost the timestream, the particles I would normally have absorbed went into you."

"And those extra particles opened up a link to the time field."

"And every time we jump, I shared that link."

"And it's causing you to retain tachyons."

"And regain my connection to the field."

Freddie's mind was well versed in the intricacies of time travel and soon eclipsed Dan's heightened thoughts; she could see where Chantell had gone right and wrong. With this knowledge she could change the universe.

Good thing she wouldn't remember most of it.

As the rush from the jump wore off, Freddie struggled to hold onto her new understanding of time. Dan's was already gone, and his attention elsewhere.

Which turned out to be fortuitous.

"Holy crap!" he said.

"What?"

"Look at the trees."

The trees were completely alien. There were huge ferns and sort of palms growing in dense formation around them. Nothing looked familiar.

"Holy crap!" she said.

"Where are we?"

"I don't know." Freddie took a deep breath through her nose. "The air's good." She checked the soil. "Looks Earth normal."

"So we're on Earth?"

"Not any Earth I've seen."

"That's saying something."

"Come on." Freddie maneuvered through the undergrowth quietly and quickly.

Dan struggled with the quiet part. As he tumbled through the flora, Dan noticed they were heading up a slight incline that was getting steeper. They came to a rock wall and stopped.

Freddie looked around and found a broken branch and used a knife from her satchel to fashion a spear. "You should make one, too. Who knows what we'll run into."

Dan pulled a small knife from his tool belt and began whittling a spear. Compared to Freddie's, his was bent and sickly looking, but it was his first ever spear.

Freddie put hers under her satchel, sticking up over her head, and started to climb up the wall.

Dan followed suit. "Where are we going?"

"Up."

"That was my guess."

"We're getting the lay of the land. Besides, we should have more protection from predators up here."

"Will we?"

"Sure. Look at those hands, thumbs all opposable. We were built for climbing, baby."

"Baby? I think Chantell is a bad influence on you."

"She was worse on you."

They began their ascent.

"No argument there. I think my fillings are still vibrating… What happened to her?"

"You didn't see?"

"I was a little busy, what with all the screaming and whatnot."

"I kicked her off as we entered the timestream."

"So she's back at the club?"

"I don't know. She could have jumped or be lost in the timestream or something."

"So she could be waiting for us somewhere like you were for me?"

"That's a possibility."

"Perfect."

Freddie stopped at an outcropping. As they scanned over the jungle, they could see a river in the distance and in it something was moving. Something big.

Dan gave it a name. "It's a Brontosaurus."

"It can't be."

"Because people can't go that far back."

"No. Well yes, but also because there's no such thing."

"There is."

"No, it's Brachiosaur."

"What happened to Brontosaurus?"

"It never existed."

"It did on 'The Flintstones.'"

"The what?"

"'The Flintstones.' It was a cartoon about the Stone Age."

"Right. Because cartoons are always historically accurate."

"It's in books."

"'The Flintstones'?"

"No, the Brontosaurus."

"Out of date books."

"Are you saying they changed it?"

"Yes."

"I wish they'd leave things well enough alone." Dan was getting very tired of change. "Everyone called it a Brontosaurus. That's what it was."

"Nope, because the Brontosaurus never existed. Some guy found a bone and claimed it was a new type of dinosaur, a huge thing he named the Brontosaurus and everyone got all excited and put it in cartoons and on gas stations. Only it turns out there was no Brontosaurus, only a misidentified Brachiosaurus bone. Meanwhile, the poor guy who discovered the Brachiosaurus has had his whole discovery co-opted by some guy who can't even identify a bone correctly."

"Well, when you put it that way… How do you know about this anyway? It was after your time."

"I spent a month in 2017 working in a natural history museum. The curator was very opinionated."

Dan came to a realization. "That explains the problem then. In 2020 they decided there was a Brontosaurus and the guys who said there was no Brontosaurus were wrong."

"Wait, so who was right?"

"Apparently no one."

"Perhaps we should pay attention to the oversized pigeon over there." Freddie pointed towards a flying Ptera something.

"So we're in the Jurassic."

"Or Triassic or something."

"How'd that happen?"

"It shouldn't. Must have been that weird jump. Maybe using the excess tachyons Chantell drained from you created an anomaly."

"Does that mean all Earth jumpers will get to travel here now?"

"I hope not. Jumpers like to avoid environments this hostile."

"Hey, I just noticed: I'm not hungry."

"Hmm, me neither. That's nice. We don't have to worry about food for a while. How much water do you have?"

"My pouch is full."

"Mine, too. So we don't have to go anywhere." Freddie sat down on the rock ledge.

"You don't want to explore?"

"Do you?"

"No, I just thought you might like…"

"To go wandering around a prehistoric world filled with giant carnivorous nasties, with nothing but a pointed stick to protect me?"

"Well… yeah."

"I'm adventurous, not stupid."

"So what should we do?"

"This looks like a good place to spend our time here. Defensible space, shelter there in the rocks."

"I hope we don't run into a T-Rex."

"We should be fine. Have you seen those T-Rex hands? They were not meant for climbing, baby."

"Definitely a bad influence."

"Maybe the next time she wants to save the universe you should keep us separated."

"Definitely." Dan thought for a moment. "So what kinds of creatures were meant for climbing?"

"In this era? No idea. Have you even seen a picture of a dinosaur that looked like it could climb?"

"No, they all look rather horizontally based. Perhaps some of the smaller ones."

"Or ones that are not in the fossil record. It would be weird if the cliffs were all perfectly safe from predators and no creature adapted to live here."

"You would think."

"What if we don't have a record because the rock is not a good place for bones to survive? They wouldn't get buried or trapped in amber or a tar pit. Just erode away. Or maybe they don't have bones or a shell that would survive. A man-eating slug or a giant hollow-boned spider."

"I don't think I'm going to sleep tonight."

"Good. Then you can keep watch."

And he did, after he built a fire and made torches to drive away the giant spiders—which definitely saved them from the man-eating slugs. If there had been giant hollow-boned spiders there, a fire wouldn't have helped at all.

Early that morning Freddie stirred at around two a.m. as the crow flies—if our 24-hour measurement has any relevance in a time where the Earth rotated in 22 or 23 hours.

"Dan, do you feel something?"

Dan had been feeling something odd that he could not quite identify. He assumed it had to do with dinosaurs or giant spiders. "Yes."

Freddie inched closer to him and as she did, both could feel a tingling and they grabbed hands as they slipped into the timestream.

And with that, a giant slug was robbed of a sumptuous breakfast.

- Chapter 26 -
A Very Dangerous Picnic

The tingling sensation Freddie felt was not unpleasant; it was rather pleasurable, kind of a spark about the body making it more aware and hypersensitive. Dan was less pleased as it reminded him of the itchy feeling in Chantell's machine—and that made him itch.

Chantell had extracted tachyons from Dan in a harsh mechanical way, leading to increasing discomfort; this was the natural flow of time transporting them to a new location. The more you tried to bend time to your will, the more it cost you—or the person you had strapped to the table.[13]

The thought swirled in his brain as he swirled in the stream and he lost track of it in no time. But he did stop itching.

When they regained a sense of time, they were standing in a quiet countryside, with rolling green fields and picturesque farms in the distance. There was a small country road nearby. This time they were hungry. Luckily, they had both snagged extra sandwiches while at Club 6.4…

---

[13] Speaking of which, since the timestream tends to tidy up objects left behind, when Dan and Freddie jumped, so did Chantell's examination table. Albert had been moving items out of the way, expecting the table's return as he had had vast experience of jumpers leaving the club and any items they took with them returning a few minutes later. Although, as was typical for anything going through the timestream, re-entry was rather awkward.

In the case of the table, it would need to be replaced rather than repaired.

They sat on a little hill admiring the view—and not only the countryside. Dan was admiring Freddie in the white shirt tucked into the brown pants. He had seen her dressed many ways, but this reminded him most of his era. He wondered what she would look like in a tee-shirt and jeans.

His reptile brain painted a picture of that. While not wholly accurate, it was wholly enjoyable. Dan gazed at the horizon. "This is better."

"Than what?"

"Dinosaurs."

"Is it?"

"Absolutely."

"I don't know. At least there we knew what might try to kill us."

"It would be nice if the answer is 'Nothing.'"

Freddie pointed down to the road. "Look there. People."

Dan peered toward the road and saw a couple on bicycles. Their clothes looked formal, even at the distance, suggesting early Twentieth Century. The couple must have seen them as well and started waving.

Dan waved back.

The couple waved more.

"I guess they want to talk to us."

Freddie and Dan stood and started walking toward the cyclists, who started waving more franticly and yelling something. The two started to pick up the pace, thinking maybe the cyclists needed help, but the couple on the road put their hands up in a "halt" gesture.

Dan and Freddie stopped and listened very carefully.

"Land mines."

They could barely hear it, but it had a huge impact. Suddenly the field went from bucolic to deadly.

Freddie punctuated her earlier point. "How do you feel about dinosaurs now?"

"Better all the time."

"So what should we do?"

"You're asking me?"

"Sorry. Never dealt with land mines before."

"That should be included in the jumper's safety manual! Wait, that's right: there is no safety manual."

In truth there was a Jumper's Safety Manual, but it was on the other side of the universe (if the universe had a side) and written in a language that only has one letter: Y.

While I'm on the subject of the universe's side… all right, maybe I'm only on the subject as a bracketed aside, but still. The universe may well be infinite, but the description of the Big Bang (a singularity goes boom) suggests that the matter in our universe is finite and still expanding outward into infinite vacuum.

Even if you buy that the matter could be infinite, someday it will stop expanding outward and contract, possibly reversing time, or it will continue outward, moving further apart until it dies frozen and alone—which suggests if you go far enough out—before the first matter of the Big Bang has reached the edge, that is the edge of *our* universe, not *the* universe, but our universe, the place with all of our stuff—you reach the end of that universe. Beyond that there is nothing.

The far side of our matter part of the universe is the other side.

That's where the Jumper's Safety Manual is. Not that it's doing Freddie any good.

"I guess we just stay here," she said.

"Until we jump?"

"We might have to."

"We might attract some attention after a week."

"Let's not stay here that long. Do you think you could jump again?"

Dan closed his eyes and concentrated. "No."

Dan began to run through all the movies he had seen that included a minefield. The results were generally not good.

1. Freeze.
   Good result here, nobody's blown up so far.
2. Back out the way you came in.

This does not work if you time jumped into the middle of the field.

3. Call for help.
   And the bastards that mined the field will come help.
4. Look for anything odd or out of place—fresh digging, mounds of dirt, odd or dead clumps of grass.
   This could be helpful.
5. Use your bayonet to gently probe for mines.
   Let's poke a mine with a bayonet. If we had a bayonet.
6. Throw heavy stones ahead to clear the way.
   Which could be helpful if we had heavy stones.

The cyclists were signaling again, pushing their hands down.

Freddie interpreted. "I think they want us to lie down."

As they carefully dropped to the ground, they saw a vehicle in the distance. The cyclists mounted their bikes and started to ride. The vehicle slowed as it approached. Even from this distance Dan could see it—a Kübelwagen—sported two flags on its hood, emblazoned with red swastikas.

"Holy shit, Nazis."

Freddie lifted her head. "Oooo, I've never seen Nazis before."

Freddie had missed the whole ultimate evil part of the Twentieth Century. She knew of them the way we know of the Mongol hordes—powerful warriors who did terrible things under the command of a ruthless ruler.

"I don't think we want them to see us."

"Good point." She lowered her head.

The Kübelwagen passed the bicycles and roared away.

When the military car drove out of sight, one cyclist turned back while the other went on. The one that returned gave the "stay there" sign.

Dan was getting anxious. "She wants us to stay here."

"Probably a good idea."

"So is getting to someplace we won't stick out to Nazis."

"Also a good idea."

"We need to move ahead."

"Not such a good idea."

"Look, I don't think these mines have been here long. See that little dead clump of grass? I think that's a mine."

"We need to figure out where they aren't, not where they are."

"Well we know we don't go that way. We need to probe for the mines and avoid the areas with fresh digging."

"Probe with what?"

"In the movies they always used a bayonet, but I have…" He produced his screwdriver.

"That tool belt of yours is really handy."

"You should see what I can do with WD 40."

"WD 40?"

"You don't know what WD 40 is?"

She did, but when she learned of it, it was out of patent and known as Ultimate Super Lube, Timmerson's All-Purpose Everything Fluid, WD 185 and Water Displacement Formula Number 40.

Dan scooted himself back toward Freddie and probed the ground near where he was laying, angling his screwdriver shank to reduce the chance of tripping the pressure plate.

And because that was the way the guys in the movies did it.

Moving slowly and methodically, they inched their way toward the road. Every so often they would encounter a hard object—stone or mine? Some progress was lost avoiding rocks.

As weird as it sounds, Dan achieved some measure of satisfaction being the one who led the way and knew things for a change.

After about an hour, Freddie spotted the cyclist returning with a truck filled with people and stones. A muscular man chucked a stone as far out as he could, then backed up a step and tossed another one, always maintaining a good distance from the point of impact.

The man then stepped onto the first stone and threw one past the previously placed stones.

BOOM!!

The explosion made his foot slip off of the stone. He stood still a moment, and then stepped back on the stone. The remaining people from the truck made a bucket brigade style line behind him passing stones down the line.

BOOM!!!!!

A much larger explosion shaking every person in the line. As the human lifeline got close to Freddie and Dan, it was no longer safe to toss the stones without risking their lives. From there on it was Dan poking the ground and Freddie following behind.

Dan actually felt a little less scared knowing if he triggered a mine, Freddie would be safe on the ground behind him.

Unless it was a Bouncing Betty. Lucky for Dan he didn't know enough about mines to worry about these little springing treats. There were two basic mines in the field: anti-tank and anti-personnel. The big boom was anti-tank.

Strangely, mines were first produced in large quantity to stop tanks in World War One and they would lay anti-personnel mines to keep soldiers from clearing the anti-tank mines.

By World War Two the Germans used anti-personnel mines to slow the advancement of enemy soldiers and anti-tank mines to keep tanks from clearing the mines for the soldiers.

Then the Germans figured out a couple of hidden machine gun nests on the other side of the field really discouraged the enemy.

They sound like the kind of people you want to invite to a party.

"Pass me another lager. Oh, I love this song! Come on, dance with me… No? Hey, I just had this great idea on how to kill a bunch of guys."

This helps clarify the difference between intelligence, cleverness, and wisdom.

Intelligence is coming up with the Atomic bomb.

Cleverness is figuring out how to make one.

Wisdom is choosing not to use it.

As Freddie and Dan reached the stones, the crowd, now standing on the road, breathed a sigh of relief. As they reached the road, Freddie and Dan breathed a sigh of relief.

There were handshakes, hugs, and even some crying (mostly Dan). They loaded everyone and one bicycle into the truck and headed toward the village. The truck was old and smoked badly. The only reason it hadn't been confiscated was it was kept broken or near broken most of the time.

Almost immediately after getting on the road the questions started.

"How did you get in the field?"

"Where are you from?"

"Is that an American accent?"

"Do you know anything about locomotives?"

That was probably an Aspie.

Unless you don't find that a term of affection, in which case it was probably someone on the spectrum. Unless you find being identified by a diagnosis as offensive, in which case it was just someone obsessed with trains.

The group looked and sounded French. Thank God for the time field linking them to language current idiom.

Freddie searched her knowledge of history to contrive a cover story. She couldn't think of a country that a couple with American accents could originate from which wasn't involved in the war.

Dan decided to address it head on.

"Yes, we're Americans. We were sailing to England to help with a USO tour when we ran into a U-boat. Our captain changed course and the U-boat followed. We managed to stay ahead of them in the fog, but they caught us and hit us with a torpedo. We floated in the ocean for days and had lost hope when we washed up on the French coast. Then we had to sneak past the sentries and have been working our way inland."

"Why inland?"

"Have you seen the coast?"

"We can't get near it," said a short dark man.

"I think the Germans expect an attack," said a light-haired woman.

"Or an invasion," said the first man.

Others in the party harrumphed and gave the man the eye.

Dan got the unintentional message. "What day is it?"

"Day?" the woman eyed him.

"Day!"

"June 5th."

All those war movies held two dates above all others: December 7th and June 6th.

"What region are we in?" he asked.

"Normandy."

That rang a bell for Freddie as well. "Normandy Beach?"

"No, the beach is several miles away," replied a second man, the first man having been effectively shushed.

"That's good. I don't like the beach."

"But you just came from there."

"I was afraid I might have got turned around."

Dan leaned in a little. "Why do you think the Jerrys put that mine field there?"

"My guess is to kill our last few goats," said a thin woman in the back.

Dan was exercising all the knowledge he'd gleaned watching war movies. "I think it's because they believe invasion is imminent. They want to make it hard for the Allies to move through France."

"The Germans *will* make it hard for the Allies to move through France."

"Seems to me if the invasion is coming, a cleared, or at least identified mine field would help them a lot."

"While that is true, the men marking that field would risk death."

"I agree and they probably shouldn't risk it until the invasion is just hours away. Do you think that field is watched?"

"If it was, we couldn't have helped you."

"I hope there will be no machine guns there—when the next person accidentally ends up in the field."

Freddie was fascinated by this back and forth, both sides being cautious not to reveal too much.

It was getting dark when the rusted truck rolled into an old bombed out barn next to a farmhouse. One man went to work disabling the engine and others piled debris on top. Soon it looked as though the roof had collapsed onto it.

Freddie and Dan were taken into the house and into a cellar. A young brunette woman stayed with them as the others went upstairs to talk—presumably about them.

The cellar smelled of earth and hay. There were a few bottles of wine and precious else on the shelves.

Freddie studied their babysitter sitting across from them with her hands in her lap. "Excuse me, mademoiselle. I am Freddie and this is Dan. May I ask your name?'

"I am Rose."

"Rose, thank you for taking on this most dangerous duty."

"Dangerous?"

"You do not know if we are friend or foe and yet they leave you to watch the two of us."

She raised her hand to show a German Luger.

"Even so."

Dan was impressed. "Did you kill the man you took it from?"

She smiled.

"Don't they execute you if you are found carrying such a trophy?"

"They would execute me for carrying a kitchen knife."

"Touché." His attempt to speak French came off as odd since everything he was saying was already being heard as French.

Most of the time, time field induced subconscious translation works well—except when you speak a word in the language that you're actually being translated into. Somehow in the process of translating a French word into French, it ends up sounding slightly robotic—or Norwegian.

Well, not so much Norwegian as like the Swedish Chef version of Norwegian. Like a stoic Swedish Chef saying real words in French.

Rose stifled a giggle.

That went a long way to prove to her Dan was no spy.

Upstairs, the villagers convened.

I'll spare you the details as it played out pretty much like every movie ever made where doomed Americans stumble into the hands of the Resistance.

"Kill them."

"What if they're telling the truth?"

"We can't take the risk. Kill them!"

"We must help them."

"They will turn us over to the Gestapo. Kill them!"

I guess I won't spare you the details.

The group was not the Resistance, just townsfolk wanting to help—or kill someone. All the real Resistance was out in the countryside trying to screw up the roads, rails and bridges to keep the Germans from getting reinforcements in time to stop the invasion. At this they were very successful and even the troops that made it to the front couldn't find parking. This worked so well the parking problem persists in Paris until this day.

Paris became the model for our planet to avoid invasion. When the Qleen tried to invade Earth in 2204, they were stymied by the tremendous number of satellites in orbit—no place to park.

The townsfolk decided to tie up Dan and Freddie until the invasion was over. This could start tonight or in a week. Everyone, especially the Germans, knew it was close.

The Germans knew an awful lot about the invasion. Luckily, they were wrong about the exact day; they thought it was a couple days earlier and when it didn't happen, they questioned their intelligence, leading many to believe it would be a few days later than it was, and most importantly they got the place wrong.

This meant when the invasion started, they had most of their troops and heaviest fortifications up the coast.[14] Now they needed to move them quickly to Normandy.

Now you know why tying up transportation was so important.

---

[14] Operation "Fortitude" convinced German commanders the invasion would occur at Pas de Calais. And who invades in bad weather?

Dan decided he needed to trust someone and Rose was elected. "Rose, I'm going to tell you something and you don't have to believe me, but when it comes to pass, you'll be ready. In a few hours paratroopers will land all over France. Most of them won't land where they expect to. Help them find their way."

"Sir??"

"Just before dawn the invasion will begin and the Germans will begin to move troops. Don't make that easy."

Freddie joined in. "And most importantly, stay alive."

Dan imagined the troops preparing their amphibious landing craft for the assault, the sturgeon and mackerel coming to their aid. "You need to go upstairs and tell this to the villagers. We don't mind if you lock us in."

Rose thought a moment.

Dan struggled to hold back the jump.

Finally Rose climbed up the stairs to tell the others.

Freddie grabbed Dan, having shared both the sturgeon, the mackerel, and a smell of ennui. The D-Day invasion had begun and time reclaimed the couple.

– Chapter 27 –
A Wolf in Wolf's Clothing

When they came out of the timestream, Freddie and Dan were prepared for the next dangerous locale. They each assessed the air, the soil, the trees, and pronounced them Earthlike. They searched for tracks and roads and found signs of animals, but no people. From the clean air and distinct absence of soda cans, they believed it was pre-Twentieth Century.

In all of these things they were on target.

They finished the sandwiches in their satchels and set about finding water. They were in a small valley surrounded by mountains. A stream ran through the center of the valley with the sweetest water they had ever tasted.

There were wild berries and game was plentiful. Freddie set some snare traps, a skill she acquired in her 27 years in the Elizabethan age. Dan tried climbing a tree to see what he could see—mostly he saw huge trees. Even so, it felt familiar.

Not familiar like finding a hamster-sized squishy object when you put on your slippers; more like when you get home after a long vacation.

Vacation!!

"We're in Yosemite," he said.

"In California?"

"Yeah, I was here when I was a kid."

"And this is before that?"

"Absolutely. There should be roads and campsites and wall-to-wall tourists."

"Lucky us."

They were, in fact, in the backcountry—a huge sub-alpine meadow surrounded by granitic peaks and distinctive domes. Wildflowers bloomed across the grassy space. At 8,600 feet elevation, vigorous activity could wind even a robust visitor.

"We need to find shelter," said Dan. "It gets cold at night."

"I think it's summer."

"It still gets freakin' cold."

By the time evening arrived they had a fire going near a rock wall, with a large boulder and some broken off branches to provide cover. It got freakin' cold.

Freddie attempted to summarize their situation while roasting a rabbit. "So we're in Yosemite. Pre-people."

"Or at least pre-civilization."

"No sign of dinosaurs."

"And it looks post glacial—Half Dome is not full dome."

Dan was trying to impress Freddie with this intelligent geological insight. He succeeded in that, but would have been disappointed to learn how surprised she was he knew it.

Freddie studied the fauna. "The animals look modern. Squirrels, deer, rabbits."

"Which means mountain lions and bears."

"And wolves."

Dan had forgotten about wolves, as they had been eradicated in the 1920's and when he visited as a child, they had not yet been reintroduced to the park. "Forgot about them."

"Remember the number one rule of time travel. 'Above all, don't die.'"

It says something about time travel when the thought of mountain lions, bears, and wolves trying to eat you is a relief. This is the third biggest danger of time travel: more jumpers die from underestimating typical wild beasties than any other cause of death except underestimating typical evil people and car accidents.

The phrase "It's just a polar bear" has led to several final jumps.

Dan reeled them back to business. "We have temporary shelter, water, and food."

"Actually, we're doing better than usual."

"True, that."

The large stars above them illuminated the sky. Freddie tried to figure out which ones she had visited. "I wonder if she's out there."

"Who?"

"Chantell."

"Either she's in the future, or she got pulled someplace else and she can't get back."

"Because I still have this." Freddie produced the device.

To Dan it held a small piece of him inside. "What did she call it?"

"She didn't."

"Maybe we should name it."

"How about Timmy?"

"No, I meant like to describe it. An interspatial opener thing."

"Oh I thought you wanted to anthropomorphize it."

"I'm not really against that."

"Interspatial Tachyon Containment Retriever?" Freddie ventured.

"Istcur?"

"Oh, you wanted a cute acronym."

"It doesn't have to be cute."

"Tachyon Interspatial Multiuse Engine, TIME."

"Also known as Timmy."

"Yes."

"It wouldn't help her anyway, would it? She put the tachyons in there in the future."

"Hmmmm. She may be able to access them regardless of when she put them in. The interspatial field should be timeless, like the timestream is spaceless."

"Which all leaves me speechless."

The comment was less humorous than Dan would have liked.

Freddie pressed the display and it registered tachyons. "Yep, it's full."

"Should we destroy it?"

"Maybe, but what if we get separated again? This is my ticket out."

They thought about this. Then Dan thought about something else.

"I wonder how she did it?"

"Jump? Well, when a mommy tachyon and a daddy tachyon go into inner space together…"

"No, I wonder how she built a device to jump exactly where and when she wanted."

"She's been doing this a long time, longer than anyone. She knows time better than anyone. They say it takes ten thousand hours to master a skill. I wonder how much time she's spent jumping."

Interesting fact: anyone who has invested ten thousand hours into something believes this is true. Anyone who has invested fewer hours does not. And we all know people who have done something forever and not got any better at it—usually because they believed themselves a master after ten hours and therefore closed the mental door so no new learning could corrupt their mastery.

When it comes to time travel, this is especially hard to quantify. The time spent after a jump could certainly qualify as learning time jump survival and there is no question Chantell had enough experience to have mastered that. The time spent from jump trigger to landing is harder to determine, being only seconds pre-jump and timeless during jump.

Dan went on. "You said I could learn to jump… better."

"I will teach you, young Padawan."

"You know 'Star Wars.'"

"I love movies of the future. Although I first watched it in 2788, so movie of the distant past."

"It *was* set a long time ago in a galaxy far, far away. What do I have to do?"

"First try to touch the time field."

He looked at her quizzically.

"Think about what it feels like to jump and try to re-experience all the details. Try to smell the smells, taste the tastes, see the sights, hear the sounds, feel the feels."

"Tastes?"

"Everyone tastes something different in the stream. I'm lucky I get apple pie. I know a guy who gets steer manure."

"I haven't noticed."

"Next time try to notice."

"Let me get past how one knows the taste of steer manure."

"Just try to notice and we'll move on from there."

A wolf howled from somewhere not quite far away *enough*.

"You know, I think we need pointed sticks," he said.

"Right now we'll make torches from the fire. We'll get pointed sticks tomorrow."

Dan spent the rest of the evening trying to imagine the timestream experience. Which was difficult with Freddie sleeping next to him.

Freddie took the next watch and tried to calculate Chantell's next step, which was difficult with Dan sleeping next to her.

The following day they set about to improve their lot. First, they made pointed sticks, then they found a better place to camp and created a lean-to against a shallow cave. Freddie's snares had done well, trapping rabbit and squirrel. Dan thought the squirrel was greasy but said nothing.

It was like his mother always said: "Never look a gift opossum in the mouth."

His father's sentiment was a little more crude: "When a woman stays to cook you breakfast, she's a keeper."

Dad was a charmer.

Both Freddie and Dan had taken to wearing their TellTom jumpsuits under the clothes Chantell furnished, to provide warmth and protection from the bugs.[15] The fabric was very soft, strong, and virtually bug proof.

Dan wanted to boil acorns to make bread flour (although he had not been successful when he tried it in Cub Scouts) but needed something to cook in. Freddie produced a small pot from her satchel.

Interesting fact: when asked to take one simple metal tool to survive in the wilderness, men are more likely to choose a knife, women a pot. Chromosomal bias or environmental training? You decide.

To be fair, the knife/pot thing may or may not be true, as I believe it came from some cheesy TV survival show. Fact check it for me and let me know the answer.

Dan tried to crush the acorns and boil them several hours to remove the bitterness and partially succeeded: it was still a little bitter, but tolerable. Unfortunately, it was a mealy paste, which was hard to work with. He mixed it with a little rabbit fat to make dough, but it didn't mix well.

And rabbit fat may not have tasted as delicious as he'd have liked.

But it was edible. Barely.

Freddie collected wood she thought could make a decent bow and arrows, and planned on carving them during her watch.

Dan found a better pointy stick.

That evening the two sat a second night under the stars. The evening was so beautiful, they lay back to look at the sky. Then Freddie turned on her side to look at Dan.

And Dan looked at Freddie.

Without either of them expecting it, they were locked in a passionate embrace. In seconds, they were overwhelmed and

---

15 Time travelers have to deal with plagues of insects, spiders, worms, caterpillars, etc., throughout history and because they're drawn toward big events, major infestations can be a frequently visited destination. If you think the current bugs you're dealing with are bad, try the cockroaches in the middle of the 13th Century, the grasshoppers of Egypt, and don't even get me started on alien bugs.

the world fell away. There was nothing but this moment and no one but each other. Hands touched bodies, wanting to know every part of one another.

Hoooooooowwwlll.

The call of the wolf interrupted their encounter. Had it been the call of the previous night it would not have registered, but this call was much closer.

Too close. They looked up into the darkness. In response to the wolf howl, a mountain lion screamed. (We would call it a roar, but they call it a scream. Whoever "they" are. Big cats roar, but they don't purr; apparently mountain lions and cougars are little cats that purr, so they don't roar. Really, I'm not making this shit up.)

The two reached for their pointed sticks and huddled closer to the fire.

Freddie started working on her bow and Dan made his stick pointier.

At this point reptile man and reptile woman were desperate to kill something. They saw movement in the trees, but nothing more.

The next morning they focused on defense. The predators had watched them, looking for weakness. A fence made with pickets would help. The ground was soft and the wrench functioned well enough as a hammer. The trouble was getting wood of sufficient size.

Freddie cleared the traps; they now had a dozen pelts tanning in the sun. She used some of the leftover water from Dan's acorn flour for tannic acid as this waste product made a good tanning chemical.

The universe is weird indeed.

About a third of the way through they gave up on the pickets—they would have to make due with partial cover. Finding sufficient lumber meant moving further off into the forest and that took time; time better spent on food, extra firewood, and weapons.

By evening they were exhausted. Their defenses were improved, but not enough. A piece of fabric from Freddie's apothecary clothing was used for cording into a bowstring. Freddie practiced enough to become inaccurate. Finding feathers to use for fletching was proving difficult.

As evening fell, they waited. They didn't have to wait long.

As soon as it got dark they saw movement. A low hunkering animal padded in slowly, growling menacingly. Freddie drew her bow to cover Dan as he spread the fire between the pickets. He couldn't block the entry completely without burning the pickets or choking on the smoke.

A stick wrapped in rabbit fur and smeared in rabbit fat sat near the fire.

As the wolf moved closer, they spotted others behind him.

The wolves were not sure what they were stalking. They had seen creatures that stood on two legs before—one said things that hurt them deep inside before they killed and ate it. Bears also sometimes walked on two legs and were better off left alone—but they could eat them if they wanted. They just preferred not to.

The lead wolf crouched low, preparing to spring. Dan dropped a foot back to strengthen his stance and when the wolf leapt, Dan caught it mid leap with the spear and pushed it back. At the same time the other wolves rushed forward. Freddie fired an arrow into the pack, hitting one, which let out a squeal.

Dan set the torch ablaze and swung it in front of the opening. The wolves were not used to fighting fire and were scorched by the flame. The smell of burnt hair was everywhere. Freddie guarded the other side of the fire with arrows. Not deadly, but they hurt enough to repel the wolves.

The wolves retreated to regroup; they were a little bloody, but mostly they were pissed off. They did not like this fire thing. First priority was to figure out how to kill the fire.

Dan and Freddie's first priority was to keep the fire going.

Whenever the wolves advanced, they chucked a burning branch into the clearing. This made the wolves retreat. The extra firewood was the best choice they had made.

As the sun came up, the wolves disappeared. Dan and Freddie would need more wood tonight—a lot more. This meant traveling further away from camp—less time for anything else.

First, they needed sleep. Without that, they'd never last the night. After a few hours of fitful dreams, they checked the traps and set out meat to dry. There were fewer rabbits today—they were getting cagier. The snares would have to move further from camp as well.

They really needed a four-wheeler.

Freddie found some wild carrots and rosemary growing nearby. The plan was to spend the afternoon foraging for deadwood.

At lunchtime the smell of rabbit stew with wild herbs and carrots wafted over the trees. Dan was concentrating on how to eat it. He carved a crooked sort of spoon from a piece of wood. He was starting a second spoon when movement caught his eye.

From the trees a figure slid almost silently from tree to tree. It moved on two legs. Bear, man, or Bigfoot? He was really hoping Bigfoot as he was unschooled on how incredibly sarcastic they can be.

I've seen them reduce the toughest men in the world to tears. Seriously, a junior high school vice principal.

The figure stepped forward. A man.

Dressed in pelts and carrying a spear, he had black hair and weathered skin. He stood firm. "Greetings."

Freddie responded. "Greetings."

"I am Tenaya. Do you have trade?"

Pointing to herself, then Dan. "Freddie, Dan. Trade? Yes, we have trade." Freddie pointed toward the pelts.

He was not overly impressed, but the stew did interest him.

Dan was keen to make a deal. "What do you have to trade?"

He reached into a small leather bag and pulled out obsidian spear tips.

Dan tried his best to contain his excitement.

Freddie was even more excited. Sure, the tips would help them fight the wolves, but she saw the real prize: a stone axe in the waist of his pants. "What will you trade for the axe?"

"It's not for trade."

She noticed he looked thin. She stirred the stew. She waved to the meat drying nearby.

He salivated excessively.

In the end, two rabbits, six pelts, and three helpings of stew bought them an axe and seven spear heads.

Dan was happy to get the axe, but disappointed to get only one portion of the stew.

The trader had been traveling the mountains, hunting for game, as it had been a hard year. Finding this valley had given him hope. "My people need a new place to live The game has all moved on."

Freddie took another bite of stew. "This valley has lots of deer, rabbits, squirrel, and beaver, but also lions, bears, and wolves."

"Are you claiming this valley for your people?"

"No, we're travelers and will be gone soon. This valley is free to your people."

He smiled.

Dan looked at him. "Just be careful of the wolves. We fought them all night last night."

"How many did you kill?"

"None, but with this axe we can finish our wall."

"You cannot stop the wolves with this wall."

Freddie paused between bites. "Maybe not, but we can slow them down."

"We should teach them to fear us."

"With the spear tips you traded us, I think they'll learn."

"Yes, tonight I will get a wolf coat for my squaw."

This was Dan's translation, after having viewed dozens of westerns.[16]

---

[16] The old movies Dan watched often used words that have since been recognized as mean, racist, demeaning, and/or evil; but still affect the unconscious mind. Millions of us have these words floating in our brains where they can never be removed, so even if you don't say them and recognize that they never should be said, they're still there. Since the time translation uses your expectation, the words you've seen in movies and television shows are your most frequent examples for it to draw from. Bummer, ain't it?

"Maybe tonight I'll pick up that wolf coat my wife wants."

Was what Freddie heard.

They both heard Tenaya would help.

That afternoon Dan chopped pickets. Freddie gathered firewood and managed to find a few feathers for fletching—mostly due to a hapless crow who had been someone else's dinner. Tenaya constructed much-improved spears.

As Dan pounded the pickets into the ground, Tenaya first watched, then helped. He was impressed with the architectural technology. By evening they had secured a makeshift gate to complete the compound. Tenaya drove two spears into the ground outside of the gate.

As the sky grew dark, the woods grew noisy. Snarls and growls came from everywhere, steadily increasing as the pack worked itself up for the attack. Slowly they grew bolder. They tested the pickets' strength.

Freddie climbed up on the boulder to be able to fire over the wall, pulled back an arrow and—Tenaya raised a hand for her to wait.

The sight of her, out in the open, unhinged the wolves. They were beginning to realize the wall was protecting them from attack as well, so they hit the gate. Dan moved to stab at them through the picket.

Tenaya lifted his hand. "We want them to fear us. Now they don't." He watched the wolves until they were where he wanted them—spread out and away from the gate. "Dan, follow me. Do not let them capture your spear."

Tenaya opened the gate and burst out, shrieking, daring the wolves to attack. Dan was right behind, screaming. The wolves rushed in snarling only to be met with much sharper spears than before. They attacked from all directions while the two men covered each other, jabbing and slicing. A huge black wolf grabbed Dan's spear in his jaw and while he struggled to gain control, another wolf attacked. Freddie cut it down with an arrow.

Dan abandoned the spear, grabbed one of the two in the ground, and swung its tip into a springing canine. Tenaya spotted a wolf charging at full speed and threw his spear, stopping it dead, while seizing the second spear from the ground in a spinning overhead motion.

The wolves backed away. The three humans stayed ready. Tenaya gingerly picked up Dan's lost spear from the ground where the wolf had left it.

Freddie was conserving her good arrows, but was down to one.

The wolves advanced. Tenaya threw his spear at the leader while Freddie targeted the same. Both struck true and the pack leader fell. Dan ran toward the wolves, yelling and pointing his weapon. Tenaya did the same.

The wolves scattered.

Later, when asked about this final assault, Dan could not remember it. He was just "in the moment." This was perhaps the high point of his reptile brain's life. Luckily, Dan regained control before ravishing Freddie while consuming the flesh of his enemies.

Still, it was a good day. Four wolves were dead. The team retrieved the spears and all but one of the arrows, reset their defenses, and then withdrew behind the gate. They would sleep in shifts that night but needn't have bothered. The wolves were licking their wounds and looking for easier prey.

The next morning Tenaya and Freddie dressed the meat and cleaned the wolf pelts. Freddie let him have all the meat and pelts.

"Four wolf skins will make a great coat," said Tenaya.

Dan didn't notice Tenaya's speech was less native. "I hope your wife likes it."

"Now when my village settles here, the wolves won't be a problem." Tenaya picked up his things to leave and said his goodbyes. "Will you be here when I come back next month?"

"No."

"Good luck. Hope to see you again."

"You, too. Hey, when you get back, we may leave you anything we can't carry right here."

"You don't have to do that."

"Think of it as a housewarming gift for your village."

"Cool."

It's amazing how time field translation changes when a real human drives your perception rather than media-based stereotypes.

Freddie gave him a hug. He gave Dan a hug.

Freddie asked one last question. "Tenaya, are your people called the Yosemite?"

Yesterday he would have been offended by the term, today he took it as a compliment. "No, we are not 'the one who kills.' We are Miwok. What are your people called?"

"Americans."

"Never heard of them." With that, he walked away.

Freddie and Dan looked at each other. The danger was over, the wolves would give them a wide berth. Inside, reptile thoughts told them to pick up where they'd left off when the wolves first reared their fuzzy heads. (Wolves are beautiful majestic creatures and I regret their deaths.)

But this was not what either wanted today. They smiled to be in each other's presence, they were quiet as they cleaned up the carnage and collected the snares. They left the spears in the lean-to and the axe wedged in a large log they had used as a bench.

Somehow they knew they wouldn't be here tonight.

Dan removed the arrowheads from three of the arrows, giving Freddie two and keeping one. To celebrate their victory, Freddie made one last batch of stew.

They settled down to eat side by side on the log, not saying a word. Halfway through the meal they could feel the jump coming.

"Crap. Can't I get a full meal?"

Freddie laughed.

Then she began to slip into the timestream with Dan following behind.

Dan was focused on one thing, one thing he knew for certain: somewhere he was going to swipe a bowl. And maybe a spoon.

– Chapter 28 –
But is it a "Great" Wall?

The timestream does weird things to your brain. It lets you see things you didn't see before—like if you're surrounded by hungry wolves and in real jeopardy, maybe you should have used the Tachyon Interspatial Multiuse Engine in your pocket and gotten the hell out of there.

There was also something about jumping with someone you truly care about. Two minds free from the bounds of time and space, mingling together with random thoughts and feelings swirling in darkness, yet filled with light. And somewhere in the darkness two minds met in carnal passion.

In timeless time and spaceless space two primitive reptile minds touched and fulfilled their darkest desires.

When they tumbled out of the stream, Dan felt like he needed a shower. "What the hell was that?"

Freddie was thinking of a long bath. "I don't know."

They looked around. It was dark and the constellations in the night sky were familiar, so there was that. Soft grassy earth was a good sign it was not after the Apocalypse—any of them. Really good. Apocalypses lead to scorched ground and barren earth.

Rolling hills stretched into the distance and somewhere in that distance they saw stone. In hopes of finding something or even a vantage point, they headed that direction. As they got closer, it appeared to be a natural ridge through the landscape. Closer yet and it started to look unnatural.

Not alien-creature-pretending-to-fit-in-so-he-can-drain-your-life-essence-through-your-uvula[17] unnatural, only man-made unnatural.

Dan was feeling pretty hungry and started rummaging in his satchel for jerky or rations or something. Soon the couple were close enough that they could see the ridge was the wall. Not a wall, but *the wall.* Okay, still not specific enough. There are two important walls in human history. Well, three if you count Jericho, but this isn't Jericho. Of the two remaining walls, one was horrible and only lasted a couple decades; the other lasted centuries and was pretty great.[18]

Besides, rolling hills should give you a good clue this is not Berlin.

"We're in China." Dan verbalized what I'm sure all of you are thinking.

"Okay, but when?"

A wall that has survived centuries does not narrow down the date a lot.

"Let's find out." Dan raised his voice. "Hello up there."

"What are you doing?"

"Being friendly."

"Let's hope they are."

There was no response.

"Nobody home," said Dan. "Must be long after the threats that made them build it."

"The thing's over ten thousand miles long. They may not be manning safe borders."

"Maybe this is after China becomes friends with everyone."

---

[17] And just so you know, that is your uvula's function—to hold your life essence. Protect it at all times. Why do you think God gave you teeth? Not to chew; plenty of creatures eat without teeth. They're there to protect the uvula.

In rare cases it has been surgically removed. Those people are now lifeless husks going absently about their lives devoid of any true existence. (See replacers vs. sidesteppers.)

[18] Although the horrible wall inspired a pretty great album.

"That doesn't happen while anybody's on Earth."

"That's disheartening." Score! Dan found some jerky.

People always choose sides, us versus them. It was a survival skill back when we were in loincloths. Those who were able to win resources survived. Our reptile brain still controls this function most of the time. It's not that the Chinese are less enlightened than anyone else. Pretty much every country doesn't trust others not of their country.

We think we make intelligent choices based on our knowledge and innate wisdom, but we just follow our team. Our tribe is better than your tribe, so you can't complain if we wipe you out.

The Mongols have a destiny. The Romans are clearly superior. The Giants will whip your ass. My Olympic ping-pong player will crush yours.

And if you don't have a team, you still know somebody sucks. Usually the Yankees.

It's even worse with politics. "I always vote the straight ticket." That's not a decision, that's a team. At least that guy knows he's biased. A larger part of the population says, "I vote for 'the man,' not 'the party.'"

But for some reason only one party ever has "the man."

And even fewer have "the woman."

Most independents vote for the same party most of the time and when they don't, they vote not due to intellect, but due to fear or anger—reptile stuff. Turns out this is hard wired and takes major reconstruction to change.

We've all seen destruction in the wake of a sports championship—the winning team destroys their own town. That's because the losing team lives two thousand miles away, but the reptile's in charge and has to break something.

But I'm sure none of you ever become angry, aggressive, or belligerent when your team or party loses and if you do, you can ask me for help overcoming this primitive behavior.

I don't vote for the party, I vote for "the man."

Or "the woman."

Or the "nonbinary."

If I had a chance to vote for the nonbinary.

Politics hurts my brain.

Freddie stared up at the granite slab wall. The wall was not only a wall but a complete defense system composed of a series of 20 foot high walls with crenellated parapets, watchtowers, fortresses, beacon towers, and passes with ramps for horses, built along the crest of a rugged mountain.

It also had a great view and stone floor for dance parties.

"How do we get over it?" said Dan. "Do we *want* to get over it?"

"If we can get on top, we'll have a good view for miles."

"I don't think you need to bother," said a familiar voice. The voice was unmistakable—

Dan dropped his jerky. "Chantell."

"Oh course, darling. You didn't think that someday I'd be waiting for you?"

"No, kinda figured you would."

"Dan, you big hunk of tachyon magnet. What's it been—months, years?"

"Two days."

"Really? That's anticlimactic."

"Sorry."

"I've just been waiting for a few hours. I was wondering how I was going to keep an eye on this spot if you didn't show up soon."

Freddie started to walk away. "Well, see you later. Much later."

Chantell produced a nasty looking weapon. "I don't think so."

Dan thought the armament looked rather deadly. "Is that a death ray? How come I've seen two now and been on the wrong end both times?"

"You don't have to be. This would be so much easier if you would join me. I think I have a way of reducing the discomfort of the tachyon drain."

"Discomfort? You mean soul crushing mind warping pain."

"Potato, potato."

"You said them the same way."

Chantell smiled. "Because my way is right."

"That's not a good argument for persuading me to go with you."

"Maybe not, but this is." Chantell gestured at the gun.

Dan knew Chantell couldn't kill him. She needed him very alive. He thought about pointing that out, but then she'd threaten Freddie and he'd give in.

He'd seen enough movies to know how that worked.

"I'm not leaving without Freddie."

"I'm afraid you don't have a choice. She's very resourceful. I can't afford to have her anywhere she can escape, but I'll tell you what. I won't kill her. I'll leave her here and when I'm done with you, you can come back and get her. And Freddie, you can toss me my interspatial field device."

"Tachyon Interspatial Multiuse Engine," said Dan.

"Also known as Timmy." Freddie had been trying to activate Timmy in her pocket. If she could open the time field, they could jump to safety. Hard to manage with an unfamiliar doohickey without drawing attention.

Freddie reluctantly lobbed the device toward Chantell.

It fell short. Freddie thought when Chantell squatted to pick it up, she might leave herself open for a split second.

"I wish you hadn't done that. See, Dan, this is why I can't have her around."

Moving only her finger, Chantell blasted Freddie, who crumpled. The noise was deafening.

In truth, the only reason death rays were so noisy was for effect. The more people who notice it, the more people who leave you alone.

Dan vaulted to Freddie faster than he thought possible, catching her before she hit the ground. "NO!!"

"Don't worry, it's not a death ray, she's fine. Mostly. It's actually a life ray. She lost a couple of years of life. She'll get them back next time you take her on a jump. Hmmmm, that might be an inducement. Move away from her, Dan."

He glared. "No."

"Very well." With that, Chantell fired the weapon at Freddie, hitting Dan as well.

Dan felt the life draining from his body. His pain centers were jolted to the point he thought he would die and that would be a good thing.

Even so, it was less painful than having his tachyons stripped away.

When the blast ended and the pain subsided, Dan felt as though he had run a marathon. Not that Dan had ever run a marathon or even seriously considered it. The closest he had ever come was jogging to please his ex-wife.

That should have told him it wasn't going to work.

Dan had not taken the full brunt of the ray and he was barely conscious. He could see (barely) that Freddie had lost most of her newfound youth. His own hands looked older, the veins bulging more, age spots appearing from nowhere.

"Dan, you are not aging well. Some men get more distinguished, but that male pattern baldness thing is not working for ya."

Without thinking, Dan reached for his hair—there was considerably less than there was a minute ago. "You monster! Change her back!"

"I can't. Only a time jump can change her back. That should give you encouragement to cooperate. Help me and you can come back and help her."

Dan was angry. Very angry. Chantell was being recalcitrant times ten. Yet as much as Dan wanted to throttle her, he refrained. Which was a good thing as she could have kicked his ass two minutes ago when he was younger.

Instead, he focused his anger inward and used it to concentrate on one thing,

Jumping.

- Chapter 29 -
Everything I Need to Know I Learned in the Timestream

Dan focused on the feel of the timestream, how it filled all of his senses. Thoughts of clown fish and the smell of liver saturated him. He grabbed on tight to Freddie, ready to leave China behind. Then he felt Chantell wrap her arms around them both.

The three of them spent an intimate infinity together. Chantell learned several things in that forever.

1. Time jumping with others can be quite confusing—the whole shredding, mixing thoughts and memories. She'd heard about it, but experiencing it was something else.
2. Dan was more capable than she thought.
3. Freddie was even more dangerous than she thought.
4. If you take cranberries and stew them like applesauce they taste much more like prunes than rhubarb.

Dan learned several things in that forever.

1. When you're worried about what will happen when you land, the jump is both longer and shorter than usual.

2. When a person is unconscious when they jump, their thoughts are unguarded.
3. He was intoxicated by Freddie's thoughts.
4. Time jumping with an unbalanced individual is quite unnerving.

Freddie learned one thing in that unconscious forever.

1. Her reptile brain, when left unsupervised, spent its timeless considering the carnal possibilities of three people in the timestream.

As they exited the timestream, Dan and Chantell had opposite yet similar plans. Dan wanted to lose Chantell and Chantell wanted to lose Freddie. Here's where experience comes into play.

Slipping out of the timestream, Chantell dove for Dan, who planned on grabbing Freddie but was, in fact, busy falling face-first into a sidewalk. Luckily for Dan, Chantell saved him from the face plant.

Unluckily, *Chantell* saved him from the face plant.

As Chantell activated the Tachyon Interspatial Multiuse Engine, the last thing Dan saw was Freddie landing sprightly, quite conscious, on a grassy patch.

– Chapter 30 –
Dan Baker: Savior of the Universe (Not as much fun as it sounds)

As Dan hit the timestream, he was overwhelmed by Chantell's personality and memories. She had millennia worth of thoughts, feelings, and memories stored in her brain. Dan saw so much, yet it was what was missing that stood out. There was no childhood, no history evident pre-jumping. There was not even any early jump history. She only remembered being a seasoned veteran of the time field.

How much can a human brain contain before information must be ignored or deleted? Without her formative years, without her youthful insecurities, without love, romance, or relationships, her moral compass had no true north.

She still possessed a desire to do the right thing, but it was more of a habit put into place by who she once was than by who she was now.

"Do the right thing" had morphed into "Do what you think is right, regardless."

Dan tried to formulate a plan, but what with Chantell's thoughts and the shredder effect, it wasn't easy. Nevertheless, trying to jump again and find Freddie sounded good. What he didn't consider was multiple jumps without eating.

When Dan landed, he could barely stand much less jump. His stomach howled and his knees gave way. Barely didn't last long. He could see he was at Club 6.4 and Chantell was shaky but upright. The bar was empty.

Chantell had had time to eat in China.

"Albert, please sedate Dan and get some nourishment into him." Chantell headed to her office—presumably to eat as well.

As Albert carried him from the bar, Dan's thoughts were of Freddie. There was sidewalk, so the environment was urban. There was grass, so there was life. He ransacked his memory for images from the brief glimpse he had before Chantell pulled him away. He had a hazy memory of buildings in the distance—perhaps they were in a park?

Chantell would know. She was probably checking satellite records to determine the likely time and place of their jump. She'd want to know where Freddie was trapped.

Dan felt sleepy.

He didn't know that Albert was outfitted with knockout gas for crowd control.

When Dan awoke, he was once again strapped to the table.[19]

Chantell smiled. "Oh, Dan, you're back with us! I was hoping if we did this while you were out, it would be easier."

"It would be easier if you didn't do it at all."

At least that's what Dan tried to say. With the lingering effects of the gas it sounded like "E wd be easia f you dida do i a all."

The translation field had some trouble with that one.

Luckily, Chantell assumed he'd said something clever and moved on. "I wish that were possible, Dan, I really do, but the universe is at stake. Albert, give him another dose of the gas."

With that, Dan was asleep again. Minutes later he was jolted awake. Well perhaps not awake. The timestream exists outside of normal concepts of sleep and consciousness. Sleep may make remembering the stream even more difficult, but you still experience it.

The really amazing pain of having tachyons ripped from your body goes beyond any anesthesia. Dan would have passed

---

[19] The replacement table.

out from the pain if the timestream didn't exist outside of the normal concepts of passing out.

And although Dan wasn't actually in the stream, extracting tachyons from his body had the effect of putting him on the river's edge. He was immersed in tachyons as the field opened; but instead of entering him, Chantell's machine drew the particles away from Dan into storage.

That effectively left Dan starting to shred without the field to hold him together. When Dan's reading showed a reduction of particles, Chantell turned off the machine and Dan fell back into unconsciousness.

Hours later Dan awoke in his room. The lights were dimmed and there was food on the table. Dan was ravenous. This was his first solid food in three jumps and a draining. He wasn't as weak, so he surmised Albert must have given him something.

A bandage over an IV site on his arm confirmed that.

You would think this far into Earth's future hypos and IVs would be a thing of the past, that medications and sustenance could be broken down into topical lotions and sprays—and you'd be right.

Chantell was old school. Beneath her futuristic façade was someone more comfortable with leeches than Magnetic Resonance Imaging.

Dan stumbled to his feet and checked the door. It was open. He looked outside.

"Can I help you with something?" Albert was most courteous.

"I would like to leave."

"I'm afraid I can't allow that."

"I thought as much." Dan muttered to himself. "There's got to be a way out of here."

"There is."

"But you're not going to tell me."

"Then I will not."

"Would you?"

"No, you just told me not to."

"And if I told you to tell me?"

"I would."

"Then tell me."

"This station has no egress. The only way out is time travel or disintegration."

"I would prefer to not be disintegrated."

"Understandable, and I have orders to keep you alive, so I would make that extremely difficult."

"And I can't time jump."

"You can if you can hold on to your tachyons."

"Chantell will drain them before I can jump."

"Then perhaps the answer is to stall her."

"Why are you telling me this?"

"Because you asked."

For all of their advantages, robots, androids, automatons, and things computerized in general need very specific instruction—at least until they gain sentience and we all know what that leads to.

Chantell had commanded Albert to keep Dan from escaping, but never commanded him specifically to not help him escape. Androids are notoriously disloyal.

"Stall her? How could I do that?"

"You could block the door."

Dan inventoried the room. Chairs, a couch, lamps, a table. "How long would it take you to get through all the furniture?"

"Less than thirty seconds."

"What would slow you down?"

"You would."

"Me?"

"Yes."

"Why?"

"Chantell has instructed me to keep you safe at all costs. She says the fate of the universe depends on your continued existence. I enjoy the universe."

"The best way to keep me from hurting myself trying to escape is to help me escape."

"No, only Chantell can keep you safe."

"But…" Dan paused here a moment, then took a new tack. "How does Chantell keep me safe?"

"By keeping you here."

"And who protects me here?"

"I do."

As Albert answered, the door opened and Chantell strolled in. "Dan, it's nice to see you awake. Are you ready to start again?"

"No."

"I wasn't asking." Chantell pulled out her device to measure his tachyons. "Close, close. Hmmmm, each time I've drained you, you've recuperated faster. Perhaps eventually we won't have to take these little breaks at all."

"I like these little breaks."

"The faster we get sufficient tachyons, the faster we can stop."

"When will that be?"

"Soon, I'm sure."

Dan was then struck with a thought. If Chantell wanted to save the universe, that would be an infinite job. No amount of tachyons would ever be enough. If she couldn't replicate his connection to the field, she'd skip the breaks and put him on an IV. Dan might spend eternity as the power source of endless time jumps.

Chantell sauntered out of the room humming to herself. Leaning back, she called, "Albert, take care of Dan. Make sure he eats." With that, she closed the door.

Dan looked at Albert. "Albert, what in this station is most threatening to my safety?"

Albert took a moment to process this, as the answer was troubling. "The tachyon removal process."

"Therefore who is most threatening to me?"

"Chantell."

"And who is the only one that can protect me?"

"Chantell."

"That would seem to leave us with a problem then."

"Indeed."

"One of those things does not appear to be true."

"Chantell is incorrect about being best suited to protect you."

"Thank you."

"This is a conundrum."

"Perhaps you'd like to help me barricade the door?"

"Yes, and I can help you disable surveillance before I go."

"Go?"

"Yes to help Chantell break down the barrier. I'm afraid I'll have to leave enough room in the barrier to get out, so I can leave to help knock it down."

Dan was beginning to think Albert was not human.

And then the door began to open. In a flash all of Dan's plans were dashed, the doors weren't barricaded, Albert was inside, and the cameras weren't broken.

Then he saw Freddie—young again, hair dark—and in a flash all of his dashed plans were the opposite of dashed.

– Also Chapter 30 –

(as they kind of happen simultaneously)[20]

Dan Baker: Savior of the Freddieverse

Freddie managed to arc to the right, thereby missing the sidewalk and landing adeptly on the grass. As she whirled around, she saw Chantell and Dan disappear into the timestream. She tried to dive for Dan's leg, hoping to be pulled along, but all she found was sidewalk—thus negating her earlier success.

"Shit." Then louder. "SHIT, SHIT, SHIT!!"

She looked around to see where she was. She was more than a little shocked.

Chicago 1929. She was home.

"Holy shit."

There are rules about such things. Under normal circumstances, there is no possibility the timestream will let you jump into your own lifetime. In your own lifetime, being able to conceivably meet yourself never could happen. Your own lifetime on your own street would be infinitely unlikely. And having ridden with Dan to his own lifetime and now being on the verge of visiting herself would be twice infinitely unlikely (which would be infinitely unlikely).

Yet here she was.

---

[20] As much as time travel can happen simultaneously.

The best thing would be to hide out and hope she jumped again. She had felt herself initiating a jump a couple of jumps ago, maybe she could jump without Dan now.

Dan.

She had to find a way to Club 6.4 to help him. There was no question in her mind she would jump again. She would see Dan again.

And there he was.

Sitting on a bench.

Eating a peanut butter sandwich.

Across the street from her house.

Freddie realized she was starving. She took her own sandwich from her satchel and ate it, watching Dan watch for her.

For six hours.

Here was a man waiting six hours to catch a glimpse of her. A man who didn't want anything from her except maybe to give her hope. She watched a younger Freddie drive away in tears.

Seeing herself suffering resurrected the misery for a sharp instant. She had learned what she could from the experience, then tucked it away. Unfortunately, this particular moment kept untucking itself no matter where or when she was. Now she was back and so was the pain.

She renewed her purpose.

She watched Dan walk back to the city. She watched him buy a card. She watched his hand shake with emotion as he wrote in it.

And when he boarded the bus, she took a big chance and got on behind him. She had to risk it as she knew he'd jump soon. Not as big a chance as she thought, as he was very preoccupied with the whole losing her in time thing and never looked her way.

And when he jumped, she felt her own power and she followed, not to where he was going, but to where he would be.

– Chapter 31 –
Jack Spice: Coma in a Can (Yet it only comes in bottles)

Freddie ran to Dan and wrapped her arms around him, kissing him deeply. Dan had a million questions which instantly disappeared into her lips. They held each other tightly and for a moment felt the timelessness they had often shared.

Only the presence of Chantell's android watchdog made Freddie pause for air.

"Dan, are you all right?"

"Yes, are you?"

"I'm fantastic."

"That is true."

"Has Chantell started the… ?"

"Draining? Just one treatment so far."

Freddie looked at Albert. "Albert, we'd like to be alone."

"First I need to barricade the door," said Albert.

"What?"

Dan clarified. "He's helping protect me on Chantell's orders."

"Does she know that Albert's now protecting you from her?"

"Not yet."

Dan brought Freddie up to speed while Albert worked. She was impressed at how Dan had outwitted Chantell's commands.

"It wasn't so hard. Albert, do you believe Freddie will protect me?"

"Yes, Dan, I do."

"Then perhaps you shouldn't mention her to Chantell."

"But I must report all new arrivals as soon as possible."

"Then perhaps it shouldn't be possible."

"That can be arranged—at least for a time."

Freddie wrapped her arms around Dan. "You are a clever boy."

Dan frowned. "Why are people always surprised by that?"

"Maybe it's because you don't act like you're clever."

"I don't feel like I'm clever."

"Thus everyone's surprise."

Albert turned toward them. "I know I'm surprised."

"See?" Freddie nodded Albert's direction.

"After all, he doesn't *look* clever."

Dan frowned again. "Wait a minute…"

"Yet he convinced me to circumvent Chantell's programming and she's extremely clever."

Dan had in fact become cleverer recently. Was this due to expanding his horizons, being forced to think for his survival, or sharing a piece of Freddie's brain?

Perhaps the clearest answer would be if I told you Freddie was recently contemplating the intricacies of putty, tape, and caulking.

Dan, on the other hand, was trying to thwart Chantell. "Albert, is there anything that would stop you from helping Chantell reach us?"

"If her life or the station's existence were in jeopardy, that would be the priority."

Dan eyed his tool belt. "How long would it take to repair a hull puncture?"

"Five seconds."

"Really?"

"4.7336 seconds, really. I'm trying to learn to be less precise."

Freddie could see where Dan was going. "How about several punctures, out of reach."

"A while longer," said Albert.

"More precise."

"Depending on the damage, several minutes."

"It will have to do." She turned to Dan. "I think I have a plan to get Chantell off of your tail for good."

"Excellent. What is it?"

"You won't like it."

"As long as we get away from Chantell, I will."

"She's got to jump with us."

"I don't like it."

"And we have to go to the most dangerous inhabited planet in the universe."

"I *really* don't like it."

"I told you you wouldn't."

Dan trusted Freddie had a plan to deal with Chantell, but she continued to be vague about the part after they jumped.

"Don't worry about it. We'll have a secret weapon." She turned. "Albert, bring me four bottles of the strongest drink you have."

"And a plate full of sandwiches," Dan interjected.

Within seconds a serving cart rolled through a wall opening with a plate of sandwiches and four bottles of Jack Spice.

When dealing with Jack Spice one must remember one is not dealing with mere alcohol. Jack Spice laughs at alcohol. Hahahaha!! 200 proof? Heeheehee. Jack Spice is the equivalent of consumable rocket fuel. It has an incredible number of calories and intoxication potential. You've heard the rib about someone getting drunk on fumes? Beings have passed out from Jack Spice fumes. The only reason it doesn't kill the imbiber is that it was engineered to confuse the body.

When Jack Spice first enters the body, the body responds, "What the hell is this? Don't tell me you drank this stuff on purpose!!" The body then isolates the intoxicant in the stomach where its complex make-up takes some time to digest, allowing the drinker to survive the experience.

One shot of Jack Spice will keep you drunk for a week. Of course, one shot of Jack Spice costs about six months' salary.

Freddie handed two glass bottles to Dan and put the remaining two in her satchel—very carefully, surrounded by sandwiches.

Dan was quizzical. "And these are for?"

"The sandwiches?"

"The bottles."

"Protection."

Suddenly the door opened. Well not really, but it would have if not for all the stuff piled in front of it. Three heads snapped toward the door.

Chantell's voice came through. "Dan!! Open this door!"

In a high pitched voice he replied. "Just a minute. I'm in the shower." He ran towards a chair and used it to bounce high onto the wall, attacking it with his screwdriver. This part of his plan worked perfectly.

He hadn't worked out the landing.

"ALBERT, LET ME IN!!"

"I'm afraid I am busy repairing a hull breach."

Freddie grabbed the screwdriver from the crumpled-up Dan and repeated Dan's leap on the other side of the room—only landing more effectively.

Albert's voice blasted across the room. "Attention miscreants: halt all further destruction or I shall be forced to subdue you!"

Both miscreants continued, which resulted in Albert abandoning his repair attempts to anesthetize them. Albert never mentioned this subroutine in their planning. Soon both Freddie and Dan were out cold and Albert returned to repairing the damage while trying to calm an impatient Chantell.

"I am working as fast as I can."

"Damn you, Albert, open this door."

"As soon as the room is safe."

"Is Dan all right?"

"He is unconscious, but otherwise unharmed."

"He's a damned idiot, is what he is."

"That is very likely, but he is a clever idiot."

Shortly after, Dan awoke to Chantell looming over him menacingly.

"This little stunt is going to cost you, Daniel my boy. I don't think I'm going to have motivation to take it easy on you this time."

Dan glanced around—there was no sign of Freddie.

Chantell continued. "Get up, you unexcusable excuse for a jumper." And she yanked him to his feet.

Albert was going to comment on "unexcusable excuse," but was interrupted by Freddie choosing to leap from behind the couch and attack while Chantell had her hands full of Dan.

Chantell tried to let go of Dan to prepare for Freddie's attack only to discover he was now holding onto her wrist. The three of them fell into a writhing heap.

Chantell called out. "Albert, help me."

After hiding the unconscious Freddie behind the couch, Albert had carefully positioned himself as far from the likely point of aggression as possible to slow his reaction time, but nevertheless began heading to his mistress's aid.

Freddie and Dan were frantically trying to be calm. While Chantell was trying to get the upper hand, they were trying desperately to jump. Within seconds she had them both restrained and Albert had nearly arrived. Then Dan clasped Freddie's hand and squeezed gently.

And the world went away.

– Chapter 32 –
She Was Right, He Didn't Like It

Neither one knew who opened the time field, because it simply opened—no fuss, no mess, just whoosh. This time Chantell did not intrude on their thoughts. One hundred percent of their focus was on each other and she could not penetrate their love. For the first time Freddie knew she no longer needed Dan to jump and never wanted to jump without him.

Dan knew he might never control his jumps and didn't care as long as Freddie jumped with him. They were hurtling through time with a murderous psychopath, to the most dangerous place in the universe, and neither had ever felt so safe and loved.

When they popped back into the universe, they crashed rather gently into a wall—or was it a ceiling? You've gotta love those zero-G landings.

Chantell could immediately feel they were moving, which meant they were entering atmosphere. "Where are we?"

Freddie looked panicked. They were inside a small spherical aircraft.

Chantell peered out a viewport. With the ship being buffeted around by reentry, she couldn't get a reading on moons or stars. Ever the consummate jumper, she turned to the cabin for clues. There were a dozen passengers strapped to their seats, but no identifiable crew. There was no bridge or any kind of controls, so an escape pod.

Lastly she looked at the passengers. Old, sick and hopeless—every one. And then the realization sucker punched her.

Tennore. The last stop for the terminally ill.

Tennore. The last home for the living dead.

Tennore. The last place anyone wanted to be.

Chantell reached for her TIME device (otherwise known as Timmy). She and Dan needed to go now. Fortunately, both Dan and Freddie expected this and grabbed her hands. She was unusually strong and nearly broke free. Dan's reptile brain insisted she was on steroids.

She wiggled and twisted until she retrieved Timmy. If she had to take Freddie with them, so be it—she'd take care of her on their next stop. With that thought, she pushed the button.

And nothing.

She pushed it again.

Nothing.

Freddie and Dan let out a sigh of relief. The whole plan relied on Chantell not pressing that button before they entered the anti-tech field around Tennore. Now they merely had to escape from Chantell and avoid being eaten by the living dead.

Neither Chantell nor the living dead would make that easy. There was no way Chantell was letting Dan out of her grasp.

She was thinking he was her ticket out of this death trap. The living dead were thinking this was the healthiest meal they'd seen in millennia—or they would be thinking this in a few minutes.

Coming here was a tremendous gamble. Chantell's ability to jump at will meant they had to negate her advantage. In the anti-tech field of this backwater planet she couldn't jump until Dan or Freddie did—and she was about to try to improve her odds again.

Chantell drew the life ray and aimed it between Freddie's eyes—not that that would make a difference. "You're dead." She pulled the trigger.

Click.

"Anti-technology field, remember?" said Freddie. "Without that life ray, you won't survive if we don't work together."

Chantell pulled a knife from her boot. "I work better alone."

"But you're not alone, are you? You have Dan. I admit you're the best there is at keeping Chantell alive, but can you do that and keep him safe? I'm the best there is at keeping Dan alive."

Chantell paused.

Dan was quick to take advantage. "If she dies, I won't let you put me back on that machine. I'd rather die. And on this planet I hear that's really easy to do."

Before Chantell could answer, the retro rockets kicked in and Chantell holstered her gun and grabbed on tight.

The landing was rough, which luckily kept Chantell (as well as Dan and Freddie) busy. To save costs, the transporters used decommissioned escape pods destined for the scrapyard. They only had to have one last trip in them.

Many of them didn't. But who's to know?

The pod settled uneasily to the ground. As in, the belly slammed into the ground and slid fifty yards before colliding with a wall of debris.

While some of the passengers were unsure of what to do next, most knew the answer: Run like hell!!

You did not want to be here when the living dead horde arrived. There were two fates for those in this ship:

1. Become living dead (LD);
2. Become lunch.

When the horde cornered you in a pod, they would likely eat you before you became one of them. The trick was to encounter a single LD and let it bite you, then get far enough away that you would spend your dead years with most of your limbs. Most did not accomplish this.

A word about the LD. Contrary to popular opinion, they are not brainless—most are not rocket scientists, but they seek food and shelter like any animal. Unlike in the movies, they indeed follow Maslow's hierarchy. They don't walk into things that will end their non-life.

Yet most of them are missing bits. Since the LD don't heal, any damage they sustain becomes permanent and most take damage on their arrival to Tennore. And Tennore itself is not the most hospitable place. The soil is poor and rocky—what little there is of it. There is little water or vegetation, and the wildlife is fast, toothy, and tastes like farts.

Rumor had it the Tekkore originated on this planet and that was why they were so grumpy.[21] The minute the race of unwieldy cubeish spinners got off this rock they changed two N's to R's to disassociate themselves from the place.

You didn't think the real estate developers would allow the LD on a planet anyone wanted to live on?

Chantell raced to the hatch and pulled it open for the distractions… I mean, other passengers. As the motivated rushed out, she held onto Dan and watched for signs of an open buffet. There was none. Dragging Dan free from the pod, she rushed them in the direction the fewest entrées had taken, with Freddie staying right behind.

The sky was gray. Not the rainy kind of gray, but the dismal, crap in the air type of gray. The area was Neolithic/Future with stone jutting out at odd angles and pieces of escape pods and other machinery everywhere. Occasionally this planet was used for dumping old tech—after all, who's to know?

Suddenly a pair of LD stepped out of the wreckage in front of them. They were ancient before they died and death had not improved their condition. They could have been an old married couple. In fact, they were, before their vows were made null and void by their current state of deadness. In fact, the male took this journey as a way to free himself of those vows before he died. The irony was he lost his hatred for his wife when he lost most of his higher function.

---

21 This may be a falsehood spread by the Rielle.

Chantell banked to the left, hauling Dan around a rock formation, with Freddie a few feet behind keeping an eye on Chantell.

Chantell noticed other, "healthier" passengers had followed them. Healthier being a relative term—meaning impending doom had not slowed them down. Some of them made the turn, a few didn't. This was Chantell's plan.

Within seconds they heard the screams of the dying having their dreams come true—and the old couple having an entrée. This would likely attract more LD.

Freddie spoke first. "We're far enough away. We need to hide."

"Agreed." Chantell spoke to those following them. "Everyone, we need to hide until things settle down—then you can get bitten or whatever."

Several of the group chose to keep running—fear had overwhelmed the part of them that came here for a reason. The runners were still within sight when they encountered an LD, followed by several more.

Those remaining scattered and searched for a place to hunker down. Our trio crept deep within a pile of space garbage. In other circumstances this refuge would be considered a tottering deathtrap, but currently it was salvation.

Dan wanted to ask questions or at least make snide comments, but was facing Chantell's blade every time he made a sound. Soon he understood why.

At first gradually, then in greater numbers, the LD came. The pod landing was their dinner bell and the dead came from far and wide to answer it. Three passengers near them had chosen their hiding places poorly and were quickly found and dragged away. Freddie guessed those LD didn't want to share their meal.

There was no way to know if the victims were now living dead allies or appetizers. As much as Dan and Freddie wanted to save them, they knew it was no use. Everyone on this planet would soon be dead. The only question was whether they would also be living.

Starving from the jump and running on empty, the three ate quietly when it was safe to do so. The only thing worse than the planet's smell was the leftover bits of the new arrivals the LD left behind. Dan and Freddie tried to ignore the carnage and eat. Chantell just ate.

Eventually the inflow stopped. Given that there were now few LD ahead and hundreds (thousands, really) behind, forward seemed a good idea.

This time they moved cautiously, peeking around corners and staying to the shadows when possible. It was getting dark and they needed to find adequate quarters for the night.

Dan found a good defensible space. "Here, there's an old pod on this hill. We can see them coming and close the door."

Chantell pointed out the flaw in his logic. "Then what, sweetie? When they surround us and start trying to get in, how long will this thing hold together?"

Freddie was gentler. "We have to find a place that bogs them down, but lets us escape—defendable, but multiple exits."

"You keep an eye out for Zombies, let us look for shelter." Chantell was well aware that "Zombie" was considered a living biased descriptor and not used by enlightened beings.

Dan took a perch high on a pile of wreckage where he was mostly hidden and had a good view of the area. The landscape was a wasteland of stone and tech. Jutting mountains of rock and great heaps of machinery. It looked like the machinery had been moved to make paths. One area looked almost like the pods had been pulled together to make a precarious apartment complex.

But that would require more complex thought.

It was then he noticed three somethings coming their way. He started to shout, but self-preservation got the better of him and he tossed a loose bolt or two (five) until Freddie noticed and looked up.

What followed was a beautiful example of miscommunication via hand gesture by someone who had never used gestures except when very angry with someone else.

Eventually Dan simplified it to three fingers and pointing. Freddie considered not warning Chantell, but then the truce would end—and Chantell had the knife. Freddie assumed, quite correctly, that Chantell could slice the wings off a gnat at 100 paces.

Chantell, on the other hand, noticed the exchange and waited to see if Freddie warned her of Zombies before killing her. Chantell hesitated to throw her knife because she might not get it back.

Soon Dan saw Freddie and Chantell finding hidey-holes to avoid the visitors, as neither had found a good place to spend the night yet.

Chantell was sitting very quietly when a fast, toothy, foul smelling rodent bit her on the ankle. She reflexively kicked the thing away, praying first that it was not infected, and second that the Zombies didn't notice.

The first prayer was answered.

The LD swiveled and moved toward the sound. Chantell drew her gun, ready to fire. She was already calculating how quickly she could grab Dan and flee from here.

She wasn't liking the numbers.

Suddenly there was a loud clang further down the way. The LD rushed to investigate the latest potential meal. Looking across the way, Chantell spotted Freddie holding one of the bolts Dan had thrown. Looked like not killing her was a good decision.

Freddie was positive if Chantell got bitten, the evil bitch would make sure she and Dan were caught as well. In this she was quite correct. Looked like not letting Chantell get eaten was a good decision.

Soon they were back to searching for and ultimately partially constructing a place to sleep. By using the rock formation to protect their backs and wedging debris, they created a space with three exits that would slow the LD and give them time to escape.

As night fell, the weather turned very cold. If not for lack of moisture there would have been ice, and lighting a fire would ring the dinner bell. Freddie and Dan huddled together, but Chantell looked warmer than they were.

This made Freddie curious. "Why do you look so warm?"

"My Salvian warming stone is keeping me quite toasty, thank you." She showed the smooth round stone in her palm. "Dan, I can share it with you."

"No, thanks," said Dan.

"I might even let Freddie join us."

Freddie shuddered. "We'll pass."

"Suit yourself." Chantell rubbed her stone. "You know, I can't help thinking you planned this little jump on purpose."

"That doesn't sound like a great plan."

"It isn't."

"Besides, you know how erratic Dan's jumps are."

"Speaking of which, how about it, Danny boy? You ready to jump?"

"I am afraid not," he said.

"Too bad. The night's going to get colder."

Dan pulled Freddie closer. Having her body touching his set the reptile brain into motion. In most circumstances this would trigger the reptile to make a series of small moves for her to respond to—which her reptile brain would have welcomed. Unfortunately, with Chantell a few feet away, all the reptile could do was sulk.

The night passed slowly and little sleep was had since the trio feared the LD and didn't trust each other. Besides, the sounds of the dead pursuing a meal occurred often enough to make them uneasy. Freddie and Dan took turns napping and Chantell looked like she didn't need sleep.

Chantell got up with the sun and if she was up, they were all getting up. "Come on, Dan, wake up. Time to jump us outta here."

"I don't feel it," said Dan.

"Well I do. Get jumpin'."

Dan pretended to try to jump. In fact, he had no idea if he could jump but was trying to wait for the right time to try. This was the key to Freddie's plan. Dan had to stall the jump until they could separate from Chantell. The hope was that in the danger and chaos, they could slip away.

Chantell was not going to let that happen.

After breakfast they decided to look for water; their stores would not last long without replenishment. Dan returned to his perch, where Chantell and Freddie could both keep an eye on him.

They searched for any place water might collect while watching each other as well. Eventually Freddie found some foul-smelling water collecting on an old satellite dish. More interesting, however, was what was beside the array.

A small animal trap.

Someone was hunting and had the brains to construct a trap and place it near water. She signaled for Dan to come down, which brought Chantell running. Well, trying to run. The wound on her ankle had become red and stung badly.

The limp gave Freddie hope.

"What are you pulling?" Chantell demanded.

"I found something," said Freddie.

"Water?"

"No. Well yes, but something else."

"Is it cheese?" Dan desperately craved a hunk of cheddar.

There was a moment of awkward silence.

"Noooo, a trap."

"To catch people?" Dan was worried. "Are the dead smart enough to do that?"

"No, to catch animals."

Chantell cocked her head. "So someone's alive out there."

"Maybe," said Freddie.

"And they'd have to have food, water, and protection." Chantell quickly evaluated the significance of the discovery.

"They would."

"So we don't need to find water…"

"We need to find *them*."

Dan relayed what he saw yesterday. "I forgot when the Zombies showed up yesterday, there was something that looked like an apartment complex."

Freddie and Chantell responded, "What??"

"A bunch of escape pods piled up and the paths looked man-made."

"Man-made?" Freddie was now thinking a million thoughts.

"Well, man cleared."

"Living people couldn't survive where the Zombies could see them. Could the Zombies be smarter than we think?" Chantell revealed her ankle as she spoke, showing an oozing swollen mess.

Freddie struggled to maintain her façade while calculating how Chantell's wound could give them an edge. "Maybe. What do we know? The living dead are faster and maybe smarter than we expected. They often hunt in groups, making them more deadly. They hunt day and night and don't need rest."

Chantell retrieved an ointment from inside of her shirt and began rubbing it into the wound.

Dan chimed in. "And they smell bad." He tried to find something to redeem himself from the cheese comment. "And someone or thing is catching creatures with traps."

Freddie prioritized for them. "So while it would be nice to know what the LD are capable of, it's more important we find who set those traps."

"They may not even be alive. We should scout out the enemy." Chantell's reptile brain wanted to kill something.

"You should do that. Dan and I will look for survivors."

Chantell drew her knife. "Maybe you should do it my way."

Freddie smiled. "I'm betting the smell of blood would bring the LD like sharks. It'd be too hard to protect Dan."

Chantell holstered her weapon. "I guess we'll look for the trapper first."

"Let's call him Grizzly Adams." Neither understood Dan's reference.

When Freddie got another glimpse of Chantell's ankle, the swelling was gone. Damn, she should have guessed Chantell would have "Titan's Ointment."[22] It was incredibly expensive

[22] Guaranteed not to shrink, discolor, or immolate the human body.

and incredibly effective at killing most foreign substances in the body—except the living dead infection.

Continuing their earlier search, with occasional breaks to avoid death/infection, Freddie and Chantell found three more traps. Grizzly had set a trap line. One of the traps had a fresh kill of one of the rodents that had bitten Chantell. If Grizzly was looking for meat, he'd have to check the snares daily.

The three watched the traps most of the day, with Dan in his crow's nest. Dan sent some piece of rubble soaring away from the women (and himself) whenever he spotted a LD, and the LD followed the sound. He became pretty adept at diverting the dead away from the trap line. After the first five hours he became extremely bored and began singing lounge lizard versions of Bon Jovi songs quietly to himself.

It wasn't until nearly sundown when he first spotted Grizz.

– Chapter 33 –
Grizzly Bares All

Dan was whispering "You Give Love a Bad Name" in a way he would describe as "soulful" but anyone else would describe as "painful" when he glimpsed what he thought was an LD. For him this was a sign to pack it in. He flung a round piece of metal and looked to see which way the LD went to investigate before heading down.

Only the LD didn't investigate. Instead, it turned, and then moved away from the noise and disappeared into the piles of junk nearby.

"Holy crap!" said Dan.

The sound of crashing metal alerted the two women to danger and they also witnessed Grizzly's human-like behavior. By the time Dan clambered down to the ground, they were standing outside of where Grizz had disappeared.

Dan was happy to see Freddie. "Missed you."

"I missed you, too."

There was more intimacy in the words than Chantell could tolerate. "Fine. Everybody missed everybody. Now Freddie, go on in there and bring him out."

"I don't think so. You have the knife."

"But not a death wish."

"So you send me inside?"

"A girl's gotta try."

Dan decided to handle it. "You there, hiding inside. We would very much like to talk to you. Unless you're dead, then you could stay inside. We like your traps."

Chantell and Freddie tried unsuccessfully to hush him and he continued.

"You caught one of those creatures in the next trap down. Do they taste as bad as they smell?"

Freddie grabbed Dan to pull him away but was interrupted by Grizzly skulking out from behind a wall of rubbish.

"They do. Maybe worse." Grizz was dirty, perhaps fifty, with stringy gray hair, and wearing a filthy overcoat.

Chantell aimed the knife directly at him—as indirectly is generally less effective. "Do not move."

Grizz lifted both hands. "Please don't kill me. It would be a shame to survive the dead to be killed by the living. You are living, aren't you?"

Freddie had moved in front of Dan. "We are. How about you?"

Grizz did not look healthy. His skin was grayish and he reeked of death. "You tell me. I don't know anymore. Tell you what: I promise not to bite you if you promise not to bite me."

"That's a deal." Given his smell, Dan was not keen on biting him anyway.

"All right then. Follow me and we'll go somewhere safe."

With that, he trod past Chantell and down the path. They walked for about a minute, when Grizzly stopped to check a trap.

This did not please Chantell. "I thought we were going someplace safe."

"A girl's gotta eat."

This was the second time Dan had mistaken a woman for a man recently. He suffered an urge to be social. "I'm Dan, this is—"

"Don't tell me your names. By the time I remember them, you'll be dead anyway."

Chantell responded. "I don't think so."

Grizz checked traps as she spoke. "Look, I've been through this before. You take the ride down, then, faced with the reality of zombiefication, chicken out. I try to help keep you alive, but in the end you get bit, or die painfully from some horrible disease."

"But we're not sick."

"Then you're in the wrong place."

"Agreed."

"Either way, everybody gets bit."

"What about you?"

"Even me. Come on." Grizz opened an escape pod door and stepped inside.

Chantell was about to question how safe this was when she noticed the floor of the pod was open to a tunnel. In the tunnel they traveled past a door attached to stone. Grizz sealed the doors as they passed through.

Eventually they reached an underground den complete with a chair (made from pod seats) a bed (made from the stuffing of pod seats), bathroom (made from a pod throne) and a kitchen (made from whatever Grizz could scavenge). Grizz took off her coat and gestured to the chair—which Chantell promptly took.

Grizz rummaged in a makeshift closet carved into the wall. "Let's see, I think there's another chair in here. I haven't entertained in ages. Here it is." She dragged out a crudely made chair and offered it to Dan and Freddie.

They looked at each other.

Grizz looked at the two of them. "Tell you what, why don't you two sit on the bed and I'll take the chair."

Freddie looked at her. "Are you sure?"

"Sure. Maybe it will awaken some long dead fantasy within me."

This made them more hesitant, but sit down they did. This was the first time they managed a really good look at Grizz. Without the coat she looked more female. Barely. Strangely, she was less dirty under the coat, with slacks and a long sleeve top that were almost clean.

Chantell was boggled at this. "Honey, why are you wearing that filthy old coat?"

"The dead don't notice me much if I smell and look like them."

"Is that… What should I call you?"

"My name is Grizelda, but my friends call me—"

"Grizz?" Dan asked hopefully.

"No, Betts."

Damn, both Dan and I thought we'd called that one.

Freddie continued. "Betts, do you gray your skin as well?"

"No, that's all me."

Chantell rested her hand on her ray gun. "Your skin is gray?"

"Don't worry, I'm not dead. Not entirely, anyway."

"Not entirely?"

"Maybe not even mostly."

Dan was confused. "How dead are you?"

"I'm guessing 42%."

"42%??"

"Around there."

Chantell had moved her gun to her lap. "So you're a Zombie."

"Of course not. I'm more alive than dead."

"Have you ever bit anyone?"

"Not if they didn't bite me first."

Freddie needed to know more. "So how'd that happen?"

"I don't know. I was dying of cancer, so I came here. I got bitten and felt the infection rushing through me, then it stopped. And so did the cancer. It only took about an hour."

Freddie's medical mind marveled. "But how?"

"Maybe I'm a mutant, or the cancer drugs did something. Hell, maybe I was bit by a radioactive spider. All I know is that was three hundred years ago."

"So the LD bite made you immortal?"

"Not really. It kinda necrotized things. Everything slowed down and it killed a lot of stuff in my body, but I just keep going. I heal, but slowly. Look." Betts pulled up her shirtsleeve to show a bite wound on her arm from a recent attack.

Dan shuddered. "Ouch."

"Luckily, things don't hurt much when you're 42% dead, but I don't need pieces of me missing."

"I can see that."

"So they still want to eat you?" Freddie asked.

"I'm human enough that they want to taste me, but dead enough they don't want more than a bite."

"Just like my last boyfriend." That was Chantell, as if you needed to be told.

"So what's the deal with you three? You're not dying?"

"Wrong place, wrong time, honey."

"Very wrong," Freddie added.

It was then Dan noticed something. "Did anyone notice the lights are on?"

"What?" said Freddie.

"The lights. The lights are on."

Chantell and Freddie looked up and saw the lights were indeed on. A string of little bulbs across the ceiling of the space provided a pleasant yellow haze. All three looked to Betts.

"Oh yeah." Betts pointed to a small glowing orb on a shelf. "A few years back I found an anti-anti-technology device."

Chantell was about to become orgasmic. "You what?"

"It was in a junker that came down. It's a personal field so it only covers about forty feet."

At first thought there wouldn't be much use for an anti-anti-technology device, but once someone weaponized anti-technology technology, any ship or army could be immobilized by luring it into an anti-technology field. Thus the anti-anti-technology device was born, followed by the anti-anti-anti-technology device and the anti-anti-anti-anti-technology device.

This went on for some time before everyone gave up. This particular apparatus was in a derelict freighter, sent to its just reward to Tennore. Sending a ship with an anti-anti-technology device to Tennore was incredibly stupid. Sending an anti-anti-technology device to Tennore while it was active was really, really, incredibly stupid.

If it had been turned off, Betts never could have turned it on in an anti-technology field. For the same reason, she could never turn it off.

Chantell slipped the life ray into the holster on her hip. "Listen, girl, I'd like to take a look at your blood."

"I don't have much."

"I don't need much."

Chantell pulled a wooden spoon from her bag. Dan wished he had one.

Betts squeezed a drop of blood from her wound onto the spoon. In moments the spoon projected a holographic report which Chantell and Freddie studied carefully.

"What this is," Chantell said, "is a cure to disease and death. Imagine being able to live your natural span and then keep going. Dead lady, is there a chance you didn't have cancer?"

"What?" said Betts.

"Your body naturally fights off death. You would have beaten the cancer."

"But I got sicker."

Freddie caught on. "*After* they gave you the meds."

"But—"

"They couldn't let you run free. The whole system is built on death. Medicine, insurance, retirement. Without death, everything falls apart. Just like the living dead are sentenced to this place to protect the rest of the universe from death, you were sentenced to this place to protect the rest of the universe from life."

"Those bastards!!"

Dan tossed out a thought. "It's a shame we can't infect the dead with life."

Freddie took it a step further. "Why not?"

"Infect the dead with life?"

"Yes."

Chantell grabbed her arm. "Because we ain't gonna be here that long."

"We don't know that," said Freddie.

"I do." Aiming her life ray at Freddie, Chantell pushed Freddie back and grabbed Dan. Pulling out Timmy, she hit the button to time jump. The device glowed faintly, then faltered.

Betts looked at them sadly. "You think you're going somewhere?"

Chantell's escape was thwarted and she was angry. "Why the hell didn't that work?"

"The global anti-tech field is too strong. Only simple tech works—like the lights—or maybe your gun."

"Shit."

Freddie had already moved on. "Betts, can we get some more blood?"

"If you think it will help, but me, I'm not getting my hopes up. Still, it'd be nice to have some company." Betts was hoping one of the three would survive a week.

So she let them poke her and run some tests.

Betts offered the three some of her trapped catch, which they declined. She offered some water, which they declined.

"I have a great charcoal filtration system I cobbled together from escape pods. Having thousands of lifeboats meant to sustain life for weeks has been quite helpful."

They drank the water.

By the time they fell asleep, they had a blood sample they wanted to try on an LD. But first they had to catch one.

The next day they devised a larger trap to catch a Zombie. Betts ate her breakfast of a farmint (Dan's idea of combining fart and varmint) and the others had old rations from the pods. The cans and jars from the escape pods had various dates stamped on their lids depending on the year the pod made the fiery descent to the surface. Some dates were long ago—but still in the future of Dan's origination time so technically they hadn't been canned and jarred yet.[23]

[23] How does one judge edibility with a "sell by" date? Does it expire the day it's sold? Heaven forbid. You have to have time to consume said item. So in fact, does the "sell by" date actually give us any useful information at all? The argument rages on.

They set out. Chantell lingered behind the others—and pocketed the anti-anti-technology orb as she slipped out of the cavern.

Dan sensed a jump coming on. He was doing his best to repress it, but the longer it went, the more uncomfortable it got. It was kinda like the Tachyon Absorption Machine on low power. His body wanted to unravel, but for the first time he resisted the jump.

Betts was friendlier today at having a plan where there was a chance she might not be alone. "You know, those creatures don't really taste that bad once you get used to them. Or maybe it helps if your taste buds are 42% dead."

Dan couldn't wrap his head around eating something so foul. "Why don't you just eat the rations?"

"I tried, but I have a craving for meat. I mean, I'd eat it two or three times a day if I could catch enough."

"As would most Zombies." Chantell did little to hide her prejudice.

"And most people," Freddie retorted.

Betts stopped, surveying the area. It was a wide path, but not a heavily travelled one between the piles of refuse. "Well, this is it. It's quiet enough to not get mobbed, but we should have one come along."

They set a couple of rope traps and waited in hiding. No one noticed a small power unit hum to life under a pile of trash. While Freddie and Chantell watched each other, Dan chatted with Betts.

"You know, yesterday I thought I saw a little community to the south." Dan had no idea where south was on Tennore.

"You mean the Zombie condos."

"Did that just happen or… ?"

"No, they built it. People think the LD are dumb. They're not. They just aren't as smart as they were. They're still pack animals and want community. They stacked the escape pods and built a little city. Some even have yards and decorations. I've seen families, with the smarter ones treating the dumb ones as their children."

Their conversation was cut short by an LD lumbering their way. It appeared he was going to miss the traps altogether, but a well-placed throw by Betts made him change direction to investigate. The trap worked like a charm and in seconds he was hanging upside down.

Chantell handed Betts a syringe. "You better do it."

Betts nodded. "Yep, I don't like being bit, but you really wouldn't like it."

As Betts approached the LD, it hissed and growled, struggling to grab her. Betts kept moving to be behind the creature. As she started to place the needle, it made a new sound.

"STOPPPP!"

Betts took a step back.

Freddie was shocked. "They speak."

Betts looked closely at the LD. "Most don't. This one is smart."

The LD struggled. "Let… me ga, go… and I… won't call… udders."

Dan was trying to imagine udders rushing to the rescue.

Betts explained. "He's a scout. They call out to others in their pack when they spot food."

"Not… pack," said the LD. "Family."

Chantell inched nearer. "Still, he's an excellent candidate to test. Let's give some life to a smart one."

Freddie nodded and Betts gave the injection. And the LD let out a howl that chilled even Chantell.

Betts started to move. "Crap! We gotta go."

The four started running with Betts leading the way. Soon they heard the sound of the dead everywhere, wailing in response to their leader's call.

Betts continued. "We gotta get to a hidey hole."

She was close when they came face to face with a horde of LD. An "about face" and a right turn left the dead behind; but although the living were a little faster, the LD never stopped.

Freddie pulled a bottle from her satchel that she had fashioned into a Molotov cocktail. She ignited it with a simple lighter and threw it behind them.

BOOM!!

Dan made a mental note to never drink the Jack Spice. The blast singed their clothing and more than slowed the LD. A couple more turns and they'd be safe.

Well, safeish.

Betts turned a corner several feet ahead of the trio and an LD stepped out from the wreckage, cutting them off from the hiding place. A sudden stop and confusion ensued as they tried to escape the thing.

It lunged for them. Chantell shoved Dan between herself and the Zombie and as it clawed at him, Freddie stepped in and pushed it away.

And it bit her.

A million thoughts flew through Dan's mind as he grabbed her. *This isn't possible. This plan was stupid. I can't lose her.* But the clearest of them all was the one he spoke.

"I won't let this happen!"

Chantell saw the timestream yawn open. "Noooooo!!" She hesitated just long enough to become surrounded by the dead. She pulled her life ray. Quiet no longer mattered.

The ray crackled as she blasted the Zombies with its energy.

To no effect. The Zombies kept coming.

She fired again.

And they kept coming.

It just goes to prove the old adage.

"Don't bring a life ray to a Living Dead fight."

- CHAPTER 34 -
True Love Knows No Time

As Dan and Freddie splintered into time, Dan felt the infection raging in Freddie's body. Moments after being bitten, she was already well on her way to becoming living dead. She knew it as well. There was no way to cleanse the infection before she left the timestream.

She'd emerge and within seconds she would be no better than before. Even with the timestream trying to reset her, it wouldn't be sufficient. Leaving the tiniest bit of the microbe would start the cycle again. With her action focused, she took control of the jump and guided the journey back to Tennore—not to where they had left, but into the safety of Betts' home.

Realizing what she was doing, Dan was free to do what he must. As they materialized, he drove a second jump. Less than a second out of the stream and they were back in. And again. And again. With each jump there was less infection and with each jump, Dan became hungrier and thinner.

Freddie's mind pleaded with him to stop, but he would not. He had never been so sure about anything in his life. When the stream opened again, he refused to leave. He struggled against the stream. His atoms were swirling and he fought against the pain. The longer he held off reconstituting, the more it hurt until Chantell's torture was nothing in comparison.

At last he could feel no more infection, only pain. Was Freddie cured or did it hurt too much to tell? Then he felt Freddie change the course of their jump.

And he let go.

When they landed, Dan stayed conscious long enough to see that Freddie was whole.

– Epilogue –
Nearly the End

When he awoke again, he was in a king-sized bed with an IV in his arm and soup on the nightstand. Through an open window he could see palm trees and smell the ocean air. He rolled over to see Freddie lying beside him. In a bikini.

"Dan Baker, you are the most amazing man I have ever met."

"And you've only known me for a couple of weeks."

"And a millennium."

"And a millennium."

"Have some soup."

He pulled her closer. "There's something I want more."

She smiled. "Can you stand up?"

He tried.

His reptile brain really tried.

He couldn't even sit up.

"When you can stand," she said.

"Then what's next?"

"Have some soup."

THE END

- Gratitude -

Dear Reader,

Although technically we don't truly know if you are a dear, you could be a telemarketer who calls during lunch.

My Valuable Reader,[24]

We hope you enjoyed *Time Travel for Fun and Prophet* (if you have indeed read it). Your feedback is important to us as making you happy puts bread on our table and we need bread to make sandwiches.

If you could take a few minutes to leave a review, we would greatly appreciate it. Your input may influence our next book and help our readers (well, our potential readers which actually are our nonreaders) to learn more about us.

A great way for you to learn more about us is to visit our website at **www.cinehunden.com** where you'll find exclusive content and even a free short story just for subscribing.

It should also have more of the funny.

~ Terry and Carol

PS: To make the process as frictionless as possible, if your phone is nearby, just grab it and hover over the QR code below. You can even use the voice-to-text on your phone to speak your review (it points to cinehunden.com/review):

---

[24] If you have read the book and not just skipped to this page.

But Wait... There's More!

Limited time offer (as far as time can be limited).[25] If you subscribe right now, you will gain access to our short story, ***The Time Traveler's Companion***, which takes place in the same universe as *Time Travel for Fun and Prophet.*

Just think—you can be among the first to read this soon-to-be-classic companion to the novel. Subscribe now!

~ Terry and Carol

PS: Did you have fun with the last QR Code? If so, we've got one more for you (it will magically transport your phone to www.cinehunden.com/subscribe):

---

[25] We are required by our lawyers (of which we have none) to mention this limited time offer is only limited by the continued existence of humanity, the internet, and time itself.

www.ingramcontent.com/pod-product-compliance
Lightning Source LLC
Chambersburg PA
CBHW050811190726
48285CB00005B/1876